SAPLING

OTHER BOOKS IN THE WHITE OAK TRILOGY

Acorn *out now*

White Oak *anticipated September 2023*

SAPLING

The White Oak Trilogy, Book 2

KELSEY PARPART

For Mom, my most enthusiastic reader

CHAPTER 1

It was still dark when Erica's phone buzzed from somewhere underneath her. Half asleep, she grabbed it from where it poked into her ribcage and swiped to snooze. As her eyes adjusted, the outline of a pair of shoulders came into view. Erica ran an index finger down the long, bare spine and whispered, "You have to go."

Xander sighed, rolled onto his back, and pulled her into him. This was something she could get used to, spending every morning waking up slowly in the place and with the person she loved. She draped herself across his chest and gently stroked his side as he made the happy little humming noise she could only get out of him when he was too tired to be self-conscious. They were dangerously close to falling back asleep when the alarm went off again. Xander made fun of her last night when she set it, but she knew they were already on the verge of getting caught.

"Seriously. Out," she said, giving him a light shove. The thought struck her, as it had several times since Xander defied death and returned to her, that she was so lucky to have this moment. After thinking she lost him for good, every second with Xander was precious. Every detail she learned about him, like how slow he was to get up in the mornings, felt like it needed to be bottled up and stored forever in the warehouse of her mind. Unfortunately, they had to share shelf space with other memories she would never forget. Memories drenched in blood.

Xander threw his long legs over the side of the bed and searched for his t-shirt somewhere on the floor. The elastic of his boxers hung low on his hips. His summer tan was fading, and his back glowed pale in the moonlight. Erica loved watching him, the way his bones slid under his skin as he slipped his shirt over his head. He leaned over to kiss her before getting off the bed and ever so quietly opening the bedroom door to sneak downstairs. Erica listened to the stairs creak faintly with each of his steps and waited for the soft metallic click of the latch that meant he'd made it safely to the room under the stairs, the room that used to be her uncle Keith's. Only then did she shut her door, hoping that Granny was still sleeping soundly at the end of the hall.

Xander had been staying with them since he showed up at the cemetery hill five days ago. His own uncle, Alden, made it very clear to Xander that he could forgive him for his part in bringing down the bear tree but that forgiveness did not extend to Erica. Erica understood that her betrayal of Alden ran deeper than that single incident. She was also responsible for his and Xander's secrets getting out beyond her family to people they weren't sure they could trust. She hoped that the conversation she and Xander were supposed to have with Kyle and Derek that afternoon would help to ease her fears as far as that was concerned. She had texted them both after Xander came back, but she selfishly wanted him to herself for a few days even if they deserved some answers about what she got them involved in.

Erica tried to fall back asleep but Xander's scent—a mix of wildflowers and newly turned earth—haunted her pillows. She let herself drift in and out of consciousness, wafting between anxiety at cutting Xander off from his only family and the less than chaste thoughts that filled her head every time she smelled him on her sheets, until sunlight came through her window.

Because no one else was up yet, Erica decided to shower before she started clattering around the kitchen. Once clean, she stood in front of her dresser and contemplated what to wear. She chastised herself for not having the foresight to pack warmer clothing when she came to Juniper Falls back in August.

As she put on leggings and a fuzzy cardigan she usually only wore around the house, she resolved to text her mother a list of things to bring down from Portland when they met up at College of the Cascades later in the week for orientation. Erica had tried to insist that Danni's presence was not required but, as was typical with her mother, she lost that battle. *If I'm going to spend tens of thousands of dollars on your education, I want to know what I'm getting,* Danni told her on a phone call while planning their trip.

Erica also knew that a not insignificant reason her mother insisted on accompanying her was to make sure she actually went. Though Erica's anxieties about college and, more importantly, what she was going to do afterward, had been easing during her time in Juniper Falls, it was unclear whether that was a result of actual emotional progress or if those concerns were merely forced to take a backseat to all of the unbelievable things going on around her. Then there were the ten days she went dark. Ten days that she didn't answer her parents' calls. Ten days that, despite being so recent, Erica could hardly remember. She knew she had Granny to thank for keeping her mother off her back during that period when she wasn't sure if she had lost Xander forever. If a little hovering was the price of having him back, she was happy to pay it.

Erica went downstairs and paused at the front door where Tulip lay on the welcome rug. She bent down and rubbed the old dog's ears. Tulip registered her presence with a sigh but otherwise didn't move. Erica proceeded to the kitchen to rinse yesterday's coffee out of the pot and fill a fresh filter with grounds. She took an English muffin out of the tin breadbox and popped it in the toaster, then rooted around the pantry for some peanut butter.

She jumped when she felt something on her waist and spun around to find a sleepy Xander wrapping his arms around her. They had not been able to keep their hands off each other since being reunited. His near-death had pushed them past the awkwardness of their new relationship, and touch had turned from a want to a need. She hadn't thought twice about sneaking him into her bed that first night so she could lay her head on his chest and listen to his heartbeat.

"Did you sleep after I left?" he asked. His breath was warm on the top of her head.

"Sort of. Did you?"

"I don't think I ever fully woke up."

The toaster dinged. Erica slipped out of Xander's grasp, though he left his hand on the small of her back as she slathered her muffin in peanut butter.

"It's weird that you sleep so much but you don't eat."

Xander shrugged. "I don't think I have to sleep either. The hangover after indulging just isn't as bad. Alden and I would—," he trailed off. Erica saw the pained look in his eye that showed up every time he mentioned his uncle. She laid the muffin on the plate and held him.

Pushing her face into his chest, she whispered, "I'm sorry."

"How many times do I have to tell you that it's not your fault?"

"Until I believe it."

They stood in the kitchen, in their bare feet, neither willing to let go until the smell of peanut butter got the better of them both.

"You better eat that before I do, and that is something I won't forgive you for," Xander said, attempting to diffuse the mood that settled upon them.

He followed her to the table, unlocking his phone to start his daily scroll of news stories. This was part of the morning ritual they were developing—her sitting down to a light breakfast while he relayed highlights from the articles that caught his interest. For someone who was so resigned to his fate of being forever stuck in the small town where he was born, Erica admired how hard Xander worked to know about the world.

Having him here, in her house or following her around like a puppy when she worked at the store, had taught her more about him than the previous two months. She thought she knew him well enough to tell him that she loved him but living with him was a new experience. Erica was beginning to understand that she had only scratched the hard, gray surface of the geode that was Xander Reed, and that each new day was bringing her closer to the lustrous purple center where his real self lived.

The feelings she had originally professed to his damaged, unconscious body the day they took down the bear dryad were not untrue, but every time Erica repeated them they meant a little more. She created a catalog in her head of every look, every commonly used phrase, and every fact about him as if by knowing him fully she could figure out how to keep him safe, how to craft the emotional bubble that would erase how hard his life had been to this point.

She was staring at him again and barely noticed Granny walk past the round oak table in her ankle-length quilted bathrobe on her way to the kitchen. Granny smiled at Erica and shook her head, and Erica knew they had been caught. Now that it was once again safe to do so, Granny liked to lightly tease her about her inability to keep her infatuation with Xander off her face. Erica let her because Granny had been so understanding and welcoming about letting him stay with them.

"Good morning, Vivian," Xander said, respectfully putting down his phone as he did whenever Granny came into the room. He was so determined to make her like him, no matter how much assurance Erica gave him that she already did.

"You know you two don't need to sneak around on my account. I'm not a prude." Granny was pouring herself a cup of coffee in the kitchen and couldn't see the blush that rose on Erica's cheeks and, for Xander, ran from his low hairline to below the collar of his shirt. Erica and Xander couldn't meet each other's eyes. The truth was much less scandalous than Granny was insinuating. Yes, they slept every night in a tangle of limbs. Yes, they kissed until their lips hurt. Yes, Erica could draw a map of every muscle of Xander's chest. But there was a cautiousness to their affection that was new since Xander came back.

It wasn't that Erica didn't want more—every nerve ending in her body begged her to move things along—but she was nervous. In part because, even though she had some experience, she didn't know how to have the passionate, world-bending sex she saw in the movies. She was scared that she would disappoint him or herself, and this spell of pure bliss she had been living under would be broken. She knew this was ridiculous because, though they hadn't talked about it specifically, Xander's isolation over the past ten years meant she was undoubtedly his first for everything.

More than that, Erica couldn't shake the vision of a bloody Xander, ripped through by five enormous claws. She couldn't forget the shreds of skin hanging off that chest she loved so much, the white ribs peeking through, the smell like raw beef that filled her nostrils as she laid on top of him, waiting for the nightmare to be over. Erica had not registered these things in the moment. Fueled by adrenaline, she had been focused only on the big picture—cutting down the tree and protecting Xander. Then she had been numbed by grief.

Having his body back in her hands—smooth and flawless as if nothing at all had happened—brought back memory after memory that her brain tried so hard to suppress. Erica was terrified of compromising this miracle, wary of leaving the tiniest scratch or bruise.

She knew this too was stupid. If Xander couldn't be permanently harmed by an overgrown, bulletproof black bear, there was nothing she could do that would leave a lasting mark. But logic didn't enter the equation when it came to him. For now, she treated him gingerly, as though he was made of precious glass. Something to cherish, not manhandle.

Not to mention she was never sure what was going through Xander's mind when they were alone together in the dark. Erica's previous experience with teenage boys didn't recall words like *restrained* and *respectful*. She knew that he wanted her. To date, though, he had kept his hands—and everything else—frustratingly above her hips. In this as in so many other ways, Xander continued to prove to be an anomaly among his peers.

Not that she could say any of this to her grandmother. As Granny came back into the dining room carrying a full cup of coffee and a croissant, Erica watched Xander open his mouth to protest her assumptions. Erica kicked him under the table and shot him a warning look. Xander furrowed his forehead in confusion, his thick eyebrows forming a chocolate-hued caterpillar above his dark eyes.

Granny chuckled at their silent lovers' quarrel but did not press the topic. She asked if they had plans for the day.

"We're meeting up with Kyle and Derek," Erica said as if this wasn't the first time the four of them would be in the same place since that day. As if she didn't have a myriad of reasons to be nervous.

Granny nodded, leaving space for a further explanation that Erica did not provide. Xander glanced between them, his forehead having let up slightly to reveal the signature deep line between his eyebrows. Erica longed to reach over and run her finger down the bridge of his nose until the crease released, but she didn't want to give Granny more fodder to tease her with.

She turned to Xander. "Do you want to go get dressed? We should leave in a few minutes."

Xander gestured to his t-shirt and basketball shorts. "I am dressed."

"It's November. You might want to look like someone who gets cold."

Xander shrugged but got up from the table to at least, Erica hoped, put on a sweater. To avoid any further line of inquiry, Erica also got up, grabbed her plate and mug, and patted Granny's shoulder on her way to rinse them.

Granny grabbed her wrist. "You're bossy."

Erica winced at the chastisement. She pulled her hand away and put her stoneware in the dishwasher. She returned to the table and took a seat beside Granny.

"Is it bad?" Erica had noticed that her anxiety about Xander spread beyond the bedroom. She had a newfound need that everything around her, particularly as it pertained to him, be perfect. She wanted so much for him—friends, a job, an education—everything she took for granted.

"He's had a lot of big changes. Just remember to be supportive. A helping hand instead of a guiding one, perhaps?"

Erica nodded, and Xander came out of the downstairs bedroom wearing his maroon hoodie. He had put on white crew socks but was still wearing his basketball shorts. Erica looked at Granny who gave her a smile and a little shake of her head.

"What?" Xander said, looking down at his outfit. "This doesn't work either?"

"It's fine." Erica went to him and, standing on her toes, kissed the tip of his nose. She would save her fashion advice for another day when the agenda wasn't as packed.

Kyle Zukowski's house was a compact brick ranch close to the river on the way out of town. He shared it with his father, Joe, now a partner at *Juniper Falls Farm & Feed*, the store founded by Erica's family. Kyle's mom had left when he was a toddler and, to Erica's knowledge, neither he nor Joe had heard from her since. The house remained a kind of monument to her. Items only left the house when they were too worn or broken to repair. Erica hadn't been inside since she came back for that long summer three years ago, but she expected it would look much the same.

Erica pulled her car into the gravel driveway that so far was only occupied by Kyle's beater pickup truck. Xander had been quiet on the drive over. The previous night they had discussed their expectations for what information was on- and off-limits. They knew they owed Kyle and Derek some explanation for what Erica had gotten them involved in, but they set boundaries. They would guard the location of Xander and Alden's trees, hopefully allowing them to continue to hide in plain sight. They would try not to let too much slip about what all Xander was capable of. Erica was worried about her ability to walk the line between saying enough to be seen as trustworthy and revealing too much. She knew she couldn't stop herself from asking Derek a million questions about himself, and it was unfair to expect him to reveal anything if they didn't share in return. Erica had to remind herself, as she had dozens of times over the last two months, that the secrets she kept weren't her own.

They also talked about Xander's useless posturing. What the four of them went through in the woods was enough to count them all as friends. She could forgive to a certain extent, Xander's possessiveness that day. She rationalized that he was protecting himself as much as her. Moving forward, he had to trust her. Xander was upset when she brought this up, but she assured him that if he couldn't see how much he meant to her, he was an idiot. One date with Kyle was nothing compared to what they had.

"Should we go in?" Erica asked. They sat in the car, both staring at the door painted terracotta red. Xander sighed. As nervous as she was about how this conversation would go, at least she knew these people. Xander was only just getting used to talking to more than one person at a time.

Erica did her best to comfort him by smiling at him, perhaps a little too widely, and squeezing his hand. "It'll be okay. You won't be the only—," Erica trailed off, searching for the right word.

"Weird one?"

"Special one. Derek has secrets too. He can turn into a bear, Xander. That's way weirder than anything I've seen you do."

The corners of Xander's mouth twitched, and he squeezed back. Erica took this as a good sign and got out of the car. Xander caught her hand again as they approached the door. She knocked twice and held her breath.

CHAPTER 2

Kyle opened the door, his blocky shoulders taking up most of the frame. Erica had a suspicion that he had been lurking behind the tinted picture window watching her and Xander as they made their way inside. He wore a plaid flannel button-up and jeans, the uniform for men in Juniper Falls during the colder months. He had a beard coming in that Erica thought brought some definition to his bulldog-like features.

"Hey," Erica said, hoping her voice sounded open and unguarded.

"Hi," Kyle replied. He stepped aside and let them into a living room with dark, paneled walls and overstuffed furniture. There was a cut-out in the wall to their left that looked into a white kitchen—white cabinets, white appliances, white tile floors. Erica's hunch had been right. Nothing about this place had changed since her childhood when their families would visit each other for barbecues and birthday parties.

Xander and Kyle were doing their best to avoid making eye contact with the other. Erica leaned into Xander, pushing him forward and willing him to make peace. "You remember Kyle."

"Hey, man," Kyle said, offering his hand. Xander stared at it. Erica was about to knock him with her shoulder again when Derek walked in through the still-open door. Unlike the others, Derek's demeanor was relaxed as he kicked off a pair of well-worn black canvas loafers.

"Hey, guys." Derek was wearing his usual black-on-black attire that matched his dark, messy hair. Derek stood more than a head shorter than Xander, and, even in grizzly form, had a loose quality to his movements. He looked between them, reading the mood of the room. "Let's sit down, yeah? Lots to talk about."

Erica gave Kyle a sidelong glance to see how he felt about being invited to sit in his own house. His expression was blank. She waited for him to take over playing the host, but when it didn't happen, she led Xander to a couch.

"Actually," Kyle said, remembering himself at last, "do you mind taking your shoes off too?"

"Yes! I forgot!" Erica said. She and Xander pulled off their shoes, and Erica crossed the room again to place them next to Derek's onto a mat by the door. "Your dad likes to keep this place pretty spotless. Probably sick of the dust after spending all day at the store."

This was a sad attempt at conversation, and Kyle didn't take the bait. He sat down, ramrod straight, on one end of a tan microfiber couch while Derek sprawled on the other side as though each of his limbs needed to be as far away from the others as possible. Erica joined Xander in the middle of the opposite couch, an exact twin of the first. She draped herself over him as she had gotten so used to doing recently but straightened up after seeing the annoyed look on Kyle's face.

"So. You're looking good. Considering," Derek said, with a nod to Xander.

Erica and Xander looked at each other, eyes wide, and laughed. She slipped her arm through his and patted his forearm to let him know that she agreed, he did look good, and not just considering.

Erica liked Derek more every time they met. She could like anyone who could get an honest laugh out of Xander, but her appreciation ran deeper than that. She had judged him during their initial meeting at the bonfire, with his greasy hair and hand-rolled cigarettes. But since then he had proven himself to be calm and caring, perceptive and pacifying. She harbored the hope that he would be a willing addition to Xander's limited social circle.

"Thanks," Xander replied.

"I'm surprised you're walking already after that," Derek said.

"I'm lucky that way." Xander looked down at his hands and added, "Erica said you don't heal?"

"I heal, dude, but just, like, normal. Not put my organs back inside healing."

Xander blushed. "I don't remember any of it."

"That guy—your uncle—he pushed us out of there. We got the basics of it but *what happened?*" Judging by the emphasis Derek put on the last two words, he was ready to move on from the small talk. From the way Kyle leaned forward, he was as well.

For all the talking Erica and Xander did heading into this conversation, they didn't discuss where they would start. But for Erica, Keith's disappearance marked the beginning of so many things.

"You know how I came down this summer to help Granny with the store after Keith went missing? After they found his body, Xander and Alden reached out to me. They were worried that Keith might have left behind clues about them. He did, sort of. Xander helped me look into what Keith had put together, and that led us to the bear."

Erica paused and looked at Xander for approval that she hadn't said too much. Xander nodded. Derek and Kyle exchanged a look that Erica couldn't read.

"And?" Kyle asked.

"And you were there for the rest."

There was an awkward silence during which Kyle clenched and unclenched his fists. When she didn't offer more, he spoke through gritted teeth, "I've been goddamned patient with all of this, but you're going to have to connect the dots for us better than that. It's literally the least you could do after all this crazy shit."

Erica eyed Derek, hoping to find an ally in someone else who also had more of a story than he had led them to believe.

But Derek made no attempts to save her. Xander looked at his hands. It was on her, then. Again.

"Our uncles were friends," she explained. "They met while investigating Kriners. Remember when we met for coffee, and I was asking you whether strange things were going on at the logging sites? I was asking about the bear, though I didn't know it then. The bear, well, the bear killed Keith."

Kyle deflated at this revelation and dropped his head into his large hand. "I knew it."

Erica forgot until that moment that Keith and Kyle must have been close. Joe and Keith had worked together for more than twenty years, and Kyle himself spent almost five years working at the store. She wondered why they hadn't talked about him more when they were almost seeing each other. Maybe neither of them had been willing to face the loss. But now that things were somewhat resolved—Keith was at peace, and they knew what happened—it had become as real for Kyle as it had for her.

Erica got up off her couch and sat gingerly next to Kyle. She knocked her knee against his. "I'm sorry. I should have told you."

"There is a lot you should have told me," he said with a pointed look toward Xander. "Like what he has to do with that thing."

"I—," Xander said, struggling to find the right words.

"They're similar. They're all—."

"Dryads," Kyle said. "You told us back in the woods. But there isn't much information about dryads, is there? Unlike mister were-whatever over here."

Derek put his hand to his chest in a gesture that said, *Who? Me?* "That's werewolves, man. A whole different thing. Bears are born not bitten. You can't always trust the lore."

Kyle snorted and shook his head. "I just don't get it. I asked my dad about the Reeds, and he said Xander's uncle would be in his sixties if he was still alive. That blonde guy that showed up looked my age. And I knew Xander as a kid. Do you guys just stop aging after high school?"

Xander took a deep breath. Erica returned to the opposite couch. She leaned against him and wrapped her arm around his again, this time with her hand on his bicep. This was the point at which she had promised not to talk for him, but she also knew that Xander tended to shut down when things got difficult.

All their eyes were on him, and she felt him tense. She squeezed his arm and gave him what she hoped was an encouraging smile. He didn't relax, but he did start talking. "Me and Alden, we have nothing to do with the bear dryad. We think the increase in logging activity around Juniper Falls made it more active. When the weird stuff started happening, we didn't know what it was. We heard about the same stories you did about the broken equipment and dead animals. But Alden didn't find its tree until after Keith shot it."

"Why didn't you cut it down on the spot?" Kyle asked. "It sounds like the lore has that part right."

"We didn't know how," Erica pleaded. "And it was possible Keith was an accident. He was tracking it. It could have just been wrong place, wrong time."

"But you didn't do anything even after I told you guys were dying on the job. You two knew—you ran out of the fundraiser when I told you. But it took that thing tearing up downtown to do anything about it. And then you made us do it." Kyle pointed between himself and Derek. "You didn't even have the balls to do it yourselves. Derek almost got ripped in half."

Erica looked at the floor. They had no defense. Even if she told Kyle that she had made those same arguments, that Xander had done his best to track the bear and stop further attacks, it wouldn't be enough. He would have had to have been there, to see how Alden's face crumpled at the idea of killing something he wanted so desperately to understand. Something that he thought could tell him more about himself than he had learned over the past almost forty years since he died and was reborn altogether different.

"We're sorry," Erica said. "We did our best with the information we had."

A loaded silence hung in the air. Kyle had scooted to the

edge of the couch, and he looked poised to jump at Erica and Xander. Erica shook her head lightly and raised her eyes to meet his anger head-on.

"That's it?" Kyle muttered. "You make us do your dirty work and then give that lame apology? I tried to reach out to you after. I've tried to be your friend. You keep pushing me away." It always came back to this with her and Kyle. Erica opened her mouth to protest, but Kyle beat her to it. "I know you want me to keep this quiet, but trust goes both ways."

Erica recoiled as if he had hit her. There was no other way to take this than as a threat. This must have been clear to Xander too because he made to get up off the couch, and she had to hold his arm in a vice grip to keep him down.

"Hey now," Derek said. "That's enough." Three heads turned toward him. "I trust all of you."

Erica could see the top of a raised scar, still red, poking out of Derek's t-shirt near his collarbone. She knew it had been self-ish to get them involved. Wasn't her generation constantly being taught about consent? And yet she led them, blindly, into a far more dangerous situation than they could have been prepared for.

"I'm so sorry. Both of you," she said. She turned to Xander, "And to you too. I didn't ask if any of you wanted to help or if it was okay to expose your secrets. I was scared and it was the only thing I could think of to do. It wasn't fair." Tears welled in Erica's eyes. Xander extracted his arm from hers and pulled her into him. "Derek, I'm so sorry you got hurt. I'm so sorry you had to, you know—."

"Erica, I was ready to go after it out in the open at *Farm & Feed*," Derek replied. "You're the one who kept telling me to keep my clothes on. It was going to happen eventually, and I'm glad it was only in front of three people instead of a hundred."

"Really?" Erica asked with a slight warble in her voice.

"Yeah. I swear."

Erica dried her eyes on the sleeve of her sweater. "You said bears are born. Have you always been able to change?" She knew she should be ashamed of herself for asking him to talk about it, but they were in dire need of a change in topic.

Derek nodded. "Since I was a baby. I'm the only one in my family, though. It skips generations supposedly. Doesn't hit all the kids."

"There are more of you?" Xander asked.

"We're not common, but yeah, there are more."

Xander shifted beside her. She could feel his heartbeat quicken. "Here?"

"No, in Kodiak. Alaska. Where I'm from."

Xander's eyes were wide. Erica thought she knew why. Derek was the only person other than Alden that Xander knew was not just like everyone else. And he seemed to know why, which was a luxury Xander and Alden didn't have.

"You didn't want to stay there? With them?" Xander asked.

Erica flinched. She knew the answer to this was painful for Derek, but his easy countenance didn't change.

"My dad is a mean drunk. He didn't expect when he headed on down to Kodiak and got married that he would get a bear for a son. I guess it's a little my fault."

"It's not," Erica said without hesitation.

Derek shrugged. "He's better when I'm not around. Not great but better. I spent a couple of years wandering around the Lower Forty-eight trying to make as much money as possible. That's how I wound up here. Logging is good money. But I didn't expect to find this. I thought I left all that supernatural shit at home."

Xander and Erica started to ask the same question at the same time. They looked at each other, and Erica let Xander talk. The answer was more important to him. "Does Alaska have other stuff? Other than the bears?" Erica knew that he meant *anything like me*.

Derek shook his head. "Just bears. So many bears. Real ones and ones like me. It's a whole—," he stopped. "Never mind."

Erica wanted to urge him to continue, but Kyle cut her off, "Plus you're helping your sister, right, man?"

"Yeah, it's on me to put her through college. My parents can't help her." Derek made a dismissive gesture as if the sacrifices he was willing to make for his family were no big deal.

Derek talked about his bookish sister, Anna. He joked about how much of a nightmare it was to live with someone who always thought they knew better than you, especially because they were right. Erica was taken aback that they moved off their main subject so quickly. She knew how uncomfortable boys usually were around crying girls and wondered if they didn't want to risk her tearing up again.

Erica used the interlude to check in with Xander. She reached up and put her pointer finger on his chin, her eyes searching his face. Disappointment was written across it after having, for a fleeting moment, thought answers about what he was could be found somewhere. In the brief time she had known him, Xander had not expressed a particular desire to understand the mechanics behind becoming and being a dryad. She could see now that the wheels were starting to turn, and she worried for him.

Erica heard Kyle say her name. She turned from Xander, and Kyle repeated his question. "I was asking why you chose Cascades. We were talking about Oregon schools."

The honest answer—the library—would land lamely in this company, so Erica told them the reasons she gave her parents. Small class sizes, compact campus, good financial aid. Close but not too close to home for holidays and long weekends. Derek asked questions about other schools she toured, and she answered them. Kyle teased her. The conversation flowed smoothly among them, and Xander even spoke up occasionally, mostly to agree with something someone had said.

Erica wanted to trust that they had come through the worst of it, that she had smoothed things over with everyone, and that Xander would be safe. She could attribute the stony expression Kyle gave her whenever their eyes met to her inability to stop touching Xander. But she knew he was the only person in the room who had nothing to lose. It made her—but more importantly, Xander—vulnerable. She would have to be on her guard.

CHAPTER 3

Two days later, on a Tuesday morning, Erica kissed Xander goodbye in Granny's driveway. The idea of leaving him behind, if only for a few days, was unbearable. She had gotten into the habit of having him accompany her to work at the store just so that she could make sure he was still there, real and whole, whenever a memory of that day came unbidden into her mind. Erica would have been willing to stand up to her mother's wrath at bringing a boy to her college orientation if it had been possible. But Xander couldn't leave Juniper Falls, and Erica couldn't stay.

As she drove parallel to the clear blue-green Umpqua River, she was mildly embarrassed about how needily she had clung to him as they kissed, balling up the back of his gray wool sweater in her fists. Just the day before, Granny had gifted Xander Keith's wardrobe after realizing he had run out of clean clothes in less than a week. Though every piece was several inches too short, Granny showed him how to push up sleeves and roll up cuffs to make it appear intentional. Erica felt guilty for stretching out the well-loved pullover that she remembered Keith wearing on more than one family holiday. But she couldn't help it. Driving away from Xander felt like a betrayal even if he did keep encouraging her to go.

The drive from Juniper Falls to College of the Cascades near the hipster town of Bend was almost as far as the one from Juniper Falls to Portland. The points of these locations formed the mountain-hopping triangle in which Erica's whole life was to be conducted. As she made her way northeast, the tall trees and fern-filled underbrush thinned out and gave way to the high desert of Central Oregon. Miles of squat, identical pines stretched before her interspersed with knobby shrubs.

Bend itself wasn't much to look at from the highway. Its charms lay off the main roads—a blend of foodie restaurants and breweries mixed with upscale housing and shopping to please the Californians who came rushing to the ski slopes to spend their tech dollars. Erica's destination lay still farther north and then west back toward the mountains, far enough out of town to not even be considered a suburb.

Erica had chosen Cascades because it felt so different from the other schools she toured. It boasted the student-teacher ratios typical of liberal arts schools while being unambiguous in its intentions to prepare students for the working world. While it offered softer subjects—Erica had spent too much of the summer drooling over their English courses—even these paths of study were geared toward future lawyers, not poets. Erica figured this was how she had gotten in with such a generous financial aid package. She couldn't remember a single week in her life when she hadn't contributed to the operation of one or the other of her family's stores. Her work ethic aligned neatly with the college's mission.

She supposed her aesthetic did too. As Erica turned her midnight blue sedan emblazoned with the silver *Juniper Falls Farm & Feed* logo onto the main street of campus, half the girls she saw walking between classes were carrying the same throwback navy backpack with a faux leather bottom that sat next to her in the passenger seat. Their puffy jackets, skinny jeans, and ankle boots matched the outfit she was wearing piece-for-piece. She was struck by the familiar feeling she had growing up in Portland of being just another moderately smart and generically pretty girl among hundreds. Pulling her car up to the administration building where she was supposed to pick up her itinerary for the next two days, she was tempted to turn around and head back to Juniper Falls, to the people who made her feel the most seen.

This feeling was not helped by the sight of her mother who was standing in front of a parking meter, her long acrylic fingernails tapping against the screen of her phone. To Erica's displeasure, Danni, in a tailored tartan jacket and leggings, stood out against the blander adults mingling around the entrance.

"You're late," Danni said as Erica got out of the car and headed toward her.

"By fifteen minutes on a three-hour drive."

"And your roots are growing out. We should do something about that while we're here."

This Erica could not argue. She and her mother had the same shade of mousey, not-quite-blonde hair. While Erica's was currently coppery after fading from a deep red, Danni's was dyed a rich caramel with expensive-looking lowlights. Only Erica and her father knew that this was the result of many years of trial and error with every brand of drugstore box dye under the sun.

After giving her daughter an appraising once-over, Danni pulled Erica into a quick one-armed hug before gesturing with her phone to the door. "That looks more like a resort than a school."

Erica couldn't tell if her mother meant this as a criticism or a compliment. She always had trouble divining her mother's intentions. It was true that Cascades did not have a traditional campus feel. Most of the buildings were huge timber structures with mosaics of windows and sloping charcoal roofs, reminiscent of the nearby ski lodges. Thick, rough-hewn beams jutted out from the building in front of them, supporting a glass and iron canopy.

"Should we pick up our schedules?" Erica asked. "What are you supposed to be doing while we're here?"

"Feeling better about how much money I'm about to give them," Danni said, as they made their way inside.

Erica sighed. She had received scholarships and grants to cover most of her tuition. Room and board weren't cheap, but she knew her parents had been saving for college since her mother dropped out while pregnant with her. Erica already felt worryingly unsure about and unprepared for choosing a major and, by extension, a career. The guilt trips, peppered throughout conversations with her mother like emotional landmines, didn't help.

Taking one more deep breath, Erica pushed the looming dark thoughts from her mind. She needed to create positive associations with this place if she was going to thrive here. This was made easier as they stepped into the airy atrium. Light spilled in from all angles, highlighting the tastefully designed mix of wood, metal, and concrete.

Erica had expected her orientation to be something like in the movies where hundreds of students stood in line to approach folding tables strung with bright banners. If she had started on time in the fall like she was supposed to, she may not have been disappointed. But winter orientation appeared to only require one table manned by two girls wearing forest green fleece quarter-zips embroidered with the school mascot, a bull elk.

"Hi!" the brunette girl said, her toothy smile on full display.

"Um, Wright," Erica said, nodding toward the milk crate of files sitting on the table.

"Right, what?" asked the other girl, a blonde.

"My name. Erica Wright." Erica looked at her mother, and they shared a clandestine eye roll.

"Oh, sorry!" the blonde apologized as she flipped through the files. She pulled out two fat manila envelopes and handed them over. She then consulted the list on her clipboard. "Erica, you are going to be rooming with a sophomore. Her name is Robin. Room 512 in Brookings Hall."

"I thought I was staying with my mom at the hotel?"

"Oh, no. Orientation is about getting the full Cascades experience so that you're ready to start in January. Your temporary room key is in your welcome packet. The first session is at two. If you're hungry, your room key also doubles as your meal pass while you're here. Same for you Mrs. Wright. I recommend the Indian place in the big cafeteria in the Student Union Building. Do you need a map?" This was a lot to take in. Erica planned on nodding, but the blonde girl already pulled a map from a pad in front of her. She drew a line in highlighter between their current location, her preferred lunch spot, and the dorm. "Any questions?"

Erica looked at her mother again. Danni shrugged. "I guess not."

"Great!" said the brunette. Erica wasn't sure if the intense smile ever left her face. "We will see you again tonight for our meet and greet. Seven o'clock. Mountainview Ballroom Number One." Seeing the look on Erica's face, the girl reached across the table and tapped the envelope in Erica's hand. "It's all in the packet."

Erica thanked them, doing her best to sound sincere rather than annoyed. She couldn't picture ever being sure enough of herself and of this place to talk like those girls did. Since meeting Xander, there had been so little time for Erica to brood over her future. Away from him, her all too familiar anxieties manifested once again. She wished he could be here. He had a way of making her feel braver than she was.

Danni led Erica across the atrium in the opposite direction that they came. They exited into a sunny and expansive commons that served as the heart of the campus. As Danni tried to get their bearings on the map, Erica checked her phone. A text from Xander read: *Hope you made it safe. Don't forget to take pictures of the library for me. Love you.*

Erica must have been grinning, prompting a rebuke from her mother. "Unless you have nav up on that screen, put your phone away and help me find the Student Union."

Erica texted back a quick: *Here. I will call you tonight.* She slipped her phone back into her purse.

"Tell me that wasn't Kyle Zukowski making you look that happy."

"What?" Erica protested. It took her a moment to register why her mother would even think that. Then she remembered how Kyle had been desperate for her attention at Keith's funeral. She recovered and responded, "No. God no."

Danni drew her lips into a thin line, a gesture Erica knew meant she didn't believe her. Erica could see how the vehemence of her objection was suspicious, so she decided against making any further protest. She figured the easiest way to make it through the next two days was to put on her good daughter song and dance routine. She pushed her doubts out of her mind, straightened her shoulders, and gave her mother the thing she craved most in life—someone's full attention.

They wandered through campus taking note of any location that might be important for Erica when she started living here in nine weeks. They followed paths of gray imported cobblestones from the sciences building to a row of low greenhouses so full of condensation that it was impossible to see what was within them. The grass that grew between the walkways was so aggressively lush and vibrant that Erica wondered if dryads were more common in Oregon than she realized.

When her mother suggested they visit the library, Erica declined and suggested they grab lunch after all. Danni's eyebrows shot up, but she didn't argue. Erica inherited her love of reading from her grandmother, and it had skipped a generation. She wanted to save that experience for when she was alone so that she could remember as much as possible to relay to Xander.

After their stroll through the sparsely populated commons, Erica was unprepared for the chaos of the Student Union Building. The doors must have been made from soundproof glass because the moment they opened them, they were overwhelmed by a cacophony of voices, clinking plates, and cash registers with an undercurrent of barely discernible Top Forty music. The smells were no better. The SUB's cafeteria appeared to serve food from every content except Antarctica. Nearest to the door were pizza and Chinese, which did not complement each other. She spotted a lighted sign farther back that read *Curry in a Hurry*.

"Let's do Indian," Erica said, opting to take the check-in girl's suggestion rather than try to compromise with her mother. They fought their way through the crowd and stepped into the roped-off line behind a dozen or so students.

"This is crazy," Danni said, looking around. "I hope you have other food options."

"Online it said there's another dining hall closer to the dorms but there aren't as many options."

"Might be worth it to avoid this."

Erica also found it a little overwhelming, but she wasn't going to admit it. Plus, she discovered the student workers moved quickly, as they largely were just responsible for ladling your choice of three pre-prepared curries over rice. After grabbing their trays, Erica and Danni scanned their cards at the registers and were presented with a new challenge—finding somewhere to sit. All the two- and four-tops were full. They were forced to take chairs across from each other on a long table otherwise filled with students, some engaged in shouted conversation, others pouring over bulky textbooks. It was so loud that they didn't bother trying to talk.

After lunch, their prescribed itinerary began. Danni was due to sit in an auditorium with the other parents to listen to a lecture on allowing your child to make their own decisions. Danni voiced skepticism that this would yield any value for her, but Erica hoped she would take detailed notes. Erica had to make her way quickly across campus for an official tour, which, she shouldn't have been surprised to discover, was led by the smiley brunette who had checked her in. The first thing she did was make them all put on name tags; hers read, Amanda.

It turned out that, on a campus that wasn't even half a century old, there wasn't much in the way of exciting history to discuss. No one famous had attended. No world-changing theories were discovered. The most interesting thing to note was occasionally when an alumnus made enough money to fund the renovation of a wing or two and have their name slapped on the front in bronze.

Erica tried to catch the eyes of her group of ten or so fellow enrollees, hoping to connect with at least one. Her attempts fell flat, and she found herself in the back of the group barely paying attention. At the end of the tour, when they were advised to break into two small groups to get to know each other better, Erica realized that everything she wanted to say about herself—about Keith, about Xander, about her autumn in Juniper

Falls—would come off as crazy. She focused on her life in Portland and helping her parents run the store, which wasn't nearly as interesting to her peers as the girl who had her spoken word poetry featured on NPR or the guy who was starting a quarter late after spending an extended vacation at his family's ancestral home in Greece.

Erica was thankful when Amanda broke up the conversation and herded the group into one of the timber buildings that were already blending together. They were due for a meeting with campus security for a discussion on personal safety and the Cascades code of ethics. Everything about orientation was felt like fodder for new college-related fears when Erica spotted a familiar thick brown ponytail connected to an even more familiar face.

"Cora!" she yelled, so loudly that half the group turned to look at her.

Cora scanned the crowd, trying to find the person who called her name. She pivoted on the wedge of her too-tall heels until she saw Erica. When their eyes locked, Erica thought she saw a friendly light shine through them before they suddenly went dark. Cora walked slowly over to Erica as if at any moment she might change her mind and head into the lecture hall instead.

"What are you doing here?" Erica asked, opting to punch Cora lightly on the arm rather than giving her the hug that she needed in that moment.

"If you would have picked up your phone in the last two weeks, you would have known I would be." Cora was unable to keep the venom out of her voice.

Erica froze. In the excitement, she forgot that Cora tried reaching out—multiple times—in the aftermath of the chaos caused by the bear dryad. She had been so caught up in losing Xander and then in the relief of having him back that calling Cora hadn't crossed her mind.

"I'm so sorry. Things were so crazy after everything."

"Yeah, they were. My dad, the whole town council, they had to try to keep it quiet and clean it all up. And you were nowhere to be found."

"I'm sorry. I was dealing with something."

"Something related to you sneaking around with Kyle, Derek, and Alex?"

"Xander," Erica corrected her automatically.

"Seriously, Erica?" Cora snorted like an angry bull. The last of the students had entered the classroom, and Amanda held the door open for them. Cora glared at her. Amanda took the hint, letting the door close behind her. Cora snapped her attention back to Erica. "Everyone saw you guys cutting across Main Street together. I heard that you came and grabbed Kyle and Derek out of your store where they were safe. Why?"

Erica thought hard about how to explain herself. The truth was out of the question. Unless Cora already had it from someone else. "What has Kyle told you?"

"Kyle hasn't told me shit, Erica. He said I had to ask you. Which means there is something to tell."

Erica made a mental note to thank Kyle for his discretion but part of her wished he had already fabricated a lie that she could corroborate. "I wish I could tell you. I do."

"Can you at least tell me what you know about what happened? What was that thing?"

"A bear," Erica said, but she could hear the lack of conviction in her voice.

"Bears don't make trees shoot fully grown out of asphalt."

They stood in the hall, Erica somehow feeling small despite the height she had on Cora, even wearing her heels. She wished Cora would yell at her instead of silently seething.

"What is your dad telling people?" Erica asked. It didn't feel right to keep talking about it, but she couldn't think of anything else to say.

"He only has guesses. The bear was a genetic mutant. The trees were always there, waiting for a crack in the pavement to burst out. He's telling everyone that if they say anything the government will overrun the town, and you know how they feel about the government."

"It seems like he has it under control."

"He doesn't, Erica." Cora stomped her heel in frustration.

"Mitch has it under control. He has the media contacts and the money to keep people out of Juniper Falls if he doesn't want them there."

Erica bristled at the name of the head of the Kriners logging operation. As far as she was concerned, he should be the one to deal with the fallout. It was his illegal activities that caused the bear to lash out after being dormant for who knows how long. "Well, as long as Mitchell is involved, I'm sure we're fine."

"You don't get to be sarcastic about the only person who is doing something about this. He knows you know something. I'm sure he's just waiting to see if he can figure it out first."

Cora glared at her, but Erica didn't dare to open her mouth to someone who had just admitted they were in bed with Kriners. She so badly wanted to have a friend on campus but the cost of slipping and saying something to Cora was too high. She willed Cora to correctly interpret the sadness on her face, but Cora snorted and walked right past her out of the building. Erica considered following her and trying to explain. Instead, she opened the door to the auditorium as quietly as possible and took a seat in the back. With any luck, this was just another example of Cora's notoriously hot temper. Erica hoped she would cool off and all would be forgiven, preferably before the start of the quarter.

CHAPTER 4

Erica could barely concentrate the rest of the afternoon. She sat alone through two more presentations, one focused on the groups, activities, and intramural sports teams she could join to meet people. She watched the other future students nod along as they were listed out and wished reading and working weren't her only hobbies.

After they were dismissed, she found her mother in the ballroom for the welcome banquet and mixer. Danni started making a snide remark about how much of a waste of time the day had been when they ran into Cora's parents. While Erica's mom was much younger than Cora's dad, they both grew up in Juniper Falls, which meant they were well acquainted. They fell easily into reminiscing about their shared past including her uncle Keith, who had been known to play poker with Bobby Hendricks when his schedule allowed.

Erica and Cora put on a show around their parents rather than have to explain their falling out. They sat next to each other through all three courses of the catered dinner—a wilted arugula salad, chicken in too much cream sauce, and sweaty cheesecake—and were polite but distant. At one point Mr. Hendricks vaguely alluded to the events of two weeks ago but, seeing the confusion on Danni's face, dropped the topic and moved on.

By the end of the evening, Erica was exhausted and already weary of yet another new experience. She begged her mother to let her share her hotel room, but Danni insisted she go meet her new roommate. They left the ballroom, picked up Erica's bag from her car, and walked the entire length of campus for at least the third time that day. From her tour, Erica now knew that the handful of tall, boxy buildings that looked awkwardly authoritarian next to their sleek, timber-framed neighbors were the residence halls. Their stucco exteriors were painted with multi-storied murals that tried their hardest to distract from the buildings' oppressive symmetry. Brookings Hall, Erica's soon-to-be home away from home, featured a gray-toned abstract rendering of the Three Sisters, the volcanic peaks that dominated the skyline in this part of Oregon.

"Meet you here in the morning?" her mother asked.

"Depends. Are you having breakfast in your hotel first?" Erica made sure the eye roll came across in her tone.

"Grow up," her mother snapped, her usual cattiness giving way to genuine anger. She tossed the overnight bag she had been carrying for Erica at her feet. "I'm tired of you not showing any gratitude for how lucky you are. You get to go to the college of your choice. As long as you play your cards right, you'll graduate without debt. You will have opportunities that no one else in this family ever has."

"You sound jealous."

"I am jealous, Erica. I thought I was clear about that."

Erica stood her ground and met her mother's eyes with her chin up, but she could feel hot embarrassment coursing through her. She was glad it was dark. Her mother was objectively right. Erica knew she had no reason to be as obstinate as she had been today. Everything was rubbing her the wrong way, and it wasn't anyone's fault but her own. She could have shown more interest in her peers during the tour. She should have tried harder to win over Cora. And for all her mother's flaws, wasn't she here, supporting Erica through it all?

If their relationship was different, if Erica was different, she would apologize, and they would hug. But they weren't, and Erica grabbed the bag from the ground.

"I'll text you when I'm up."

She already had the keycard in her hand, which made for a quick getaway. Without looking back, she threw open the glass door and headed toward the staircase, not having the patience to wait for an elevator.

Erica's first impression of her dorm was that it smelled like industrial-grade cleaner and was excessively beige. Beige speckled linoleum, beige walls, and off-white doors and trim. Unlike the gorgeous atriums of the administrative building and the library that she still had not visited, the ceilings here were low and the lights fluorescent. She ascended the stairs, taking note of the floor numbers as she passed them.

She pushed through the door marked with a three-foot-tall number five and landed on a floor that was much quieter than she had been expecting. Low music played from a handful of open doors. She could hear a shower running in some distant bathroom. Erica checked her phone. It was about ten-thirty on a Tuesday. Even so, she had been led to believe that this many newly emancipated young adults living in one place would be rowdier.

Erica scanned the room numbers looking for 512. The walls were crammed with cork boards and whiteboards decorated with take-out menus, long overdue reminders for scholarship deadlines, and flyers for everything from upcoming basketball games to art shows. Midway down the hall, she found what she was looking for. In addition to the brass room number, the woodgrain door was decorated with construction paper flowers that read Robin and, much to her surprise, Erica. Steeling herself for whoever was on the other side, Erica knocked lightly on the door. It flew open so fast that Erica jumped back.

"I've been wondering when you would show up!" the girl who must be Robin squealed. "Come in!"

Robin hugged Erica tightly, which normally would have made her uncomfortable. But something about Robin's body, soft in all the places Erica's had hard angles, and the mild, pleasant smell of sandalwood that radiated from her frizzy, chestnut-colored hair, made Erica relax. She hugged the other girl back as if they had known each other for years.

"Sorry I'm so late," Erica said, pulling away and peering around the room. It was as though an invisible line was drawn down the middle. The side Erica was supposed to inhabit had predictably beige carpet and walls. Its furniture—a desk, a raised bed, and a short dresser—were all a nondescript light wood and conspicuously lacking in any kind of ornament. The bed had been made with white sheets and a white duvet like a mid-range hotel room. The other side—Robin's side—was an explosion of rainbows, tie-dye, and florals from the rugs on the floor to the fuchsia mosquito net hanging over her bed. Robin's desk was wrapped in what appeared to be wallpaper that had time traveled from a living room in 1963. Glitter gel pens sprang from the horn of a ceramic unicorn next to an open laptop.

Robin must have noticed Erica eyeing her stuff. Her cheeks went pink, and she said, "I know it's a lot, but it makes it feel a little less lonely in here. My last roommate dropped out about three weeks in."

"Why?" Erica asked. She threw her bag on the bed and jumped up to sit on it. It was harder than she would have liked, and she made a mental note to buy a mattress pad.

"Oh, stuff happens. Boyfriends and whatever."

"Did she get pregnant?"

"Ha. No," Robin said as she exhaled, the blush on her cheeks deepening. "She dropped out so she could be closer to him. She said she was going to transfer to a college in Seattle."

It clicked for Erica that Robin was trying to present the facts in as non-judgmental a way as possible, and it made her like her even more. She decided she needed to take a softer approach.

"You're a sophomore? What's your major?"

"Computer science. You?"

"To be determined. But probably Business Administration. I have my first advising session tomorrow." Erica had been trying not to think about that part of orientation. She didn't want to unload on Robin in their first meeting, so she kept the conversation moving. "Computer science is cool. I wish I had the brain for that."

"You probably do," Robin said, turning her desk chair around and sitting down so they were facing each other. "Code is just another kind of language. If you can learn to talk, you can learn to code."

Erica assumed that at some point there had been a chair at Robin's desk that matched hers—a lifeless plastic swivel chair—but it had been replaced by a wide, wing-backed version upholstered in poppies on a deep teal background. The chair took up almost a quarter of the small room, but Erica didn't mind. Robin's style did liven the place up.

"I don't think most of us learn code in our infancy."

"You do when both of your parents are developers," Robin replied with a grimace. "I built my first app in middle school."

"Impressive. My parents run a small business."

"Hence Business Administration."

"It's a little depressing how much influence our parents have over us, isn't it?"

They laughed. Erica was relieved. Robin had a warm, easy energy coupled with a quick wit that reminded her of Granny but in a very different package. Erica hadn't been worrying about whether she would get along with her roommate, but she was sure she would have if she hadn't been so distracted recently.

"You're from Portland?" Robin asked.

Erica almost corrected her and said *Juniper Falls* before she remembered that she was in fact from Portland. She closed her mouth and nodded. "You?"

"Bay Area."

"That tracks. How did you wind up in Central Oregon?"

"Do you know what the population density is in San Francisco? My parents are workaholics, so I grew up right in the middle of it. My sister wound up going to school at Ball State."

"I don't even know where that is."

"Exactly."

Erica was about to ask what classes Robin had tomorrow when her phone buzzed. Xander hadn't texted her since the morning. She knew he was trying to give her the space she needed to get comfortable with the campus, and she was trying not to rub her ability to have this experience in his face. But right now, she needed his voice, his reassurance.

"I need to make a call," Erica said. She looked around the tiny room as if a private nook was going to make an unexpected appearance. "I guess I'll talk in the hall?"

"There are a couple of study carrels at the end. They should be free this late."

"Thanks." Erica checked her coat pocket for her key and slid off the bed.

Her hand was on the doorknob when Robin, failing to keep the disappointment out of her voice, asked, "Boyfriend?"

Erica understood the unspoken implication. "Yeah. He's chill, though. Supportive."

"Okay. Nice. That's great," Robin said, as if trying to make herself believe it.

Erica wasn't sure what she could say to reassure Robin. She felt the too-familiar twist of guilt in her stomach, but she pushed it down with thoughts of Xander and went in search of a quiet corner.

When Erica got back to the room after giving Xander a play-by-play of her day, Robin was already in bed with the lights out. Erica fished in the dark for her toothbrush and face scrub and found the bathroom on her own. After washing off the day, she slept fitfully on the hard mattress and woke up at six o'clock, unable to go back to sleep. She cursed herself for not bringing her laptop and settled for scrolling through her phone. Erica had never shared a room with anyone before, and she wasn't sure of the protocol. She figured deliberately waking someone before the sun was up was not a great beginning to their friendship, especially after the boyfriend conversation.

Robin wasn't in any hurry to start her day. Erica gave up on waiting when she received a text from her mother asking where they should meet for breakfast. Without replying, Erica grabbed her bag and headed to the bathrooms. She didn't want to get an earful about sleeping in when all she was trying to do was be a good roommate.

Erica walked past the toilets and the long vanity in the front of the bathroom through the swinging doors to the showers. She was immediately confronted with the naked body of one of her floormates. The girl barely registered Erica as she toweled herself off.

There were four curtained stalls with a low wooden bench in front of each. Erica put her bag down on one and pulled her towel out as slowly as she could, trying not to look in the girl's direction. The girl was not in any kind of rush, and Erica was worried that her delay tactics were getting awkward. She trained her eyes straight ahead and tentatively pulled off her pajama top.

"New?" the girl asked, as she slipped on a pair of loose basketball shorts.

Erica snapped her arms across her chest. "Yeah. Orientation."

"You get used to it," she said. Erica wasn't sure if she meant co-showering specifically or Cascades overall. Erica nodded but didn't remove any more clothing. The girl smiled and pulled a white tank top over her head without having put a bra on first. It didn't help her look any less naked. "I'm Madison. Room 504."

"Erica. I'm rooming with Robin."

"You're lucky." Madison picked up a plastic shower caddy, a useful purchase Erica made a mental note of, and threw her towel over her arm. "Robin is the best. She's like everyone's mom but in a good way. Wait until she makes you microwave brownies."

"Looking forward to it." Erica knew she wasn't coming off as sincere, but she couldn't overcome her discomfort. Madison seemed like someone she wouldn't mind getting to know better when they were both fully clothed even if she did get the feeling that she was stalling to watch her squirm.

"Okay, well, see you around," Madison said with a hint of a smirk.

Erica watched her go before quickly pulling off the rest of her clothes and darting behind the curtain with her sandwich bag of toiletries. She showered and dressed with lightning speed, managing to successfully avoid any further unwanted conversations. She all but sprinted back down the hall, her hair still wet and makeup undone, and only felt safe when she slammed the door to her room behind her. Then she gasped and turned toward Robin's bed but thankfully her roommate was already awake.

"I'm so sorry about that," Erica said, pointing to the door. "To be honest, the shower situation freaked me out a little bit."

"I heard," Robin said, failing to conceal a laugh. "Madison texted me."

"Oh god." Erica dropped her bag on the floor and sat behind her desk, her head in her hands. "I'm not sure I can do this."

"You definitely can." Robin gave her a serious look. "Give me a second to get ready, and we'll get something to eat."

"How busy is the dining hall this time in the morning? It might not be worth the stress."

"We could grab a donut and coffee at the cafe near the library."

Erica dropped her hands. "Library?"

"Yeah. Does that sound good?"

"That sounds perfect."

Erica texted her mother that she was having breakfast with her roommate. Danni could not argue about this, as it fell in line with the true college experience she had been pushing. They agreed to meet up at ten o'clock for what their itineraries identified as team-building exercises. Erica was glad to have a brief respite before what was sure to be a trying day.

She had planned an outfit for her advising appointment that would not have been out of place at a job interview. She panicked for a moment when she realized she forgot her blow dryer. Robin did not own one—her hair was wild enough without applying heat—but she was able to track one down from another girl on the floor. Erica felt confident as they left their room to head for the cafe, but that confidence withered when she realized how out of place she looked. Erica was dressed more like faculty in her pencil skirt and ruffled blouse, and she found herself wishing she could swap with Robin's comfortable overalls and pastel hoodie.

Erica was trying to swallow her nerves when they turned a corner, and the library sprang into view. Twice as big as any other building on campus, the Carter Memorial Library was an architectural wonder. The exterior was in line with the ski lodge style of the rest of Cascades, but Erica knew that inside was a white, modern, sun-soaked haven. She was drawn to the wood and glass double doors at its entrance, and Robin had to grab her arm to pull her in the direction of a little cafe Erica hadn't noticed before.

Whereas the library was defined by tall ceilings and light, the cafe was in the style of a British pub, all polished leather and wooden beams. The bitter smell of strong, black coffee hit Erica's nose as she walked in, and woke her up as much as a cup of it was likely to. The volume of students wasn't nearly as crazy here as in the dining hall but there were still more than a dozen people in line. Erica wondered if there was anywhere on campus that wasn't packed. The fact that there might not be sent a shiver up her spine.

The cafe's pastry selection was limited. Erica settled on a big apple fritter, a banana, and a drip coffee. Robin opted for a cream-filled donut and a chai tea. Her dining card didn't work here, so Erica offered to pay. Robin declined, but she could tell the gesture was appreciated. The girls settled themselves at a booth in the corner farthest from the register. The leather creaked under Erica as she scooted toward the window.

"This place is great," she said, peering out into the library courtyard where a constant stream of students went in and out of the big doors. "Thanks for bringing me here. I've spent the last few months in Juniper Falls. That's where my family is from. Only a couple thousand people live there. I think I got used to all the quiet. And the privacy."

"Where is Juniper Falls?" Robin asked, sipping her tea.

"Like three hours southwest of here in the mountains. I lived there until I was eight."

"Why have you been down there for so long?"

Erica tensed. She was dreading this part. She couldn't lie to Robin. Keith's disappearance and his obituary were in the newspapers. For all she knew Robin already completed a thorough internet search on her and was pretending she didn't know to be polite. Erica gave her the high-level version—Keith's disappearance, needing to help her grandmother, and the eventual discovery that Keith had been killed in an animal attack. She left out that there was an ongoing murder investigation and her involvement in bringing down an ancient supernatural being. Because how could you ever tell that to someone you've known less than twelve hours? It was fortunate that having a recently deceased relative was enough to stop most people from asking follow-up questions.

Robin frowned sympathetically. "It sounds like you've had a lot to deal with lately."

"I have." Erica wanted to add *more than you know*.

"Are you going back to Portland after orientation? It's almost the holidays. Your parents must want you back."

Erica shook her head. "Xander can't leave Juniper Falls, so I'm going to stay down there until the semester starts."

"Xander is your boyfriend?" Erica nodded and tore off a piece of her delicious apple fritter. "Why can't he leave?"

Alarm bells rang in Erica's head. She had let her guard down for a split second and now she had to fabricate an excuse for why Xander was stuck. She ran through plausible scenarios knowing that every second she didn't answer made her story less credible.

"He has to take care of his disabled uncle," she said, settling on what seemed like her strongest option. "The rest of his family passed away, so they don't have anyone else."

Robin made a sympathetic face. "I can see why you guys are together. You both seem like very compassionate people."

Erica's heart swelled at what may have been the best compliment she had ever received. She repaid it by asking Robin questions about herself. She learned that in addition to her older sister, Robin also had a younger brother. She was into digital art as a hobby. *Think Lisa Frank*, Robin said. Her parents were of

Irish and German descent, which meant her mother was very loud and her father was very quiet. Erica could relate. They chatted until well after their drinks had been finished and only vacated their booth after Erica got a text from her mother that she was leaving her hotel.

"Can I get your number?" Erica asked before they parted.

"Of course!" Robin took Erica's phone out of her hand.

"And, um, can I text you? Like if I have any questions before January?"

"Yes," Robin said, a slight edge of exasperation coming into her voice.

"No, sorry. It's fine."

"Erica," Robin said, handing her back the phone and grabbing her wrist. "We're friends, okay? You can relax."

It was like letting go of a breath she had been holding since last night. Erica hugged Robin, as tightly as the first time they met. "Thank you. I need that."

"We both got lucky. The truth is my last roommate was terrible."

"I knew it," Erica said smiling.

Robin smiled back. "I'll see you tonight?"

"Definitely."

Erica watched Robin walk back toward their dorm room and found herself processing the idea that she might be excited to start school. It was a warm, comforting feeling that could only be improved upon by a long-awaited visit to the building in front of her.

CHAPTER 5

Stopping in the library was going to make Erica late to meet her mother, but she couldn't wait until the afternoon. She was riding high on how well she was getting along with Robin, and she wanted to stretch that feeling as far as she could take it. Erica waited for a throng of students to enter before approaching the massive doors. On her first visit to campus, she stumbled into the library from where it connected to a cluster of other buildings. She had missed out on the work of art that was the main entrance. The doors were made of oak and carved to resemble the raw material from which they came. A thick trunk started at the ground and was split in half where the doors met. Asymmetrical branches wove out from the trunk up to the frame. The negative space was frosted glass against which the dark wood stood in highly polished relief.

Erica snapped a picture for Xander. Even though they could find beautifully lit, professionally produced photos of every inch of this campus online, Erica wanted him to see it through her eyes. She made her way through the doors ahead of another group of students that was threatening to push in from behind and landed in the room that sealed her fate as a future Cascades student. It was an overcast day, so the light wasn't as perfect as when she first saw it, but the effect was still stunning.

The main wing of the library was built around a four-story atrium crowned with a glass dome. Rows of books extended out in every direction like the spokes of a wheel. There was an enormous window and a couple of tasteful chairs where each row ended. Students sat casually in these chairs as if they didn't look like they were posing for a catalog. Erica searched for a directory and found a sign advertising an app that would let her identify the location and availability of any book in the library. This unfortunately required her to log in using her student identification number, which she was due to set up later that afternoon. It wasn't like she was looking for anything specific anyway.

Erica wandered through the stacks, taking general note of the layout. She was used to local libraries, which catered largely to entertaining children and the elderly. This was a college library, and the books were of a much different variety. The first floor was dedicated to the sciences. Erica ascended the spiral staircase up to the second floor, which focused on history, philosophy, and periodicals. She texted Xander a picture of a whole row of biographies. He responded right away.

Xander: You're bringing me back some of those, right?

Erica: I can't check anything out yet!

Xander: What is the point of having a fancy college girlfriend if she can't hook me up with books?

Erica smiled and continued to the next floor where she found the fiction she craved. It was a much smaller portion of the library than she had hoped and focused primarily on works she imagined would come up on the syllabi for literature courses. She ran her finger along the spines and breathed in the musky sweetness of the fading paper all around her.

Her phone buzzed again, and she checked the screen hoping to see Xander's name. It was her mother telling her that she had better see her face in the next ten seconds because she wasn't going to do these stupid icebreakers without her. Erica sighed and descended back to the ground floor. Before leaving the atrium, she took one last look and promised herself that she would never study anywhere else on campus.

Heading back through the oak doors, she picked up her pace so that she was only a few minutes late for a visualization exercise being led by Amanda. She was lucky that the silence in the room as parents and students meditated on their expectations for their first semesters meant that her mother was confined to making her displeasure known through glares. When they were asked to share their thoughts with those around them, Erica turned to pour her heart out to a guy with acne scars and a boy band haircut, forcing Danni to interact with the boy's father.

After their joint morning exercise, Erica was shuffled to a computer lab to get herself officially set up for registration following her advising appointment. She wasn't sure what Danni was signed up for the rest of the day, but Erica was trying to avoid having to talk to her until lunch when she knew she would have to play twenty questions about Robin. While her parents had made their expectations known regarding her major— something that sounded like a job title—her mother ultimately seemed most concerned about the peripherals. If she could hold off on spilling roommate details, she might not have to give a play-by-play of the academics.

At last, Erica was headed to her advising appointment. She expected to be led into one of the tiny offices that made up the top floors of nearly every building she had been in the last two days, each door bearing a name starting with the title of *Dr.* She imagined being asked to sit and having to first move a stack of half-graded papers from the chair. Her advisor would be older, gray, and bespectacled. They would tell her exactly what she needed to hear to know that she was heading in the right direction.

To her dismay, she and her cohorts were guided back to the ballroom where they had dinner last night. The round tables they sat at were still there, but the crisp, white tablecloths were replaced by pieces of paper with a large number printed on them. A person was stationed at each table with a laptop and a stack of papers in front of them. The blonde from check-in met them just inside the door. She took their names and pointed them toward their advisors.

"Wright," the blonde said when Erica approached. "I remember. Table three."

Her table was almost smack in the middle of the room. It was manned by a young woman who looked like she had maybe five years on Erica, which did not inspire much confidence. She was dressed in an argyle cardigan over a turtleneck, her copious hair in a messy bun. Erica sat down and placed the planner she received earlier that morning in front of her.

"Hi, I'm Grace. And you should be—." She consulted her notes.

"Erica."

Grace gave her a polite smile and referenced her laptop. "My records say that you plan to pursue a degree in Business Administration."

"Yes," Erica said, fighting to keep the hesitation out of her voice.

"What drew you to that major?" Grace's fingers were poised over the laptop, ready to take notes.

"My parents own a small business. It's a branch of my grandparents' store."

"And you want to take over the family business?"

"Oh hell no," Erica said, letting out the type of nervous laugh reserved for when nothing is actually funny. She realized her mistake when she saw the frown on Grace's face.

"What are your plans for after graduation, then?" Erica stared at her. She wished she knew. Grace tried again. "What is it that you like to do, Erica?"

The thought passed through Erica's mind that they could rescind her acceptance if she was too boring. She was embarrassed by how long it took her to formulate a response. "I don't know. I read. I used to swim." This was ridiculous. There had to be more to her existence. Erica sighed and threw her hands up. "I work a lot." It came out as an apology.

Grace took her fingers off the keyboard and folded them in front of her. She studied Erica before posing a different question. "What do you hope to get out of your time at Cascades?"

Erica inhaled as a stalling tactic. But before she could decide between telling the truth and saying what she thought the advisor wanted to hear, she was already talking. "I want to be independent. To focus on me. I want to find something I'm good at. And when I'm done, I want it to pay enough that I get to have a life outside of it." Erica said all this as fast as she could, surprising even herself with the answer.

If Grace was put off by her outburst, it didn't show. "Those are all achievable goals, Erica. They're why most people go to college even if they don't realize it while they're here. I love a kid with a passion, don't get me wrong, but only a handful of people in a lifetime get to be the president."

"I don't want to be president."

"Good for you. It's a terrible job." Grace smiled in earnest, and Erica relaxed. "I can tell there's something you really want to do. What is it?"

"I want to study English." Erica had expected to feel ashamed when she said it aloud, but Grace's placid face didn't change. "I just don't know what I would do with it."

"What do you like about English?"

"Reading. I get to put my life on hold."

"What if you created that experience for other people? Have you thought about Journalism or Advertising?"

"I don't know if I'm much of a writer." Most of the praise Erica received in her life was related to being forthright and dependable. Her grades were the result of hard work, spurred in no small part by avoiding confrontation with her mother rather than innate scholastic gifts. She couldn't recall a teacher telling her she had a particular aptitude for any one subject.

Grace went back to the computer. She clicked through a few screens and read something Erica couldn't see. She turned her attention back to Erica. "Your personal essay was good, but it's all about your parents' store. I think we could help you find your voice."

"How would you do that?"

"By trying a few things on. Why don't we put you in English 101 and a Humanities class? You should also take Introduction to Communications. Technically you should be admitted into the major first, but I have a feeling you will get something out of it."

Grace walked Erica through her course options, steering her helpfully away from classes that met too early or too late. She asked her more questions and recommended professors whose teaching styles she thought were a good match. When Erica squirmed, worried that this wishy-washy approach was going to cost her in the long run, Grace added Business Calculus.

"We pride ourselves on graduating our students on time," Grace said as she wrote out Erica's schedule, her loopy penmanship looking close to calligraphy. "This is your freshman year. Be bold. You have time."

Erica pressed the schedule into her planner, thinking about how it would look above the bed on the corkboard in the room she shared with Robin. For the second time today, she got a glimpse of what life could look like as a student, and it wasn't the worst.

"I appreciate this," Erica said as she stood up.

"Of course." Grace pulled a business card from a stack on the table. "Why don't you stick with me until you declare? Set up an appointment with me before you register for spring, okay?"

Erica thanked her again and floated out of the ballroom, not even minding that she got lost several times before finding her way out of the building. She was about to text her mother to meet her when Danni sprung up from one of the benches scattered under the eaves. She hurried toward Erica, looking around as if someone was going to tell her she shouldn't be there.

"You look happy," Danni said.

"I like my classes. Aren't you supposed to be in some separation support group or something?"

"I can't do it anymore." Danni picked at the gap between her cuticle and the start of her acrylics, a sure sign that she was anxious. "Do you want to skip the rest of this thing?"

"Mom! This was your idea."

"Yes, but I think we got everything out of it that we're going to, don't you?"

Erica had to admit that another afternoon of orientation sounded oppressive, but she was looking forward to spending the evening with Robin. She needed more information to weigh her options. "What would we do instead?"

"I was thinking we could grab lunch, color your hair, and try to find somewhere to get it cut in Bend. It's beyond time."

This was a good proposition. Her mother was happiest when they were doing something girly. "I'm in. Just let me text my roommate."

Robin was disappointed by but understanding of Erica's apology text. Erica slipped her phone into her pocket then realized that spending the day with her mother meant she wasn't going to be able to talk to Xander tonight. She shot him a message explaining the situation while her mother grumbled that she couldn't possibly have that much to say to someone she had known for less than a day.

Xander: What time will you be here tomorrow?

Erica: Hoping before noon.

Xander: Would you be up for a date?

Her heart leaped. With everything they had been dealing with since they met, the closest thing to a date Erica and Xander had been on was the hour they spent at the school fundraiser before rushing home. Going to a restaurant, ordering food, whispering across a table—it felt too ordinary to attempt, especially with someone who, as a rule, didn't eat. But if Xander was game, so was she.

Erica: Always. XO.

Erica did a little skip as she slipped her phone into her purse.

"Your mood has certainly improved since yesterday," her mother remarked.

Erica fought back a grin and lost. There was no harm in letting her mother think she was excited about college. She was. It just wasn't the only thing she had to look forward to.

The evening passed as pleasantly as Erica could have hoped considering it was spent with her mother. They found a cafe just off campus and realized too late it exclusively served vegan dishes but enjoyed their tofu stir fries nonetheless. Danni tracked down her preferred brand of hair dye at a salon supply store, and Erica picked out a deep auburn that was much more natural than her previous pomegranate. They dyed Erica's hair in the bathroom of Danni's hotel room and searched for well-reviewed salons while they waited for the color to set. Danni talked Erica into getting a long pixie with cheek-length bangs that covered her left eye.

They stayed up too late watching classic movies. Her mother bought wine at a grocery store and, after finishing a bottle herself, let Erica help her with the second. Forgetting alarms, they woke up much later than they had planned. When they were finally conscious, her mother was in a hurry to get out of Central Oregon after leaving Erica's dad in charge of the store for two whole days. Tossing their key cards on the beds, they left the hotel room and walked to their matching blue sedans.

"Are you coming home for Thanksgiving?" Danni asked as she transferred an enormous duffle bag of clothes from her car to Erica's.

"I can't leave Granny on her own to do Black Friday."

"Bring her with. That's what we promoted Joe for."

"I don't think that's a good idea, Mom." It was difficult to be back here, disappointing her mother again after such a pleasant day. But Erica had a suspicion that it had been at least a decade since Xander had a proper holiday, and she was already planning how to give him the full experience. "You and Dad should come down for Christmas like usual."

Danni pursed her lips, but she was in too much of a hurry to argue. They looked at each other. Erica waited to see if either of them would give in and make a gesture of affection.

"See you at Christmas, then," Danni said and got in her car.

Erica waved at her as she backed out, and her mother waved back with a small smile. That would have to be good enough.

CHAPTER 6

Erica had to try not to speed through the tight curves of the highway on her way back to Juniper Falls. Being away from Xander wasn't as hard as she had expected but knowing she would see him soon made the minutes feel like hours. When she finally pulled into Granny's driveway, she left everything in the car and sprinted to the door. It opened before she could turn the handle, and she fell into Xander's arms.

"Is Granny home?" Erica asked, scanning the room.

"I think she's at the store. Just me and Tulip."

Erica ran a hand down Xander's chest to the top of his jeans. She tugged on his belt loop. "I missed you."

"We said we weren't going to say that," Xander reminded her, but she could tell from the curve of his lips that he was pleased.

She kissed him, soft at first, but escalating quickly into a hungry, open-mouthed affair. Even his saliva tasted earthy, like oolong tea. She ran her hands under his sweater and slid a finger along his ribcage. She felt him shudder against her touch, and it thrilled her that she was able to have this effect on him.

Erica moved to pull off his t-shirt when Xander took a step back and came up for air. "Hang on, hang on. Our date."

"Can it wait just a little bit?" Erica breathed. She pouted playfully and peered at him under her eyelashes.

"Your hair!" Xander said in a less than subtle change of subject. He pushed her bangs out of her face with his long fingers before holding her out at arm's length to admire her new look. "I like it. You look more you somehow. Now go change. Nice but warm."

"All of my warm clothes are in the car. Where are we going?"

"It's a surprise," he said, looking mischievous. "I'll get your stuff."

Erica watched him from the window as he collected the big duffle from the trunk, as well as her overnight bag and purse from the front seat of her car. He chivalrously carried the whole load up to her bedroom. Erica made her best play to get him to stay there, laying a string of kisses from the base of his neck to his ear lobe, but he was intent on getting her out the door.

A disappointed Erica unzipped the bag full of winter clothes. She fished through it and pulled out a pair of black fleece-lined leggings and a blush, chunky knit sweater dress. Erica had forgotten to ask for a reinvigoration of her shoe collection, so she settled on her canvas sneakers. Checking her reflection in the vanity, she re-applied her tinted lip balm and fixed a smudge of eyeliner with her pinky finger. On her way out of her room, she grabbed the doorframe and retraced her steps, remembering the bracelet she bought Xander at the Harvest Festival. She had tossed it in the drawer of her nightstand during the dark days. So much had happened since then that she forgot about it entirely. Erica pulled the supple leather bracelet from the drawer and stashed it in her purse, ready to spring it on him when the moment presented itself.

Xander was waiting for her at the bottom of the stairs holding a wicker picnic basket and a bottle of sparkling apple cider. He had run a wet comb through his hair and was wearing another one of Keith's sweaters, this one an olive green that brought out the deep chocolate of his eyes.

"What's this?" Erica asked at the same time Xander said, "You look amazing." They smiled at each other. She grabbed the cider from him, and they walked out to the car after checking that Tulip was still safely snuggled in her dog bed by the fireplace. Erica was so used to being the chauffeur that she went for the driver's side. Alden hadn't let Xander take his tan pickup when he left, so they were stuck with Erica's car. Xander, however, deposited the basket in the back seat and opened the passenger door with a sweeping gesture.

"For me?" Erica asked.

"You don't know where we're going."

"Fair point."

She swapped sides with him and noticed she had left yesterday's shoes, a pair of sensible black pumps, on the floor of the passenger seat. She briefly considered swapping them out for her sneakers but caught a glimpse of the picnic basket and decided against it. Chances were they were headed somewhere that was better suited for hiking boots, and Erica admonished herself for thinking a date planned by Xander would be by the book.

As Xander drove, Erica told him all about Robin and the uncharacteristically peaceful evening she spent with her mother. She wasn't paying attention to where they were going and was surprised to find them turning onto the same forest road she had gone to with Cora when she was still unraveling the mystery of who Xander was and how he was tied to Keith. She recalled uncovering the newly cut stumps covered in salal and ferns, tall trees already springing in some cases directly from the sawdust. While this place was a piece of their shared history, it didn't strike Erica as a particularly romantic spot for a date.

Xander parked the car, and they gathered up their picnic. By now Erica was used to following him into the woods without asking too many questions. The sky was overcast, so even at the peak of the day, the walk felt ominous, the forest pressing in from all sides. Then they broke into a clearing and she saw their destination—a little gazebo, open on the side facing them, but otherwise draped in dense purple flowers.

"It's beautiful," Erica said as Xander led her inside. There she found what Xander must have envisioned were a table and low stools made of roots drawn from the ground below them. They lacked the finesse of Alden's living furniture she had seen back at their cabin, but she admired the attempt. The interior was also coated in flowers, though these were yellow and grew in little clusters. The dim light that made its way through the foliage reflected off the flowers giving the little room a golden hue.

Erica sat down, trying not to let Xander see her shift to find a comfortable position while he unloaded the basket. First came a gingham tablecloth.

"To cover up this travesty," Xander said, pointing to the makeshift table.

"It's not bad for a first try."

"The problem is, it's not my first try."

Erica laughed. "In that case, I have to tell you that I have a stick in a very unladylike location."

"I'm sorry!" Xander said, blushing. "Let me fix it." Erica stood up, and Xander ran his hand along the top of the stool. The roots snaked past each other, smoothing out the bumps and evening out their spacing. "Try it again?"

Erica sat down. "Much better."

"I swear they weren't like that when I left them yesterday. Trees seem to have a mind of their own. They don't always do exactly what I tell them. I'm better with flowers."

To prove his point, Xander put his hand on the bare earth under their feet and little green tendrils shot up, unfurling and sprouting leaves to cover the dirt floor. He put the tips of his fingers together and slowly spread them. Tiny periwinkle petals burst open like popcorn.

"Hell of a parlor trick," Erica joked. Xander gave her an exaggerated wink and returned to unpacking the basket. After the plates, utensils, and napkins came pulled pork sliders, potato salad, and a flourless chocolate cake topped with raspberries, exactly proportioned for two people.

"Those are Granny's specialties," she observed.

"She said these are your favorites. I helped her make them. It was my first time cooking."

Xander looked so proud of himself that Erica got up and gave him a loud kiss on the cheek. "You did good. It looks delicious."

Xander served up the food onto two plates as Erica returned

to her seat. Wanting to be useful, she found glass champagne flutes wrapped in dish towels at the bottom of the basket and popped open the bottle of cider. She poured the fizzy juice into the glasses and waited for the froth to dissipate before placing one in front of Xander.

It wasn't until he took his first bite of the messy slider that Erica realized how weird this was. "You're eating!"

Xander smiled, a dribble of barbeque sauce falling down his strong chin. "I wanted this to feel normal."

"You've never been on a date if you think anything about this is normal," Erica said, looking up into the canopy of flowers above their heads.

"Ouch," Xander said, but he took it like it was meant.

When the two of them were together like this, devoid of distractions, everything felt so uncomplicated and undemanding. Erica could forget that her life was on the precipice of yet another monumental change. She could focus on how Xander kept finding her legs under the table and running the balls of his feet up her calves. She discovered he would grab her hand whenever she complimented the food, so she made sure not to go three bites without saying something nice. They took a break before digging into the cake and sipped their cider like it was a fine wine.

"Thank you for this. I love it."

"And I love you."

The words came from him so effortlessly, so naturally that Erica had to widen her eyes to discourage tears. Though she read novel after famous romance novel and binged their television and film adaptations, she could never have imagined that this was what her own love story would look like. She wanted to savor every moment. She shifted in her seat intending to get up and settle herself into Xander's lap when she noticed a new expression had settled across his face.

"What's wrong?" she asked.

"Nothing is wrong exactly." The long pause after this attempt at reassurance put Erica on edge. "While you were gone, I was thinking about what the future looks like for us. I can't hide in your granny's house forever, especially after you start at Cascades."

"Of course you can. Especially if you're going to take up the cooking." Erica hoped he would let her make the joke and move on. She didn't like where this was heading.

"Erica, I'm serious. I have to figure out what I'm going to do. I don't think Alden is going to let me live with him again. Not if I, you know."

Erica did know. Xander couldn't make up with Alden if they were together. She felt deeply how unfair it was that he bore all the consequences of their relationship. Even so, she couldn't bring herself to suggest he let her go even if she knew he wouldn't. She wanted to tell him to stop, that they could do this another time. But she could see this had been weighing on him, and she owed it to him to share his burdens.

"What do you want to do?"

"I was thinking about asking Vivian if I could work in your store. Maybe take over a little bit for you when you leave."

"I'm sure she would love that." This was not what she expected, and she was relieved.

"You think?"

"Absolutely. She wouldn't let you stay with us if she didn't trust you. I'm sure Joe will do whatever she says."

Xander took a deep breath. "I forgot he's Kyle's dad."

"They're not the same at all. Joe is the sweetest. You'll like him when you get to know him."

He didn't quite look like he believed her, but Erica wasn't worried. She didn't think Joe had been rooting too hard for her and Kyle. He had always been a little scared of Erica's mother and did his best to stay on her good side. Erica was confident Joe would be as welcoming of Xander as he was of any other employee that had come through *Farm & Feed* during his long tenure.

"There's something else," Xander said. "There's a reason I brought you out here."

"Okay?" Erica picked up her fork and popped a bite of cake in her mouth. It was rich and melty and perfect.

"You know that the bear dryad regrew the trees in this area?" Erica nodded, helping herself to another bite. Xander continued, "Ever since we did what we did, I've felt uneasy. Anxious."

Erica put her fork down. "I don't understand."

"We killed it, right? Now Kriners is out here decimating the forest. What is here to stop them?"

"What? Do you want to sneak out here at night and plant forests?" Xander nodded. Erica's brain almost couldn't process what she was hearing. "That's crazy. You don't think that Kriners is suspicious as hell about what happened out here? Or what happened downtown? If you creep around their logging sites they're going to catch on. What if they figure it out?"

"How could they? Who would ever guess what I am?"

"You're playing with fire. This is a very bad idea."

"I thought you would understand," Xander said quietly. He slumped in his seat and ran his hand through his hair. In any other situation seeing Xander so dispirited would have made her give in to him immediately, but this was asking too much.

"I don't," Erica said. She had to stop herself from shouting. Xander doing anything that could result in her losing him again was beyond her ability to handle calmly. She stabbed the cake in front of her with her fork. She ate to fill the silence and didn't stop until she had made it through the whole thing. Xander didn't move a muscle until she threw the fork onto the empty plate with a clatter.

"You done?" he asked, sarcasm dripping from his voice.

"Obviously." She gestured to the empty plate.

"Since we took down the bear tree, I don't feel right. Not just because it rearranged my organs. Before, I could tap into the ecosystem when I needed to, get a little bit of a picture of what was going on. Now it's like there's a movie playing in the back of my head all the time."

"Why didn't you tell me?"

"I noticed it as soon as I was conscious again, but I was distracted with trying to heal and then being with you. But when you were gone and it was quiet, it got louder. Every time those assholes are out there with their chainsaws, I can feel it again. The way it felt to cut into the bear tree."

In all the hours they spent whispering to each other during late nights in her room, Erica had never heard Xander talk like this. She had asked him about his experience healing, and he gave her the physical details, the uncomfortable sensation of skin knitting itself together in record time. But they skirted around the psychological side effects of what they had done. She didn't give a voice to the panic that shot through her every time she lost sight of him, and he, apparently, neglected to tell her this.

"I don't see why you think putting yourself in danger is going to make any of that better."

Xander shrugged. "The forest is asking me for help. I can't just choose not to listen."

As much as every inch of her wanted to yell at him that of course he didn't have to, she knew that it would come off as sounding like she was telling him to listen to her instead. This was a part of Xander that she couldn't even pretend to relate to. She thought about trying to reach out to Alden who she was sure would also vehemently disapprove of this plan. Then an idea occurred to her, a way to potentially redirect Xander's call to action.

"I ran into Cora when I was at Cascades, and she's pissed that I haven't reached out to her or helped with the mess downtown. We should talk to Granny about how to help."

"Erica, I—."

"I know I can't stop you. But maybe the reason you feel so strongly about the tree part of you is that you don't spend enough time with the people part." Xander opened his mouth then shut it without protesting. He shrugged again, which Erica chose to interpret as agreement.

Erica cleared up their dishes, carefully repacking everything into the picnic basket. Xander watched her, unmoving, his expression unreadable. She knew she had disappointed him. He blindly supported and accepted every decision she made about her future. As much as she wanted to be able to do the same, she couldn't agree with him putting himself knowingly in the way of harm. They had found the bear dryad with a single camera. What was stopping Kriners, with all their resources, from using similar tactics to sniff out Xander?

The thought sent a shiver down Erica's spine. Suddenly she wanted nothing more than to be back in the safety of Granny's house. She pulled Xander up to his feet, trying and failing to get him to maintain eye contact with her.

"Ready to go?" she asked.

"Sure."

She gave him a quick hug that he did not return and charted the path back to the car. She thought about the bracelet in her purse, etched with acorns. It would be an empty gesture to give it to him now.

When Xander dropped himself into the passenger seat, not even helping her to put the basket away, Erica knew she had approached this all wrong. She made a silent promise to listen better and try harder to understand should he bring it up again. But she hoped that would be an if not when.

CHAPTER 7

Erica and Xander tiptoed around each other over the next few days, both careful not to make any reference to their argument. Xander's mood didn't recover, but it was unclear how much of that was related to her shutting him down and how much was adjusting back to not eating. It didn't take long for Erica to understand why the occasional indulgence wasn't worth it for him. He spent the second night after their date tossing in her bed, his stomach gurgling. When he woke the next morning, he was gaunt, tired, and unresponsive to her attempts at showing him affection.

This was the state Xander was in when he started his retail career. As expected, Granny thought that Xander working at the store was an excellent idea. So far Kyle was keeping Xander's secret. For all Joe knew, Xander was just a boyfriend who needed a job. In fact, after two weeks of Xander trailing behind Erica while she worked, Joe seemed relieved that he was finally there for a purpose. Joe put Erica in charge of getting Xander up to speed, which, in any other circumstance, would have been just another reason to spend time together. But instead of her usually mature, sweet Xander, Erica was stuck training one of the surliest teenagers she had encountered in her many years of supporting the family business. She had never known him to have a temper but little corrections like keying in the wrong code for a decorative gourd made him instantly withdraw.

It was Monday morning, and the store was quiet. Erica left

a part-timer to man the register while she and Xander worked on building out a Christmas display. She tasked him with transferring merchandise from the storeroom, figuring it was the best option for keeping him away from customers.

"You put all this stuff out before Thanksgiving?" Xander whined, pulling a flatbed trolley of plastic light-up snowmen to where Erica was clearing a space for them at the front of the store.

"Christmas starts November first in the big box stores. We're already a week behind."

"I wouldn't know."

While Xander had been snippy in general over the last three days, it was these comments that dug into Erica. She fought against the idea that his geographic restrictions had to be as limiting as he found them. Their disagreement on this topic tended to be the only real bruise on their otherwise healthy relationship. A starving and angry Xander was now determined to push on that bruise every chance he got. But years of living with her mother made Erica very good at not being baited into an argument so she changed the subject.

"Do you think we should put those cute boxes of handmade dog biscuits up here by the doors, or next to the counter?" she asked as she unloaded the snowmen. Xander gave an exaggerated shrug. Erica pitched her voice an octave and added, as sweetly as she could muster, "Do you want to grab them for me, and we'll see where they work best?"

Xander rolled his eyes at her and pulled the trolley to the back of the storeroom with all the enthusiasm of a little kid being called inside for the evening. Erica distracted herself from the show he was putting on by focusing on her display. Assembling the seasonal arrangements was one of her favorite parts of her job. Granny was undoubtedly better at them, but she had been avoiding the store more than usual lately. Erica was having a hard time wrapping her head around her first holiday season without Keith, and she imagined similar feelings were keeping Granny from wanting to be around the trappings of festivity. But when it came to working, the show had to go on, and Erica wanted to create something that Granny would be proud of.

She was mixing pounded metal lawn ornaments in with the snowmen when Kyle came through the doors. He was dressed for work in cargo pants and a jean-and-sherpa jacket. Even after everything that happened, he was still working for Kriners. Erica wished she could lay into him about it, but he was now part of Xander's safety plan. She had to play nice or at least as nice as she could manage without feeling complicit. Erica plastered on a smile and waved him over to admire her work.

"What do you think?" she asked.

"The hair? I like it," Kyle said. Then, pretending to have just figured out her meaning, "Oh? About the snowmen?"

"Ha. Ha." Erica said flatly, but she pulled her bangs into place. "Seriously, though. Do you think it's coming together?"

"Are you asking for my help?"

"You don't work here anymore, remember?"

"C'mon. You know your mom would say this is cluttered. *Not your best work*," he said in a bad imitation of her mother's high voice.

"How dare you!" Erica said, but she was laughing. Before she could help herself, she asked, "No logging today?"

Kyle shook his head. "I showed up but they had to move some equipment around and told us to come back this afternoon."

"So you thought you'd come volunteer here for a few hours?"

Kyle's face turned serious. He glanced toward where the part-time girl, a high school student a couple of years younger than Erica, stood a few feet away pretending not to eavesdrop. Kyle drew closer to Erica and lowered his voice. "I came to warn you. Cora said she ran into you at orientation, and you were kind of a bitch."

"I was not! She was super angry about," Erica checked herself and lowered her voice as well, "stuff. I tried to calm her down."

"She called me after and tried to interrogate me again about where we were while downtown was getting trashed. She's sure it has something to do with Xander."

Cora's relentlessness was one of the things Erica most admired about her friend, but she had never been on the other side of it. She knew it was in her best interest to stay out of the line of fire from people like Cora. She had to convince Xander to give up on his plans to regrow the forest. If Cora learned too much, and if she was as deep in bed with Kriners as it appeared, it was impossible he wouldn't get caught.

"What did you tell her?" Erica asked.

"Nothing. That we were just trying to stay safe like everyone else. I don't think she bought it."

A loud crash of metal against concrete caused Erica and Kyle to jump away from each other. Erica didn't have to look far for the cause. Xander was standing in front of them with a trolley full of dog biscuits, its swiveling handle on the floor, the clear source of the noise.

"It's getting cozy in here," Xander quipped. The expression on his face reminded her of what he looked like just before he shoved a chainsaw into the dryad tree, his chest puffed out and his eyes blazing with a mix of hurt, anger, and determination.

"Kyle was just giving me some news about Cora," Erica said as she deftly placed herself between Kyle and Xander just in case.

"Oh yeah? What?" Xander didn't take his eyes off Kyle.

"I'll tell you later. Kyle has to go to work."

Kyle was going to correct her, but Erica cut him off with a look. He hesitated as he made to leave. Erica marched up to him and led him by his bicep to the door.

"What's up with him?" Kyle whispered.

"He's not himself."

"No kidding. Are you okay?"

Erica looked back at Xander. Sure, he was being combative, but he was her gentle Xander who loved her. He made flowers grow from bare dirt just to make her smile. He put himself in this state trying too hard to give them—her—some sense of normalcy.

"It's fine. He'll snap out of it," she said with more confidence than she felt.

"Call me if you need to."

"I will."

Kyle opened the glass door reluctantly and left but not without getting a last nod of reassurance from Erica. Once he was gone, Erica pulled Xander past row after row of dusty metal shelves to the back of the store.

"You need to chill out. Now."

Xander just looked at her. While she couldn't be entirely sure, she thought she saw a line of vivid green shooting through his usually dark brown eyes. Erica reached out for him, but he took off back to the storeroom before they touched. She tried to decide whether to go after him or let it go. She felt a pair of eyes on her and turned just in time to see a look of pity on her employee's face. Not wanting to set the example of chasing after a jerk, she squared her shoulders and went back to her display.

Kyle was right. It was cluttered. Erica swore under her breath and took it all apart. She would put it back together, piece by piece, and it would be perfect. She could fix anything with enough time and patience. Because what other option was there.

After his temper tantrum at the store, Erica contemplated telling Xander he had to find some other way to earn his keep with Granny. When they got home that night, Erica watched movies on her laptop in her room while Xander read downstairs. She expected him to sleep in Keith's room and was surprised when he climbed wordlessly into her bed at almost midnight, keeping his back to her.

He was still in this position when she woke up the next morning. Erica reached a hand into the cold and increasingly familiar trench between their bodies. She ached to touch him but wasn't ready to face whatever iteration of Xander might show itself today. She was gathering her nerves to make the first contact when he inhaled deeply, and she dropped her hand, pretending to be asleep. She kept her eyes shut as he stirred. Then he did the exact thing that she hoped he would, that she needed him to do—he wrapped his arms around her, kissed her temple, and tucked her head under his chin. She put a hand on his chest and felt his heart beat slow and steady.

Erica inched ever so slightly out of his grasp to look at him. His eyes were closed, his expression was serene, and a smile lingered in the corners of his mouth. She gave him an off-center kiss, and he pulled her in again.

"Feeling better?"

"Mmm," he mumbled affirmatively. "Have I been awful?"

Now was not the time to get into it. "A little bit."

She folded herself into him as tightly as she could, and he stroked her side. They laid like this until Xander's hand stilled and his breathing became deep and regular. When she was sure he had fallen back asleep, Erica slipped out of bed without waking him. She grabbed his maroon hoodie off the floor, put it over her pajamas, and headed downstairs where she was glad to find Granny sitting on the plaid couch flipping through a cooking magazine. A large fire flickered in the fireplace, and the smell of smoke and freshly brewed coffee hung in the air. Erica poured herself a cup and joined Granny on the couch.

"I think Xander is back," she said, tangling herself in a plush blanket.

"Did he go somewhere?" Granny asked. She was distracted by an article about taco trucks in Albuquerque. The spread was a patchwork of bright pinks, blues, and yellows. It reminded Erica of places Xander couldn't go and things he couldn't do.

"Mentally, yes. Haven't you noticed?"

Granny closed her magazine and gave Erica her full attention. "Honestly, I don't know him that well."

"He's here literally all the time," Erica said, taken aback.

"Yes, but he's not very chatty, is he?"

"He is with me."

"I hoped as much. I didn't peg you as someone who would fall for a stoic." Granny searched her face in that knowing way that came only with age and experience. "What's bothering you?"

Erica tried to find the words. It was more than just seeing a side of Xander she hadn't expected. It was compounded by a suspicion that it was more than the food contributing to his mood.

"I guess up until now I thought of us as the same except he had this special thing about him. But the more time we spend together, it's not like this dryad thing is some fun hidden talent. Like, he's not a pro skateboarder where I can learn some tricks and try to relate. He's not—." Erica wanted to say human, but she stopped herself because saying it out loud made it real. When she promised Xander after their first kiss that she would help him find a future, her imagination could only conjure up one that mirrored her own. College, a job, and then what? Marriage? Kids? He could only fake his way through one lifetime. None of this was news to Erica. She understood it all on paper but was only just starting to see the implications in practice.

Granny squeezed the fingers of Erica's hand that wasn't holding the coffee mug. "We fall in love fast in this family. Your Grampy and I got married three months after we met." Erica's eyebrows shot up. "Don't give me that look. That's what you did back then. And your mom, it might have taken them a while to get married, but I knew she would the first time she told me about your dad."

Erica nodded, feeling somewhat reassured. Her parents and grandparents had long, happy marriages. She should trust her gut. "You're right. I'm sure it was just the food."

"That's not what I'm saying." Granny's tone became more serious. "We fall in love fast. Too fast. We don't always take the time to think it through. I never wanted to leave my family in Wisconsin. Grampy insisted on coming out here. It's always in the back of my mind what it would have been like to stay and raise my kids around my sisters. Would I have been less lonely? Had to work less hard? And your mom. Without your dad maybe she would have finished school. She might still have wound up in Portland but who knows? I'm not saying that our lives would have been any better if we hadn't settled on our first loves, but they would have been different."

Erica pulled her hand out of Granny's and wrapped them both around her mug. She sipped her coffee rather than having to answer. She wasn't offended by Granny's suggestion that her mother's life would have been easier without her—she was used to being told as much directly. But to hear that even Granny had misgivings about the course of her life, a life that until recent events Erica had thought of as fulfilled, was news to her. Was no one around her all that they seemed?

"If you guys can't get it right with regular guys, how am I supposed to with someone so complicated?" Erica mused, more to herself than to Granny.

"That's the thing, love. Maybe you can't. Xander is lovely, but if he's not the one or it's too much for you, that's okay."

The door to Erica's bedroom opened and she jumped in her seat, almost spilling her coffee. She didn't think Xander was listening to them through a potted plant but, watching him mosey down the stairs, she was filled with guilt for expressing any doubts about him. He flopped onto the couch beside her. His hair was growing out into soft waves and a dark shadow of stubble lined his sharp chin and cheeks. The glint of green in his eyes Erica had sworn she saw yesterday was gone, and they were as rich and warm as she was used to. Erica leaned into him, tossing the blanket over them.

"Good morning, Vivian," Xander said, as polite and even-tempered as before.

"Good morning, Xander," Granny replied. The smile she gave him was so genuine that Erica almost thought she had imagined their conversation.

Granny picked up her magazine and went to the kitchen to wash her mug. When she was safely around the corner, Xander nuzzled Erica's neck and whispered, "I'm sorry about every-thing. I will make it up to you."

Erica nodded. Of course he would. He was Xander. He was superhuman.

CHAPTER 8

Exactly four weeks and a day after the events at the Harvest Festival, Erica and Xander arrived downtown with Granny to help paint the grocery store. Its distinctive wood facade had been rebuilt and all that was left to do was reapply the fussy tricolor paint job reminiscent of a 1950s soda shop—a teal base with maroon and white accents around the windows and decorative panels. The grocer handed out pictures of the building in its former glory to all the volunteers, which mostly consisted of ladies over sixty from Granny's walking group.

As they waited for the woman who was bringing the rollers to arrive, Erica and Xander wandered across the newly paved street to *Falls Custom Furniture*. Alden's store was a utilitarian concrete building saved from being downright ugly by the pair of black-framed picture windows that sat on either side of heavy wrought iron double doors. The windows usually served as a showcase for some of Alden's best sellers—low, live edge coffee tables and minimalist three-tiered end tables—or, rarely, absolute masterpieces of chairs and stools crafted from the continuous root ball of a giant tree. The furniture store had suffered some of the worst of the damage, tree branches having shattered all but one pane of glass. Someone had carefully put up plywood to protect the store from the elements. Erica peered through the remaining window and thought she could make out dozens of pieces of furniture stacked at the very back of the store.

"You should call him," Erica said.

"I tried. It goes straight to voicemail." Xander kicked the concrete. "I feel him sometimes, though."

"Do you think he feels you too?"

Xander nodded. "I know he does. He's been practicing blocking me like the bear used to. He can't hold it for long."

Erica ran her hand across the metal frame of one of the missing windows, pulling it away when she hit the plywood and got a splinter. She sucked on her finger. "Why doesn't he fix this?"

"He does most of his sales online lately. Interior designers in Portland and Seattle love his stuff. He's been thinking about shutting the store down anyway, but he didn't want people talking about us. It was easier to hire one person and keep limited hours than stir up rumors."

"You think he'll close up?"

"I mean, I have no talent for this stuff. If he can't make a show of leaving me the business, he's going to have to pretend to die eventually."

Erica dropped her hand and peered into Xander's face. Dark humor wasn't his style, but he didn't look like he was making a joke. She poked him with her elbow.

"Go see him."

"He needs more time to cool down," Xander said, shaking his head. "I'm keeping an eye on him. I'll know when he's ready."

Erica grabbed his hand, and they leaned against the building watching Granny's friends unroll a canvas tarp and put out paint cans and trays. When one of them broke out a collapsible ladder, Xander rushed over to help set it up. This led to Xander being volunteered to go up the ladder and, as soon as the rollers arrived, lay down the first coat of teal on the second floor on account of how much farther his arms could reach than everyone else's. Erica smiled to herself as the ladies fawned over him, this nice young man who was so civic-minded. She had asked Granny to warn them ahead of time not to ask him too many questions about himself. Little was known about Xander and

Alden around town, and the last thing Erica wanted was for someone's undue curiosity to spook him back into hiding.

The group made quick work of the first coat. Erica found herself enjoying the constant chatter and clear direction provided by experienced, assured women. She was not particularly skilled with the roller, so they gave her the thinnest brush they had on hand and put her to task filling in corners. They bossed Xander around without compunction but, from the way he eagerly complied with each request, she thought he was having a good time.

"Has your grandma talked to you about the council position?" a squat, curly-haired woman Erica believed was called Muriel asked as they tag-teamed the door frame.

"What council position?" Erica asked, trying to remember if Granny had mentioned anything.

"Gerald Harmond had a heart attack and resigned his position on the town council. We're all trying to talk Vivian into running in the special election."

Erica considered this. Granny had been backing off the store since before she arrived. Lately, she had been keeping busy with the downtown clean-up but that was coming near the end. Granny wasn't the type to be content staying at home all day. With Erica going to college and Xander's stay of indeterminate length, Granny was about to have an empty nest for the first time in more than forty years.

Erica called to Granny who was on the other side of the building holding a paint tray steady while Xander did his best to refresh his roller that was on the end of what looked like a very long broom handle. "Are you running for town council?"

"What has Muriel been telling you?" Granny shouted back at them, but she looked pleased.

Erica got up from her crouched position and, putting her hand under her brush to stop it from dripping on the sidewalk, walked over to them. "You should do it. You love Juniper Falls."

"You could rein in Bobby Hendricks before he bankrupts the town putting in another rec center," said Muriel, who also wandered over to join the conversation.

"Or at least loosen Kriners' grip on him," Erica added. Xander nodded in agreement before heading back up the ladder to delicately fill in the very top of the pitch.

"I'm considering it," Granny said. "It's been forever since we had a municipal bond. And, sure, I think we need to pay more attention to the impacts the loggers have on the town. But I don't want to campaign."

"What campaign?" Muriel laughed. "Who in this town doesn't know who you are? *Farm & Feed* is the backbone of downtown."

Granny gave a sheepish smile. She looked at Erica and, as if hoping she was the only one who would hear, whispered, "I also don't want the pity vote."

Only the wet paintbrush in Erica's hand stopped her from hugging Granny. "Keith would never want to hold you back from something you wanted to do."

"It's true," Xander said. He hopped off the ladder and laid the roller in the paint tray, leaning the handle against the adjacent building. "Keith thought you could do anything."

"Thank you," Granny said, her voice soft. She squeezed Xander's shoulder.

"We've already told you we will help with all the logistics," Muriel said, oblivious to the moment the others just shared. "Right, ladies? We've got nothing better to do than put together a campaign for Vivian."

The women around them readily agreed. With every word of encouragement, Granny stood a little taller. Erica wanted this for her, an expansion of her legacy in this little town. Something that was all her own.

Erica dropped her paintbrush in the tray and gave Granny the hug she knew the occasion required. "We'll help too."

"For sure," Xander agreed.

Erica felt Granny's breath catch in her throat as she held her thin frame. The moment was interrupted by a couple of diesel trucks turning into the *Farm & Feed* parking lot two blocks away. They parked with no regard for the painted lines, which annoyed Erica even if it was Sunday and the store was closed.

Half a dozen men exited the trucks and unloaded construction equipment—shovels, sledgehammers, a jackhammer, and something that looked like a lawnmower but narrower. They carried their tools to the front of Alden's store and inspected the sidewalk that had been cracked and buckled by the tree roots grown by the bear dryad.

The men acted as if they were oblivious to the women standing no more than fifty feet away from them. They dug out chunks of concrete, tossing them into a wheelbarrow that they pulled from one of the alleys. Erica couldn't wrap her head around what was going on until she noted a familiar face. Even when supervising construction work, Mitchell Watters was wearing freshly pressed jeans with a crisp crease that ran from his knee to the perfectly placed break of his cuff above a pair of what appeared to be brand new leather work boots. Unlike his companions in dirty denim jackets, Mitchell wore a charcoal wool overcoat and kept his hands clean. Erica wondered if they would spray paint a Kriners logo on the fresh concrete when they finished.

A few of the women grumbled about the interruption. They were only a few rolls into their second coat of teal when the jackhammer revved to life. A startled Muriel dropped her paintbrush on the sidewalk as she covered her ears, causing a large splotch that was going to be hard to pressure wash away. Erica looked around at the other surprised faces and watched as Granny strode meaningfully toward the men. She followed, hoping there would be strength in numbers. Xander also jogged over to support, and Erica stood a little straighter.

Granny waved her arms, but the jackhammer continued until she was right in Mitchell's face. Only when it was impossible to ignore her did he nod to the operator who turned it off.

"Hello, Vivian. Nice to see you again," he said in his best preacher's voice, doing a terrible job of acting like he only just noticed her.

"We've been over this." Granny spit out his name as if she found this attempt at familiarity distasteful. "You run your big equipment on Saturdays, and we get Sundays."

"I know, I know. But we had a call from the business owner here." Mitchell pointed to *Falls Custom Furniture*. "He wanted a rush job on us fixing up this sidewalk."

"I doubt that," Xander said.

"Oh? And you are?"

"Alexander Reed," he said, using his full name for the first time that Erica could remember. "That's my family's store."

Mitchell's face, usually composed and confident, faltered as he was caught in his lie. He tugged on the cuffs of his coat, avoiding eye contact with Xander. "Well, I see. But are you sure? You don't look old enough to be making those calls."

"I'm sure." Xander pulled himself to his full height, something that he rarely did as he towered over everyone around him. Mitchell sized him up but did not look intimidated. Erica watched as he recovered his sycophantic persona and his face changed like a chameleon from genuine emotion to a mask. It unnerved her.

"My mistake then," Mitchell said. "But seeing as we're here, there can't be any harm in letting us finish up. Especially since there's no law stopping us from helping out."

"Not yet," Granny snipped. "Juniper Falls has never needed to put common courtesy into law before."

"You wound me, Vivian. We are out here doing a public service! You of all people should know how committed Kriners is to the town. We are doing these improvements on our own dime."

"You should!" Erica shouted.

"Should we?" Mitchell smirked. "We didn't make this mess."

Erica was about to explain to Mitchell exactly how he was responsible for the state of downtown when Xander grabbed her shoulder and pulled her back. She shrugged him off, then caught his panicked glance and realized that of course she couldn't say what she was bursting to. Deflated, she settled for glaring at Mitchell with what she hoped he would understand to be pure hatred. Granny and Xander joined her had similar expressions, but they had no effect on Mitchell.

"If we're done here, I would like my crew to get back to work," he said.

Erica exhaled like a bull. Looking to Granny she said, "I'll go get earplugs from the store." She grabbed Xander's hand to bring him with her when Mitchell put his arm out. Erica had to stutter-step to stop from running into it. Xander caught and steadied her. Mitchell looked right past Erica to speak to Xander.

"Son, if the furniture business isn't treating you well, we could always use strong boys like yourself at Kriners." Mitchell handed Xander a bright red business card that Xander immediately crumpled into a ball and shoved into the pocket of his jeans. Xander stared Mitchell down again, but Mitchell had regained his composure and didn't flinch. Erica tugged on Xander's hand, and he reluctantly followed her down the street.

It took them no time to reach the doors of *Farm & Feed*. As Erica took out her keys, Xander said, "That guy is an asshole."

"Yes. Yes, he is," she agreed. Mitchell was so much of an asshole that Erica was having a hard time calming down about their run-in.

She let them into the dark, quiet store. Even as she seethed, she subconsciously checked to make sure her Christmas display was still looking full and organized. Granny had called it *perfection*, which Erica didn't believe, but she cherished the compliment anyway.

"Did he seem familiar to you?" Xander asked.

"You heard him speak at the school fundraiser, remember?"

"Yeah, but I thought maybe I knew him from somewhere else."

"No idea," Erica said. "He's not from around here as far as I know."

Erica led them up to the counter where squishy, multicolored earplugs sat in a fishbowl by the registers. She pulled out a dozen pairs and left herself a note on a Post-It to take them out of inventory. She made for the door again when Xander grabbed her by the waist and spun her around to look at him.

"I thought you were going to lose it with him for a second there," he said, smiling down at her. "There's some fight in you."

Erica felt the tension and determination that had been fueling her for the last few minutes ease. "You're one to talk."

"Yes, but I have much more practice keeping my mouth shut." He stroked her short hair. "I don't think you know how much of a badass you are. I love it."

"That I'm a badass or that I don't know it?"

"Both." Xander laughed, and she relished the way it reverberated through her whole body as she pressed against him. They stood together, swaying in place, until Erica was sure she could go back outside without confronting the loggers again.

"They are probably waiting on these," Erica said, placing a pair of earplugs in Xander's hand.

They left the store, careful to lock up on their way out, and headed up the street to where Granny's friends were cheering and hugging each other. Granny was in the middle of the group, and Erica had to delicately push her way through to figure out what had them riled up.

"I'm going to run," Granny said. Then, seeing the look of confusion on Erica's face, she added, "For town council!" The women all around her cheered again.

Erica had to stop herself from rushing Granny. She settled on another hug. "That's amazing! What do you need? We'll make a list tonight. When is the election?"

"We'll figure it out," Granny said, her voice as exuberant as Erica had ever heard it. Erica thought she could feel Mitchell's eyes bore into them. She wondered if while she and Xander were gone, Granny had announced her intentions of running in direct opposition to Kriners' influence at town hall. If so, she was sorry she missed it.

Erica was about to ask when the men across the street started up another loud piece of equipment that sounded similar to a chainsaw. She quickly passed around the earplugs, but when she got back to Xander he was white, his face pinched.

"What's wrong?" Erica yelled over the noise.

He pointed toward where the men were working. Erica looked over to see them operating the tool she had thought was a type of lawnmower. She watched as they moved what looked like a circular saw blade side to side and the roots that had pre-viously been there disappeared into a pile of sawdust. It was a stump grinder.

"You can feel it?" she asked. Xander nodded and rubbed vigorously at his temples. Erica returned to Granny and shouted, "I have to take Xander home! Headache!"

Granny gave her a perplexed look. Upon seeing Xander in obvious agony, her eyes widened, and she nodded.

Erica pulled Xander down the street toward the house. He didn't seem to want to move so great was his distress. Mitchell watched them leave. His interest made her uneasy, and she did her best to get Xander to go faster. It wasn't until they turned the corner onto their street that Xander regained himself a little.

"What happened there?" she asked, slowing her pace.

Xander shook his head. "I can always feel the flora around me, but not like that. Not like pain."

"Maybe you were just too close?" Erica rubbed his back, trying to calm him down.

"I was standing right next to the bear tree when we took it down, and it was nothing like that."

They were at the foot of the driveway, and Erica had an irrational need to get him inside as if a mere four walls could shut out what he was feeling. She ushered him up the steps and through the door, where Tulip greeted them, dancing around Xander's legs. He sat on the floor as soon as he got in, scooping the little dog into his lap. She licked his face obligingly.

"You okay?" Erica asked him. "Do you want some water?"

Xander looked up at her as if to remind her who she was talking to. As if she could ever forget. Erica sat down on the floor next to him, and Tulip changed allegiances to sit on her feet. She absentmindedly petted the dog's soft ears.

"Do you think it's because of the bear?" she wondered. "It grew those trees."

Xander put his head in his hands again. "I don't know. I wish I understood more about all of this."

"You should talk to Alden."

"Give it a rest, Erica," Xander snapped. Then, in response to the stricken look on her face, "I'm sorry. I'm going to go lay down, okay?"

Erica nodded. Xander ran his fingers through his hair as he got up and climbed the stairs, shutting her bedroom door behind him. Erica stayed on the floor, scratching Tulip's side and trying not to be nervous about what just happened. Why did it seem like whenever things got a little good, they came accompanied by something worse? Erica kissed the top of Tulip's head and hoped that this was a one-off, a fluke, and not another sign that something was happening to Xander that neither of them understood.

CHAPTER 9

Xander recovered after a nap and the next week passed in a blur as he and Erica helped Granny put together her town council campaign. There was a stream of middle-aged to elderly women coming in and out of the house at all hours of the day. The old coffee pot was working as hard as the rest of them to keep visitors and volunteers caffeinated. Xander was even quieter than usual, but Erica chalked it up to being around so many strangers. At night, he held her as tightly as ever as she ran her fingers up and down his bicep until he fell asleep.

Everything about Granny's campaign felt homemade—because it was—but everyone involved agreed that added to its charm. Her friends brought cardboard, laminating machines, vinyl cutters, and any other vestige of long-dormant craft projects that might be put to good use. After one particularly long night spent debating slogans in which five bottles of wine were consumed by seven drinkers, Erica included, they settled on the very first suggestion *Schueller for Councilor* because the almost rhyme couldn't be beaten. Two days later, every stop sign in town, not that there were many, had a *Schueller for Councilor* placard next to it.

Erica and Xander spray-painted a huge piece of plywood silver, stenciled the slogan in midnight blue letters, and put the piece outside the store to surprise Granny. Smaller matching construction paper signs hung throughout *Farm & Feed*, and Granny set up regular office hours at a small table just inside the door for residents to talk to her about her platform. She fell deftly into politics, which surprised no one who knew her well. She knew there was a large contingent that supported the logging industry, so she did not make it the center of her campaign. If asked directly, she was honest that she had more interest in bringing sustainable jobs to Juniper Falls than in encouraging or subsidizing Kriners. Then she would bring the conversation around to something she knew directly affected the inquiring party like improving school lunches, siting a new dog park, or extending library hours.

The holidays were always a busy time at the store, and the influx of people coming in to see Granny or just to visit because they heard about her campaign doubled their sales volume. Erica worked around the clock between the campaign and supporting Joe in every way she could from running the register to stocking shelves to double-checking the books. Xander was by her side every step of the way. When a large batch of Christmas cacti came in looking especially parched and wilted, she caught him whispering to them as they plumped up and bloomed before her eyes. She almost interrupted and admonished him for being so careless when any of the other employees could have wandered in, but his face as he encouraged the plants was serene. He looked calmer, more at home, than she had seen him since their date, so she left him to it. The cacti sold out in two days.

Thanksgiving snuck up on Erica amid the mayhem. She rolled out of bed that morning to find Granny and Xander in the kitchen, the former with her hand stuffed under the skin of a turkey bigger than Tulip, rubbing in a mixture of butter, garlic, and herbs.

"There is nothing worse than a dry turkey," Granny was telling him. The look on Xander's face indicated that he thought dry meat was a small price to pay to never have to mimic what she was doing.

"Remind me who all is coming?" Erica asked as she edged past them to pour herself some coffee.

"Just Joe and Kyle," Granny said. She scooped another handful of the butter and continued working it into the turkey.

"And Derek," Xander said.

"Is that the boy that turns into a bear?" Granny asked with an air of nonchalance that bordered on absurd.

Erica did her best to hold in a laugh. She avoided the wide-eyed stare that Xander was trying to give her until she couldn't. The moment their eyes met, they lost it. Granny joined in and the three of them laughed until they couldn't breathe. It was a release they all needed. Each one was burning the candle at both ends, and Erica was thankful for the chance to enjoy a moment with the people she loved best.

The turkey went into the electric countertop roaster that, per tradition, Granny complained about having to store for the rest of the year. This freed up the oven for Erica's pies. Erica wasn't much of a cook, but she was a competent baker. She liked that all she had to do was follow a recipe to the letter, and she could be pretty confident it would turn out. As she collected the ingredients for her pumpkin pie filling, she instructed Xander to take out the dough for the crust that she chilled overnight. Granny walked him through how thick he should roll it out. They lined and crimped two pie plates that went into the oven for pre-baking.

They maintained this momentum, all hands on deck, for the rest of the morning. At the Schueller house, holiday meals were served at one o'clock in the afternoon to ensure no one showed up too full and there was adequate time for at least three periods of stuffing one's face: dinner, dessert, and general grazing of leftovers. Granny, Xander, and Erica got ready in shifts so that the oven was constantly monitored. In the course of the morning, Erica received a *Happy Thanksgiving* text from Robin explaining that her family's annual tradition included her dad trying at the last minute to beg a local steakhouse to send them dinner.

The green bean casserole came out at the exact moment they heard the front door open. Granny slipped the oven mitt off her hand to go greet them while Xander and Erica stayed in the kitchen to top their last dish with onion straws.

"Happy Thanksgiving, Vivian!" they heard Joe boom from the living room. Erica listened to the rustling of shoes coming off and coats being hung. Kyle came into the kitchen carrying an enormous metal pot. He nodded to Xander who returned the gesture.

"What's that?" Erica asked.

"Pierogi. Dad brings it every year." He put the pot down on the counter and lifted the glass lid to reveal what looked like dumplings. "Try one."

Erica grabbed a stray fork that was sitting on the counter and stabbed a pierogi. She bit it in half and instantly regretted not putting the whole thing in her mouth. Her taste buds popped with the savory combination of blue cheese, bacon, and garlic carried by the creamiest potatoes she had ever eaten.

"Is this what I've been missing while my mom has been bringing home the last ham left at the grocery store?"

Kyle laughed. "Keith always tried to get you guys to come down for Thanksgiving."

"I think you don't understand how much Portland loves Black Friday."

"You want to try one, man?" Kyle asked Xander. Erica gave him a dark look. She had warned him and Derek via text that Xander would be faking his way through dinner and asked that they not call attention to it. Kyle hadn't lasted two minutes into what was sure to be a very long day if they couldn't get on the same page. He quickly corrected himself, however, with, "Sorry, sorry, I forgot."

Erica doubted the sincerity of the apology, but she didn't want to pick a fight this soon. She let this first transgression slide while also deciding to keep them apart as much as possible. She grabbed Xander's hand and led him into the living room where Joe and Granny were still chatting by the door.

Joe smiled broadly when he saw Xander and clapped him on the shoulder. "Nice work this week. It's been helpful having someone again who isn't afraid of a little heavy lifting."

"Dad thinks all I'm good for is my upper body strength," Kyle said from where he lingered in the dining room.

"Well, Kriners certainly didn't hire you for your brains." This was the unkindest thing Erica had ever heard Joe say, especially to Kyle. Joe usually stayed quiet about Kriners. She wondered if Kyle had told him something about Keith's death that might have changed his mind. "By the way, Vivian, did you hear who they're propping up to run against you?"

"No, who?" Granny asked. They had known this was coming. There was no way that Kriners was going to allow Granny to run unopposed.

"Muriel Lambert."

"Muriel!" Granny cried. "She was just here on Monday helping me fold mailers. She didn't say she had any interest in running."

"That slimy guy from Kriners got to her, I guess. He really sold her on downtown redevelopment. She says he can bring a fast-food chain to Juniper Falls."

"Juniper Falls doesn't want fast food!" Granny was incensed, but Erica didn't think that was quite true. Most of the town would probably love nothing more than to not have to drive an hour to a McDonalds. At least now she understood the source of Joe's ire. She had to try harder to trust Kyle.

"Muriel said you would appreciate some friendly competition. It would make you feel like you earned it. I don't think she has any intention of winning but who knows what Kriners will do now that they have a candidate."

Granny crossed her arms and looked from Joe to Erica who did her best to be encouraging. "The election is in three weeks, and we have a jump start on her," Erica said. "Maybe we should organize a debate. It would become obvious fast if her only platform is hamburgers and not hating Kriners."

"What I don't understand is that she does hate Kriners," Granny said. "It has to be more than just a game for her."

They were interrupted by the guttural sound of a failing exhaust pipe. Erica looked out the window to see Derek parking his hatchback on the street. As he made his way across the lawn, she thought he looked cleaner than she had ever seen him. His hair was still wet from a shower, and he was wearing a navy sweater with a shell collar that hid his scar. He carried a glass dish wrapped in foil and kept shaking his shoulders as though trying to throw off some worry before making it to the porch. Erica opened the door for him as he was mounting the stairs.

"Come in!" she said. "What did you bring?"

"Cornbread," he said, his usual loose demeanor swapped for something quieter and more careful.

"Thank you, Derek!" Granny said as she stepped forward to take the dish from him. "I'm Vivian, Erica's grandma. She's told me so much about you."

Derek gave a short, uncomfortable laugh and kicked off his shoes. He knew that Granny was in on their secrets and had seemed fine with it, but today he was jumpy. Kyle came in from the dining room and fist-bumped Derek while exchanging grunted greetings.

"Well," Granny said when the room got quiet again, "should we eat?"

There was a murmur of general agreement, and they made their way to the table. As large as it was, it could barely sit the six of them and all the food they prepared. Erica steered Xander into the seat next to Derek and put herself between Xander and Kyle.

With only one person at the table that they needed to fool, it was easy to pretend that Xander was eating. Erica filled each of their plates halfway and ate off both. Kyle rolled his eyes at Erica every now and then when he caught her sneaking Xander's mashed potatoes, but he didn't draw any attention to it. Xander didn't say anything either. Erica had hoped that by seating him with Derek the two of them would have a chance to chat. But whereas Derek fit easily into the flow of conversation, Xander held back. When she caught his eye, he would give her an encouraging smile, but she couldn't help but feel that he wasn't enjoying the company as much as she had hoped.

When they couldn't eat anymore, they put their forks down to allow for a period of digestion before attempting dessert. Joe insisted that he do the dishes. He eyed Kyle who did an almost convincing job of pretending he didn't notice. Granny stayed at the table to keep Joe company. The rest of them were making their way to the living room when Kyle pulled Erica aside.

"Derek wants to talk to us."

Erica searched Kyle and Derek's faces and found them both looking solemn. She peeked in at Granny. There were a lot of dishes to get through. She might not notice if they disappeared for a few minutes. Erica nodded and waved Derek, Kyle, and a concerned-looking Xander up the stairs and into her room.

Xander sat deliberately on the bed and ushered Kyle with his eyes over to the butterfly chair on the other side of the room. Kyle made a show of not even looking at the bed and settled his big body into the too-small chair, parts of him spilling from every corner. Erica joined Xander while Derek leaned against her dresser, facing the three of them. They looked back at him expectantly as he sighed and tugged on his sparse facial hair.

"My family found me," he said.

"Oh shit," Kyle muttered.

Erica turned to look at Kyle and was surprised to find him expressing real concern. She looked back to Derek. "I know you're not close, but I feel like I'm missing something."

"What do you know about Kodiak?" Derek asked. His sock had a hole in it, and he ran his uncovered toe through the dark blue carpet, first creating a line against the grain, then smoothing it back down.

Erica was shaking her head that she knew nothing about it when Xander said, "Aren't there a lot of bears?"

"Bingo," Derek replied.

Erica lifted her eyebrows at Xander who responded with, "I saw a documentary about them. There were a bunch of tourists hanging out on the bank of a river like ten feet from these huge bears eating salmon."

"How do you think they can let people get that close?" Derek asked. He stopped messing with the carpet and made meaningful eye contact with her.

Erica gasped. "They can't all be like you."

Derek made a sound between a laugh and a snort. "No, there aren't that many of us. But we're watching from the sidelines to keep things under control."

"You can communicate with real bears?"

"Sort of. They're kind of trained. They know if they follow us that we'll lead them to the good food spots. They trust us to keep them safe."

This didn't sound so bad to Erica. In fact, it seemed like a good way to monetize an unusual skill, and she told Derek as much.

"That's the whole thing," Derek said with a heaviness in his voice. "It's all about the money. They have a few dozen weres working for them, but all the money goes to this one family who figured out how to breed the bears into their bloodline. It's lycanthropic eugenics."

"But that's not your family, right?" Erica asked. She was still trying to wrap her head around why Derek was so scared. "You said you were the only one in your family."

Derek nodded. "It's rare we pop up outside of this group, and when we do, they don't like losing track of us. My sister says dad is getting a lot of shit from the Whitlocks. If they know where I am, they are going try to bring me back."

Erica thought that Derek had a lot of the power in this situation. She wasn't sure how they were going to get a bear onto an airplane back to Alaska. But Derek looked so small and nervous in front of her that she didn't think he was looking for a pep talk. She was about to ask him how they could help when Kyle spoke up instead.

"Tell them why you really left."

Derek took a deep breath and looked at the floor. He went back to brushing the carpet back and forth with his toe. Erica turned to give Kyle a questioning look. He jutted his chin toward Derek, telling her to wait until he was ready.

After another breath, Derek composed himself and said, "There are bear hunts every year. To keep the population in check. The Whitlocks pick what bears go down. They have us get them away from the others and set them up for a good shot." Erica heard Xander inhale sharply next to her. "My buddy was going through the motions when some big money tourist literally jumped the gun and got him. They swear it was an accident, but they were so weird about it. They didn't care."

"That's horrible," Erica murmured. "You don't think they did it on purpose?"

"There isn't much up there that happens on accident. Their whole operation is set up to avoid accidents." He paused here and looked at the ground again as if trying to make up his mind what he believed and not being able to come to a conclusion. After a few seconds, he shook his shoulders again, the same way he had on his way to her door earlier that afternoon. "But anyway, I told my dad that I wanted out. But they have him convinced that all sorts of bad shit will go down if the weres leave Kodiak. He tried to get rough with me, but he was never going to win that fight. So I left."

This was the end of the story, which Derek indicated by rounding the bed and sitting down with his back to all of them. Erica looked to Kyle who seemed like he was already looped in on all of this.

"He wants us to be there when his parents show up," Kyle said.

"I don't know who they're bringing with," Derek said quietly. He twisted his torso to look at Xander. "I don't know what your deal is, man, but I might need some backup. Does your dryadness come with any perks in a fight?"

Xander looked bewildered by this question and answered honestly, "I wish I knew."

"Yeah, you went down pretty quick last time. But I bet you can do some cool stuff. It would be awesome if you could figure it out."

Derek said this lightly, unaware of the effect it had on Xander who blushed harder than Erica had ever seen him do before. In their late-night talks in the very bed they were sitting on, he had told her how powerless he felt facing the bear dryad, how he knew he had to defend them but did so entirely without a plan. He had tried to call upon the roots around him, but he couldn't wrestle control from the bear dryad. Erica discouraged these thoughts. It wasn't his fault. Why should he know how to fight something that she was sure they would never encounter again? And yet here they were, potentially facing down another, albeit very different, bear after no time at all.

Xander met her gaze, and she wished she could peer inside his brain and know what he was thinking. Derek's suggestion had struck a nerve, that much she could tell. She was apprehensive of what ideas might be gaining traction in Xander's mind.

Granny called them from downstairs. Erica turned to Derek who was waiting for an answer. She thought about dragging Derek to the bear tree, the trust he displayed as he cut it down, and how he had rushed to save them without a second thought. He was a good guy. They owed him. More than that, it might give Xander an outlet that was safer than following Kriners around like some twenty-first-century Johnny Appleseed.

"Whatever you need," she said. "We'll figure out how to help."

Erica and Xander sprang apart as Derek fell backward between them. He smiled up at them, his first true smile since he arrived for dinner. "Thanks, guys."

There was a gentle knock on the door, and Granny coaxed them downstairs with promises of pie. The boys followed her obediently out of her room as if the conversation they just had was average, everyday, commonplace. At this point, it almost was.

CHAPTER 10

Erica's parents called her late in the evening on Thanksgiving after the Zukowskis and Derek had gone home with plastic containers full of leftovers. Her mother sounded like she had made her way through the better part of a bottle of wine and was convincingly sad that Erica missed spending a major holiday with them. It was almost enough to make her apologize for not even considering going home until Danni asked her to come up and help at the Portland store the next day.

She listened to her parents wrestle for the phone before her dad came on to assuage the guilt trip. They had it under control. Of course, she should stay and help Granny. Erica was on the verge of explaining how much busier they would be than usual because of the election when Granny waved her hands and shook her head. It hadn't occurred to her until now that no one had told them Granny was running for town council. It made sense why they wouldn't. If she lost, Danni would never let her hear the end of it.

Erica assured her father that she missed him too and that she was looking forward to Christmas. She did her best to get off the phone before her mother's mood changed from melancholy to angry. This took longer than she might have hoped. By the time she hung up, Granny was opening the television cabinet and putting in a DVD. Xander had confided in her that when his own mother was alive, they would watch the old, stop-motion Rudolph movie on Thanksgiving to kick off the Christmas season. The weird little film was also a favorite of Granny's, and she was thrilled to have someone willing to watch it with her.

They settled in, all three of them on the couch under a pile of blankets. Granny had turned off all the lights, and the glow of the television made Erica feel nostalgic for a memory that wasn't even hers. She was touched by the joy written on Xander's face as he recognized scenes and lines. He would grab her hand or her thigh in excitement as she watched him smile out of the corner of her eye, not wishing to distract him from the screen.

They went to bed shortly after it ended so that they could get up and to the store well before dawn. Xander followed Erica up to her bedroom, for once not bothering to look embarrassed as they said good night to Granny and shut the door behind them. It was as though a dam had been unblocked in him, and he needed to tell Erica everything he could remember about his early holidays before everything changed.

"My mom was like you," he said, "a better baker than a cook. She loved peppermint. We would make peppermint fudge, peppermint bark, peppermint cupcakes."

Erica let Xander chatter as she lifted her dress over her head and was surprised when he swooped in and pulled her into bed. She giggled and extracted herself from the dress while Xander went on.

"She loved Christmas trees but hated Christmas tree farms. She said they were full of pesticides and poisoned the water. So, instead, we would go with Alden into the forest every year and find a tree." They were laying face-to-face, their legs entangled. He put one big hand on her stomach and, with the pointer finger of the other, absentmindedly twirled thin strands of her short hair. "Some years it felt like we walked for miles, but we probably didn't. The trees that are short enough to take into your house are usually scraggly, so it took a long time to find a good one." Erica curled into him and kissed his neck. His throat vibrated with memories. "Alden would haul them back to the truck, letting me pretend like I was helping, and we would drive home and put them up. There would be bugs all over our house for the next few weeks. Everything that lived in the trees would crawl out and find a new home."

Erica was still listening to him, she really was, but this version of Xander, so happy he was almost giddy, was irresistible. It didn't help that his hands traveled over her with a mind of their own as the words gushed out of him. She slid her own hands lower, but he grabbed them and kissed her fingertips as he told her about the year they made a popcorn garland and it was eaten by a family of chickadees they brought home in their tree. Erica wanted to be frustrated by whatever claim to prudishness or virtuosity kept holding him back, but she wouldn't ruin this moment. She sighed, turned off the lamp, and drifted to sleep, lost in Xander's deep voice and soft touch. It was enough to make her forget the strange promise they'd made to Derek earlier that day.

The morning came faster than Erica would have liked. Leaving the house in identical uniforms of blue and khaki, she, Granny, and Xander arrived at the store to meet Joe. Most of the seasonal product was already on the floor, the exception being a large batch of poinsettias that arrived too late Wednesday to go on display, which Xander took charge of. Their task this morning was to put up the traditional *Farm & Feed* Christmas decorations. Granny and Grampy had collected most of them in the 1970s and 80s, and many were vintage even then. On their daughter's suggestion, they tried updating their holiday look in the early 2000s. After weeks of complaints from the community, they went back to the old standbys. Granny secretly harbored the belief that this disagreement was the final straw in Danni's decision to uproot Erica and move to Portland—proof that she would never be a real voice in the Juniper Falls operations. But Granny had always been too afraid to open the old wound by asking outright.

Erica oversaw setting the crumbling foil snowflakes and ceramic figurines in their usual places. Granny put her artistic bent to work painting festive scenes on the windows. She and Erica had decided on a snowman theme this year despite Juniper

Falls getting laughably little snowfall. Joe took out the pieces of a twelve-foot-tall plastic tree that went up at the front of the store. After it was assembled and fluffed, he carefully intermingled the saleable ornaments featuring cardinals and old-fashioned pickup trucks with the brittle, blown-glass ones whose numbers dwindled every year as they were inevitably knocked down by big purses or over-sugared toddlers. He finished around the same time Xander completed his poinsettia display, and they helped Erica drape garlands wrapped in twinkling lights over the tops of the shelves.

Granny left early to bake biscuits that she would serve with leftover turkey and gravy. As the rest of them left the store, they shut off the overhead lights, and the barn store glowed softly in that way that is so specific to the holiday season. Erica and Xander, feeling the warmth from both the Christmas lights and their conversation last night, swung their clasped hands between them on the short walk to the house. Eager to continue recreating the magic of Xander's childhood for him, she was struck with an idea.

"We should go get a tree on Sunday. From the forest. Like you used to do with your mom."

"I think we need a permit," he replied, the way people do when they receive good news but can't quite believe it.

"If Kriners can cut down acres of trees, I doubt there's anyone out there who is going to stop us."

Xander's mind was still processing, and he answered her slowly in a series of questions. "What if we didn't cut it down? What if we grabbed one of those big metal tubs from the store and had a living tree? Do you think Vivian would mind?"

The idea was unusual but not crazy. Erica couldn't think of a reason why Granny would object. "Sure," she said. "Let's try it."

"It will be a good challenge for me, getting something that big out of the ground without harming it."

Erica wondered when this would come up. She didn't think that Derek's jab at him yesterday was going to pass without him taking some kind of action. But developing his dryad skills through Christmas tree transplantation felt as low stakes as she could have hoped. She smiled at him and squeezed his hand while he made suggestions on where to find the best Douglas firs.

Black Friday was nowhere near as busy as Erica was used to in Portland, but they had plenty of people come in search of inflatable Santas, outdoor lights, and wreaths. They were just as busy that Saturday, and Erica was glad she had the prospect of Christmas tree hunting to look forward to.

They set off early on Sunday and drove east out of town with Xander in the driver's seat of Granny's truck. When they passed approximately where she recalled Alden's cabin to be, she searched Xander's face for a change of expression and was almost disappointed not to see one. Their feud had lasted long enough in her opinion, and she agonized over Alden spending the holidays alone. He had lost his best friend—her uncle Keith—and now his only living relative in the space of a few months. Her heart broke for him, and she resolved to schedule Xander for a day at the store without her in the hopes that she could sneak off to visit Alden without him noticing.

They drove long enough that Erica was concerned they might be reaching the edge of how far Xander could be from his tree when he began looking for somewhere to pull over. Unable to find a wide enough shoulder, he pulled a little way into the forest and turned off the ignition.

"A little conspicuous, no?" Erica asked, looking back at the road. "Someone might think we got in an accident."

They got out of the car. It was just above freezing, which was cold for Juniper Falls at the end of November, and Erica was glad she wore her puffy jacket. Xander, per usual, didn't register the temperature. He held his hoodie-covered arms out wide. As he brought them closer together, the green, waxy salal that covered the forest floor crept up the back bumper of the truck until the *Farm & Feed* logo was obscured.

"Now people will think it's been here a while," he said.

Erica studied his work and nodded. She grabbed his hand

as they headed into the forest. "Tell me what we're looking for. We've always been a tree lot family."

"Not even you-cut? Your granny seems more organic than that."

"Before we moved to Portland, we all spent a lot of time together, but it was always at the store. We never had a whole afternoon to do something like this."

Xander had picked a spot with many of the correct size of tree, but they all looked sun-starved and skeletal compared to the giants that shot up around them.

"We're looking for something that height," he said, pointing to a tree just taller than him, "but, you know, fuller."

"Can't we pick one with good bones and you can embellish?" Erica wiggled her fingers and gave him a knowing look.

He laughed. "What would be the fun in that?"

They walked slowly, carefully appraising potential contenders. There was always something that Xander rejected—a good base but sparse on top, too fat, too thin, half dead.

"You're pickier than my mother," Erica said after Xander decided that one she thought for sure was a winner had what he deemed was too big of a bare spot in the back. "I don't know how my dad does it. Out of all the people in the world, to have picked someone so particular." Then she asked Xander a question that hadn't occurred to her until this moment. "What about your dad?"

"What about him?" Xander asked. He was so focused on their search that he barely registered the question.

"Do you have a dad?"

"I assume so. My mom never mentioned him. Alden said she didn't tell him either."

"Weird. I thought they were close."

"They were. Alden said it must have been a one-night stand. He says he would have known if she had a secret boyfriend." Xander seemed to register what he was saying. He stopped and looked at Erica. "She had me in her early thirties. She may have just wanted a kid. I was too young when she died to ask her about any of it. What brought this up?"

"I don't know. I was just thinking about my dad and realized you never talk about yours."

Xander leaned against the trunk of one of the taller trees. He put his hands in the pocket of his hoodie. "I used to tell Alden when he did something I thought was mean that I was going to look for my dad. He pointed out that the only way to do that was through DNA and who knows what mine even looks like at this point. If I even appear human under a microscope."

Erica walked up to him and put her arms through the triangles created by his bent elbows. She hugged him tightly. "I'm sorry. I should have known this would be a painful topic for you or you would have brought it up before."

"It's not painful exactly. It's just another shitty thing about myself I've had to come to accept."

"I promise you that there is not a single shitty thing about you," she said as she nuzzled her face into his chest. He hugged her back, and they stood there for a while listening to the wind shake the branches tens of feet above them.

"Let's head a little north then circle back to the truck," Xander suggested, landing a quick kiss on the top of her head.

"As long as you can find our way back."

"Remember who you're talking to," he said with a smile. "Do you mind if I try some stuff as we go? Flex my muscles?"

"Sure," she said. She felt the need to make up for upsetting him. "I'll keep an eye out for good trees."

"I've been looking. Like," he spread his fingers out, indicating the reach of his ability to see the forest, "and there's nothing out here."

"I thought we weren't cheating," Erica chided, trying to sound stern but also a little relieved that she didn't have to pretend they were going to get lucky.

"It was going to feel real for you at least."

He guided her toward a thicker, darker part of the forest. He asked her to walk in front of him and would shout *right* or *left* now and again to keep them going in the right direction. As much as she wanted to watch what was going on behind her, she had the feeling that Xander was looking for a bit of privacy by sending her up ahead. He didn't admonish her for peeking over her shoulder, but he didn't encourage it either.

What she did see—and hear—made her uneasy. He had taken Derek's comments too close to heart and was trying out what could only be described as a series of offensive and defensive tactics. He made multiple attempts to move or grow a tree between them as they walked. He didn't accomplish much beyond a low hedge before switching his focus. Flowering species always listened to him better, and Erica watched as dormant, thorny briars sprang to life and sprouted leaves as they shot toward dead branches and yanked them from trees with a flick of Xander's wrist. The crack of the trees was deafening against the natural stillness of the woods during a time of year when even birds and squirrels were hard to spot.

Branches bent and cracked as Xander summoned them in every direction. Erica noticed that all around him, the residual effect of his power woke up the forest from its autumnal slumber. Sword ferns unfurled and reached toward the sky, trillium flowers bloomed six months too soon, and rhododendrons doubled in size. A line of foliage, too big and too green, extended to either side of him.

Erica was thankful to catch a glimpse of the truck, still far ahead, but within sight. She didn't like how Xander seemed to have forgotten she was there, though none of his flexing, as he put it, came anywhere near her. She thought about the conversations they had before about the limits of his abilities, how he was no good at the detailed, delicate uses to which Alden put his gifts. If Alden could feel what Xander was doing now, she thought he would be disappointed or maybe even outraged. Part of her hoped he was bearing witness to this. Maybe it would force him to finally talk to Xander again.

Then the ground shook beneath her like an earthquake. Erica whipped around as she watched a huge line of trees shoot up between her and Xander. Reminiscent of when the bear came downtown, fully grown firs and cedars displaced huge amounts of soil as they climbed toward the sky. It was all Erica could do to keep her feet under her as Xander disappeared.

Erica ran toward him and fought her way through the gaps in the trees that were closing in by the second. She ignored the scrapes and welts that were forming on her arms and legs. When she reached him, Xander's eyes glowed green, and he didn't seem to recognize her. Gone was the tender, searching look he carried most of the time, replaced with something almost feral that made Erica's stomach drop. She had to snap him out of it, and she could only think of one way to make that happen. She clasped her hands behind his head and kissed him hard on the lips. To her surprise, he responded immediately. He opened his mouth and pulled her into him so that their bodies aligned.

He was frantic. He pulled at her jacket, but she pushed his hands down. "Not here," she shouted as the trees kept going up and up and up. She almost lost her balance as the dirt that was displaced by them gathered under her feet. She tried to point him in the direction of the truck, but she couldn't make sense of the landscape he had created. Xander flung an arm out in front of him, and trees went still. The two in front of them, each twice as thick as she was, dragged themselves along the ground, creating a trench of tilled soil in their wake. Xander was as motionless as the trees. Erica tried to pull on his outstretched hand, but it was like he was made of stone. She kissed him again, which woke him up enough for her to lure him back to the truck, his hands never leaving her. The truck was covered in waxy salal leaves that shrank from her hand as she moved to open the passenger side door. Xander laid a series of kisses on the back of her neck as she pulled on the handle and the leaves died upon her touch, allowing her to open the door.

Erica slid across the bench seat of the truck with Xander closely behind. He kissed her, deep and urgent, as he guided her into his lap with his strong hands. A leg on either side of him, she felt him fumble blindly for the zipper of her jacket. She let him pull the zipper down and help her out of it. Next came her shirt. She tried to be in the moment but checked the back window of the truck, hoping no one could see them. She need not have worried. Dense foliage covered the windows. As they kissed, new leaves grew in place of the ones she had destroyed.

Xander's whole body was humming. Erica went for the button on his jeans but stopped before she got to the zipper. She drew back and made him look her in the eyes. His were still green. She had started all this with the intention of bringing Xander back to her, but he looked just as wild as he had minutes ago surrounded by bushes and ferns. She had to know he was in there, that he wouldn't regret this when he was in his right mind.

She took his chin in her hand. "Do you know what's about to happen?"

Xander's lips curled into a playful smile that she recognized, and he nodded while he tugged on her waistband.

"Tell me you want this."

"I want this," he said, trying to reach up to kiss her, but she pushed his shoulders back into the seat. She stared into his eyes, which she thought might be dimming, but may have been a result of how dark it had become in the cab, how thick the cover was that surrounded it.

"Tell me you want *me*," she demanded.

He understood what she needed. His body relaxed under her, which caused her to sink further into him. This time it was he who put her face between his large hands and slowly, deliberately told her, "Erica, I have wanted you every minute since I saw you in the waterfall. Your wet hair, your legs that never end, a book in your hand. I am not a lucky person, and I don't believe in fate, but at that moment, I knew, or maybe I just hoped, that you were meant for me."

Erica couldn't breathe. She knew he meant it. His tone, his face, the way he slid his hands down her neck as he said the last syllables. This was the real Xander. They tore at their clothes, each of them high on the power they had over the other.

When it finally happened, when they came together after what felt like three long months of foreplay, it was everything she hoped it would be. Their bodies moved in sync, none of the pecking and pounding she experienced with others. One seamless motion. Xander kissed her mouth, her neck, her shoulders. When he was in the right spot, she grabbed the back of his hair which was getting messy and long. She cried out and he smiled, and she wondered how they could possibly have waited so long.

When they were done, she stayed in place, not wanting the moment to be over. They were a heap of sweat and giggles and half-removed clothes. One of the many things Erica loved about Xander was that he was never self-conscious about his body. He was sometimes hesitant about what she did to it, but after this, even that was gone.

But they couldn't stay there forever. They gathered articles of clothing, and Erica slid into the middle of the bench seat as she pulled her jeans on. Xander ran a finger over her naked hip one last time as if saying goodbye to it for now. Once fully dressed, Xander tried the car door, but it was stuck tight with salal. They both laughed, and he closed his eyes while he put his hand on the window. When he opened them, they were still deep emerald.

CHAPTER 11

Granny did not question why they came home without a tree. She sent Xander into the attic to find the artificial one, which they decorated together, singing along to old-timey Christmas classics.

Erica and Xander tried and failed to focus on the task at hand so as not to raise Granny's suspicions about what happened between them in the forest. They stole glances and touches and smiled far too often. They whispered to each other and then asked Granny questions in exaggerated voices without listening for the answers. After Erica dropped one of Granny's favorite hand-carved wooden ornaments, she shooed them outside to string warm white icicle lights from the roof. If Erica had been in charge of all her usual faculties, she would have realized how obvious they were, but she was high on Xander with no ground in sight.

Granny left a few hours later to meet her friends turned campaign managers to discuss strategy. With just over two weeks until the special election, they were going to have to pull a debate together quickly if they were to act on Erica's suggestion. Erica was supposed to attend this meeting, but Granny told her she could skip it if she and Xander promised to canvass for her a couple of days over the next week.

"You don't want my help?" Erica asked, a little wounded.

"It's not about what I want," Granny said, nodding meaningfully toward Xander.

Erica blushed to a shade of red she had not previously known she was capable of, but she didn't argue. If Granny was giving them the house, she was going to make the most of it. The moment the door closed, Erica grabbed Xander's arm and led him upstairs. They were half out of their clothes before they reached the bed.

Erica thought it felt more like a fight than an embrace as they removed the boxers and bras. She put her hands on his bare chest to push him down, but he grabbed her wrists and spun her around. The look on his face as she fell into the soft mattress, victorious and anticipatory, was worth losing to. Part of her wanted to slow things down, but there would be time for that later. Xander had nothing but time. She gave in to the rush.

If this was what love added to sex, Erica wondered how anyone did it without it. It was new to her to be this aware of someone, this present and uninhibited. To not have to wonder if he liked her, if he thought she was pretty. To know that even when she put her foot in the wrong place or accidentally bit his forehead that they could laugh together and stay focused on what was good. Because so much of it was good.

Even after was good. Xander had been in her bed almost every night for a month now, but naked Xander reminded her to be thankful for it. In the void after making love, Erica was struck unexpectedly with all the same feelings she had when Xander reappeared, whole and handsome, at his tree. She ran her hands across all of the places where there should be gnarls of scar tissue and instead there was perfect skin that became lighter every day they got closer to winter. It felt impossible that he could be real. And since he was real that he could be hers.

Erica propped herself up on her elbow and looked down at Xander's peaceful face. She ran her finger between his closed eyes and was happy to find the skin there completely smooth. She traced his cheekbones, his jaw, his forehead. All as familiar to her now as her own. Xander smiled and slowly opened his eyes. Startled, Erica dropped her hand and drew back.

"What?" Xander asked, self-consciously tugging her sheets up around himself.

"Your eyes." Erica wasn't sure if Xander had noticed the changes. He carried himself tall and straight, but he wasn't vain. She couldn't recall a single time that she saw him look in a mirror. Now was a good time for it, though. "Go look," she said and pointed to the vanity.

Xander fished around on the floor and put his boxers back on under the sheet before getting up. Erica couldn't stop catching glimpses of his eyes. They were unnaturally vivid and shone with an interior light that defied biology, like a laser through a gemstone. He had to stoop to see himself, but when he did he stepped back so fast he almost lost his balance.

He spun around to look at Erica. His voice came out raw, "When did that happen?"

"I thought I saw it a few times since you got back, but I wasn't sure. Today they've been like that since we," she faltered, "got back to the truck."

Xander was looking in the mirror again. He pulled down his eyelid as if hoping to see the line of a contact.

"After we—?"

"No. Right before that. When you were moving the big trees."

Xander sighed and ran his fingers through his hair. He sat down on the bed, gently picked up one of Erica's hands, and held it against his chest. She didn't like how quickly he resigned himself to this change. She also wasn't going to like whatever he was about to say.

"You remember our conversation when you came back from orientation?" Xander asked. Erica nodded and scowled at the memory. "I told you I wanted to help the forest. You told me to spend more time with people. I did it your way for this last month."

"And you liked it!" Erica interrupted. She wasn't sure this was true, but she needed it to be.

"I did. But this feeling, this calling, it's too much to ignore. Today out in the woods." Here Xander paused and reflected. "I've never felt that connected to my power. And it came so easily once I let my guard down and stopped doubting myself."

"You were out of it. You could have hurt me." Erica tried to pull her hand away, but he held it tight. His heartbeat was steady and calm. She knew she was grasping. She never felt unsafe when she was with him.

"No, I wouldn't have. I wish you could feel what I feel. I could see you the whole time and keep everything calm around you while making everything else explode. It was incredible, Erica. Like I was just the channel for all this energy that's always in these plants."

Xander's face was awash with excitement. He kept tugging on her arm to emphasize his point. She knew he wanted her to respond. She wanted to be happy for him. But all she could feel was loss. The emotions from the dark days after the bear bubbled up inside her and tears began to fall. She collapsed into his chest so he wouldn't see her cry. He finally let go of her hand and wrapped his arms around her.

"I don't want to lose you," Erica choked out between sobs.

"Why would you lose me?" Xander brushed her hair out of her eyes, but she wouldn't look up. She shook her head into his bare chest and cried harder. Erica wished she could explain everything that scared her. It was so much more than Kriners and fearing he would be discovered. But to say it out loud, to admit that their lives were headed in directions the other couldn't follow, felt like admitting defeat before the first shot was even fired. She wasn't ready. She may never be ready.

"I love you," she whispered into his ear. He leaned them both back onto the bed, and she settled herself in the crook of his shoulder. "Tell me more about what it's like. I want to understand."

Erica and Xander talked long past when they heard Granny come home from her meeting. She didn't knock on their door, and they didn't emerge to ask her how things went. The longer he spoke, the more Erica realized that there was no way she was going to stop him from trying to regrow the forest as fast as Kriners took it down. They established ground rules. He wasn't to go within two miles of active logging. Unlike the bear, he wouldn't leave threatening messages or harm people or equipment. They would keep what he was doing from everyone including Granny, but especially Derek and Kyle. Erica trusted Derek, but she didn't want to put him in a position where he might say something that would give Xander away.

Erica's final condition was that he wouldn't start until she went to college. They only had a month left together, and she wanted to spend as much time with him as possible. Even with conditions in place, she thought his plan was reckless. But she could feel the need radiate from him, both to help the forest and to gain her approval to do so. Even with his inhuman eyes, he was still Xander, and she didn't have it within her to hurt him any more than he already was.

The next morning at breakfast Granny handed Erica and Xander a map and a couple pages of hastily scrawled notes. They were both set to open at the store that morning. After they clocked out, they were headed to the trailer park on the edge of town to do some old-fashioned door-to-door canvassing.

"These folks are low income and lots of them are going to be super invested in the logging," Granny warned them. "That's why we're sending you. We think they might be less likely to slam their doors in the faces of teenagers."

"But also less likely to take us seriously," Erica said.

"Maybe, but I still think you're our best option. We know some of them and have written next to their address what might interest them. We can't beat Kriners talking about attracting jobs, so we have to tell them how we're going to make their lives easier. Expanded before and after school care programs and more funding for the food bank. That kind of thing."

Erica nodded. She didn't want to tell Granny that they were probably wasting their time. She was familiar enough with the residents of Juniper Falls to know that they resented the idea that they might need handouts. They would rather work fourteen hours a day breaking their backs on a logging site than try to take the easy way out. But in a town this small, every vote counted. She was willing to do her best to sway a couple in Granny's favor.

Xander was not excited about accompanying Erica on this errand. He was only just getting used to making small talk with customers at the store. Interrupting people in their own houses was a new level of social interaction that he wanted nothing to do with. Erica considered letting him bow out, but Granny made a big deal about there being safety in pairs, and he was forced to go along to atone for keeping Erica away from last night's strategy session.

At five o'clock, they walked home, swapped their *Farm & Feed* polos for cardigans, and headed out. It was the time of year when there was barely any light after normal work hours, which today was compounded by gloomy clouds that threatened rain. They drove toward the highway but took a right before the on-ramp and traveled down a roughly paved road until they came to the park. It was a mix of well-kept, vinyl-clad homes set in small patches of thick grass and tarnished, metal-sided trailers with too many cars parked around them. Erica had friends who lived here when she was very little, and back then she thought it was a fun place to grow up. The kids, grouped by age, roved around in packs, and there was a playground that had a spinner that they would take turns holding onto with their hands while they let their legs fly free until momentum made them lose their grip.

As she looked for a place to park her sedan, Erica's head-lights shone on the old playground. The paint was chipping, and the bark dust had been replaced by a rubber pad. The spin-ner had been removed. Too many broken arms and ankles, she assumed.

"You ready for this?" Erica asked. She gathered up their papers. They had a little over twenty homes to hit up, and she was hoping they would be done in a couple of hours.

"Not at all," Xander replied, but he opened his door and got out anyway.

They were late enough that lights were on in most of the windows. Erica took a deep breath and led Xander to their first door. She knocked, and they waited.

"Hello?" said the woman who opened the door. She looked

close to Erica's mother's age, but her hair was going gray at the temples. She was dressed in yoga pants and a zip-up hoodie, and Erica was suddenly embarrassed to be interrupting these people as they were clearly trying to unwind from their day. But she wanted this for Granny, so she powered through the awkwardness and started in on her script.

"We're with the Vivian Schueller campaign for town council. Are you Mrs. Lee?"

"Yeah," the woman said, wary but not angry.

"It says here that you work at a hospital in Roseburg. I was hoping to talk to you about how Mrs. Schueller is looking to secure funding to bring mobile healthcare services to the residents of Juniper Falls."

To Erica's surprise, Mrs. Lee crossed her arms and leaned in her doorframe. "What kind of services?"

Erica hadn't fully expected to get this far and had to check her notes. "Some vaccine clinics and routine physicals but mostly urgent care services. Did you know that currently the closest urgent care clinic is more than half an hour away?"

"I do know that."

"My granny," Erica caught herself. "I'm sorry, Mrs. Schueller, wants to improve the overall health of the community and that means improving access to healthcare for all residents." Mrs. Lee nodded. Erica wasn't sure where she was supposed to go from here. She saw the woman's eyes flash to Xander who hadn't said a word. Rather than get him involved, Erica handed over a business card that had the link to the website one of Granny's friend's grandkids had hastily pulled together for her as part of a Boy Scout badge project. "You can learn more about her platform by visiting her website."

"Okay. I will do that."

"Thank you so much for your time!" Erica said as the woman closed the door. She turned around and pulled Xander off the lawn and into the road before squealing in delight. "That wasn't so bad!"

Xander smiled at her as she squeezed his hand. "Hopefully they're all that easy."

They were not. Erica's flush of early success quickly dissipated after the next two houses did exactly what she expected and didn't let her make it to the end of her first sentence. They trudged on. Erica learned to offer a card first so at least if they hurried her away, they were left with something they might look at. A few women with small children listened to Erica explain Granny's plans to expand school offerings. Most of them didn't even know there was an election coming up. Erica thought this was fair. If Granny wasn't running, she doubted she would have paid attention to the signs on the road or bothered to read the flyers the Town sent out announcing voting hours.

For the most part, Xander said nothing during these interactions. He stood a few feet behind her like a bodyguard and whispered a quiet *thank you* to the people who heard Erica out. Still, his presence was comforting if only to have someone to debrief with between houses.

They were nearing the end of both their patience and the number of doors they had left to hit when they came across a particularly run-down trailer. Its dirty windows glowed a dusty orange, and she could hear a television turned up too loud inside. As they approached, Erica saw a shiny chainsaw, an almost exact replica of the one Kyle had used to cut down the bear tree, sitting in the back of a rusted pickup truck parked on what should have been the front lawn. She pointed it out to Xander.

"Maybe we should skip this one," he said.

Erica felt like she was in an old cartoon with little manifestations of her conscience sitting on each shoulder—one telling her this interaction couldn't possibly be worth it and the other telling her she couldn't let Granny down. They fought with each other as she hesitated in front of the door. Her love for Granny won out.

"I'm going to do it."

"I wouldn't," Xander said, but he positioned himself behind her, closer than he had been at previous houses.

She knocked. She could hear what sounded like glass hitting wood and rustling as a figure moved toward the door. The door creaked open slowly, leaking a stale smell of body odor and unwashed dishes. In front of them was a large man in a white undershirt. He was every inch a lumberjack down to the bushy brown beard and dirt-stained jeans. Something about him felt familiar.

"What?" he asked.

"We're with the Vivian Schueller campaign—."

He interrupted her. "Who?"

"Vivian Schueller. She's running for town council and—."

He cut her off again. "Who are you?"

"I'm Erica Wright. Her granddaughter. I'm talking to people in the community about why they should vote for her in the special election happening in two weeks." Erica already knew this was a mistake, but she couldn't just hightail it now.

"Who is he?" the man asked, pointing a meaty finger at Xander.

"Xander Reed." She felt him put a hand on the small of her back, and she took a half-step into him just in case.

The lumberjack rolled this name around in his mind before replying, "Your weirdo uncle owns that shop downtown that he won't fix." It was an accusation that took both Erica and Xander by surprise. Then she registered his face. He was on the crew of men who were repairing the sidewalk downtown when Granny decided to run. "Your grandma wants to run Kriners out of town and put us all out of a job and your uncle can't get off his lazy ass to make this place not look like a shit hole."

"I'm sorry for wasting your time," Erica said. She backed up further, putting her hands behind her to push Xander toward the road.

"I knew your mom," the lumberjack said. Erica thought he was talking to her but was surprised to see it was Xander holding his gaze. "She thought she was too good for this place, and then she tried to light you both on fire. We thought she got you for a long time too. People say you're not right in the head after that. So, are you?"

Erica heard the wet click of Xander opening his mouth to respond. She pushed him harder, and he had to shift his focus to regain his balance. Not wanting to turn her back on the man, she nonetheless faced Xander. Standing on her tiptoes, she whispered, "Not worth it."

Xander looked down at her, his newly green eyes burning. She thought he would confront the man, but he let her entwine his fingers in hers and lead him away.

"Fucking weirdos," the man called after them, not leaving his door.

There were only four houses to go but Erica skipped them. She could hear Xander breathing like a bull after a fight. They were not being pursued, but they flung themselves into the car when they reached it. Erica started it and drove them as fast as she could back to the main road.

"I'm so sorry," she said when the scene felt far enough behind them. She glanced at Xander who sat straight as a pine tree and stared out the windshield. For a long time, he was silent. She could only imagine what he was feeling. She listened to his breathing to calm until it almost stopped.

"This is the problem," he said when they were only a few minutes from home.

"What do you mean?"

"I can't be fully in your world. They reject me."

Erica's chest tightened. "That's not true. That was one guy. Think of all the people you talk to every day who like you. Granny and Joe and Derek. Customers."

"But it can't last. Someday I'll be the weirdo. Like Alden."

"Not for a very long time."

"Someday, though."

Erica reached over to grab his hand. He pulled away. It stung her to her core.

"My mom didn't mean to start that fire. It was an accident."

"I know," she said, returning her hand to the steering wheel and navigating them into the driveway of Granny's yellow house. She turned off the engine, and they sat there. She couldn't think of anything to say that he couldn't refute.

"We have time," she said finally, more to herself than anything. Xander looked at her. She fought the tears in her eyes. It was less than a day since she had cried over this exact same thing, and she didn't want to be another person who brought him down.

Seeing her wet eyes loosened the tense hold of his jaw. She inched her hand toward his again, and he took it this time, bringing it to his lips and kissing her knuckles. He dropped their clasped hands into his lap and sighed.

"Yes," he said. "We have time."

CHAPTER 12

After their experience in the trailer park, Erica was determined to talk to Alden. She knew she had been selfish to ask Xander to shut out the dryad part of himself completely. Alden had found a way to use his gifts to participate in the world even if it was from a distance. When he was tracking Kriners' movements and, eventually, those of the bear, he never interfered. If she and Alden could put their differences aside, they might be able help Xander find the balance he so desperately needed.

The question was how to reach out to him in a way that he might answer without Xander finding out. Alden was a sore spot for him, and she didn't want him to know she was meddling until she was sure it would work. She remembered the scratches on her arms that took weeks to heal after her last attempt to confront Alden at his cabin. She thought about sending a letter to his store address, but she wasn't sure if he would get it.

Thursday was the six-month anniversary of Keith's disappearance. She and Granny were taking the day off to spend together, and their plans included placing a wreath on Keith's grave. That would put her within easy distance of Alden's tree. She wasn't sure how much detail Xander could make out when he tapped into the ecosystem, but she hoped he would be busy enough at work to not be paying too much attention.

Keeping a secret from Xander was harder than Erica thought it would be. She had gotten used to sharing everything with him that being forced to filter her thoughts took serious focus. The week passed at a snail's pace. Xander called her out more than once for being distracted, so she did her best to stay in the present especially when they were alone. They had been talking less since adding a new element to their relationship after their trip to the forest, so it was easy to do.

Erica found the time to write Alden in between customers on one of the rare shifts she had at the store without Xander. She didn't think that Alden was the type to respond to too cloying a plea, so she did her best to sound sincere without begging. This required several drafts, which was challenging when it had frozen the night before and the whole town was in search of burlap and plastic to guard their landscaping. The letter was short and to the point, appealing to their mutual love of Xander.

She folded the letter the way that she and her friends used to in middle school when they would pass notes. The result was a compact square with ends that tucked in to form a diagonal line from corner to corner. Earlier drafts had included all of their names, but Erica worried what someone would think if they found it before Alden did. For the same reason, she did not address it, but instead meant to leave it at the base of his tree and hope he came for it.

On Wednesday night, Granny came home with a wreath form. She had been pressing leaves since they began falling in October and raided her stash of pinecones. Erica, Xander, and Granny sat at the dining table and assembled the wreath while telling stories about Keith. Erica had been so caught up in herself, in college and Xander, that she forgot how much she missed him. If he had been around, Alden would already have forgiven her, and the four of them would be working together to help Xander build his future.

In the morning, Granny and Erica put on nice clothes and warm coats and drove to the cemetery, Erica's note to Alden hidden in the pocket of her dark jeans.

"I can't believe it's been half a year," Granny said as they walked up the hill, past the two white oaks, and to the other side where Keith's grave overlooked the town. "It still feels like he could walk through the door at any minute."

"He loved this time of year. Fewer hikers on the trails."

Granny smiled. The headstone came into view, white granite with black letters and still too new for any moss to have accumulated on its smooth surface. They stood in front of it, silent tears wetting Granny's cheeks. "I wish I believed he could hear us."

"We should talk to him anyway."

Granny inhaled, swallowing back new tears. She laid the wreath so that it hung half over the headstone, obscuring Keith's name. Erica didn't think he would mind. They took turns telling him about their lives without him, starting with Granny.

"You would be annoyed with me, probably, for being so sappy as to decorate your grave. But I also think you secretly liked it when people made a fuss over you."

"You would be so proud of Granny. She is running for town council and she's going to make everyone's lives better."

"Erica is starting at Cascades next month, and Danni hasn't even called me this week to make sure she's still going."

"Xander asked me to tell you that he misses you."

They went on like this until they ran out of things to say. Erica felt lighter after. They stood for a few more minutes and watched the wind rustle the leaves of the wreath. She put her arm around Granny and squeezed. She was always startled by how delicate Granny was, as if she was likely to blow away any moment.

"I need to do something," she told Granny as she let go. Erica made her way to Alden's tree, giving Xander's a wide berth that she knew it was pointless. His reach spread further every day.

She put her hand on the rough, layered bark of Alden's tree. She left it there, wondering if she could feel a heartbeat in it the same way she could Xander's. But like everything about Alden even his tree was guarded. Erica leaned in and whispered, "I need to talk to you about Xander." She ran her hand down the trunk to the ground and placed her note in a fold of its roots.

In case Xander was watching her right now, she thought she should make a move to throw him off her trail. She went to his tree and kissed it lightly. It was cold and devoid of leaves but hung on to a handful of ever-present acorns. "I love you," she said, and she drew the outline of a heart on its bark with her pointer finger. Her phone buzzed in her purse.

Xander: I love you too.

No concerns or accusations. Erica hated breaking his trust, but she hoped it would be worth it. Granny joined her at the crest of the hill.

"Can they hear you?" she asked.

"Yeah," Erica replied. "I think it helps if you touch them."

"Which one is Alden's?" Erica pointed to the lighter and larger of the two trees. Granny spread her fingers and put her hand on it. "Don't be a stranger, old friend."

Erica hoped this would help her case. She looked around half expecting to see Alden make his way toward them now. He didn't, and Erica's phone buzzed again.

Derek: Fam here. Meet at coffee stop?

Erica saw it was a group text that included her, Xander, and Kyle.

Kyle: When?

Derek: Now

Kyle: OMW

Her phone was ringing now. This time it was Xander. She answered.

"Are we going?" he asked by way of a greeting.

"We told him we would."

"Pick me up?"

Erica looked at Granny. They were supposed to have lunch at Keith's favorite place downtown. But Granny was someone who didn't stand on ceremony and believed in helping friends. She would understand.

"I'll be there in ten."

As expected, Granny was happy to take Xander's spot at the store when Erica explained, in as few words as possible, that Derek needed them. When they arrived, Xander finished checking out one last customer before apologizing to Granny for ruining her plans.

"Keith would have told me I've spent too much time mourning anyway," she told him.

Xander's smile was sad, and he gave her a one-armed hug that took them both off guard. Erica took great pleasure in the bond that was forming between them. She would sleep easier at Cascades knowing he had a larger support system.

Erica mouthed thank you to Granny before Xander rushed them out the door. The energy coming off of Xander as they took the few steps toward the car was far too tense for her liking. He made a play for the driver's seat. Erica shook her head.

"I'm driving. You need a minute to chill out."

"I want to make it there before anything happens."

Erica took the keys out of her pocket and rattled them. "Not negotiable."

Xander grumbled but gave in. Erica waited until he was seated and the door was closed before getting in herself. Then she told him, "I think you're worried about nothing. They're his family, and we're meeting them during broad daylight in public."

"They might have brought people who aren't family. Other people like Derek."

"I don't think there's about to be a bear fight at the Coffee Stop." Erica turned the car on and slipped it into reverse. She wasn't driving slowly on purpose. The speed limit was only twenty-five through downtown. Xander balled his fists and kept glancing at the speedometer. Erica put her hand on his and worked her fingers between his long, thin ones until they unclenched. "I feel like you are looking for an excuse to try out your new tricks."

Xander whipped his head around, but Erica kept her face neutral and her eyes on the road. Their hands fought in silence as he tried to ball his up again and she dragged her fingers along his knuckles to prevent it. She wanted him to be worked up here in the car so that he could be calm, cool Xander when they arrived. The best thing he could do for Derek would be to lurk in the background and look imposing.

"It was nice visiting Keith this morning," Erica said, determined to deflect his attention. "I'm glad he was so close to you and Alden." She glanced at him, and he was staring out the windshield again as if willing the car to go faster. Erica decided to try again. "You know I don't believe in any kind of afterlife—."

"I felt you hovering around Alden's tree," Xander said, cutting her off.

Erica did her best not to tense up. She ran her forefinger down to his palm and back. "Granny wanted to say hi." It wasn't a lie. It wasn't the whole truth either. "It must be hard for her to have gotten an old friend back and then lost him so soon."

"It's hard for her?" Xander snapped and pulled his hand away from hers.

Erica sighed. "Yes, Xander. The last few months have been hard on all of us. No one is getting what they want these days."

"You are, aren't you? Parents off your back. Boyfriend at home. Headed to college."

"You want me to go to college! Say the word and I'll stay."

"No you won't and I would never ask you to." He slumped into his seat and exhaled a long breath. She could feel his eyes on her, searching her face for a reason she was egging him on. Emotion radiated off of him. Disappointment. Erica knew the feeling after eighteen years spent with her mother. "I need your support too, Erica. You said you would."

Every instinct in Erica told her to comfort him, to deflect, to assure him that she could be everything he needed. She went with honesty even if she could only just manage to whisper it. "I'm not sure I know how."

"I know." The tone of surrender in Xander's voice broke something in Erica. Something she wasn't sure she could put back together.

She put her foot on the gas, letting the car go ten over as soon as they hit the highway. The corners of Xander's mouth twitched in recognition as the engine chugged along. It was a little victory, a concession, an apology. But it couldn't erase the cracks that were forming.

Erica pulled into the Coffee Stop, which was significantly less crowded than when she when she was last here. There was a short line at the drive-through, but it was cold enough that few people wanted to sit outside despite the radiant heat lamps that were dotted around the tent. Erica could only make out two occupied tables through the fishbowl effect created by the tent's plastic sides. She parked next to Derek's beat-up hatchback and was relieved when Xander slowly got out of the car and waited for her instead of rushing in.

"Should we get coffee?" she asked. "Doesn't look like there's too much excitement happening in there."

"You can." Xander stared at the dark heads in the tent, the distortion making it impossible to tell where one person ended and another began.

"Right. Wait for me, though? If it's going well, maybe we can sit apart from them. Make it look casual."

"It's tense."

"You can feel it?"

Xander nodded. Erica left him positioned halfway between the stand and the tent and ordered a mocha, whole milk, at the take-out window. She was hungry, having missed lunch with Granny, but now was not the time to throw back a sandwich.

She joined Xander as she waited for her mocha to be ready. She leaned into him, and he wrapped an arm around her. "Can you make out what they're saying?"

"Not really. More just the general atmosphere."

"Do you know who is there?"

"Derek. Kyle. Three others with them. A woman, a man, and a girl." Xander closed his eyes. "There is also a couple a few tables away, but they don't seem to be involved."

Erica felt relief rush through her. Part of her wished she had ordered the sandwich. "See? It's just his family. No bears."

"Derek is scared, though," Xander said, at the same time as a barista called out, "Erica," as though she wasn't the only person waiting for a coffee.

The mocha warmed her fingers as they made their way to the tent. When Xander lifted the flap, the tent made a horrible screech of plastic on plastic and blasted the tables with cold air. Five heads snapped to look at them. Erica could tell immediately that the woman and the girl were related to Derek. They were both slight and sat like their limbs were held together with string. The man was taller and pale with hair that may have once been strawberry blonde but was now mostly strawberries and cream. His face was ruddy and bloated, and he had a hard time sitting still.

Derek was slouched so far away from the man, who Erica assumed must be his father, that she wondered how he didn't fall off the picnic bench. Kyle was doing an excellent job of looking menacing, making sure his meaty fists sat in the middle of the table as a warning. There was no room for Erica and Xander at their table, so she nodded to Kyle and took a seat on the bench immediately behind them, facing the action. Xander leaned back on his elbows and stretched his legs onto the seat next to Derek who gave him a small smile of appreciation.

"Are you that scared, kid, that you had to bring a girl?" the man chuckled.

"She's with me," Xander said, intentionally deepening his already baritone voice.

"And who are you?"

"A friend," Xander said with a cold smile. Erica felt a little bad for needling at him in the car. He seemed in control, self-assured in a way that made her wish she could kiss him. Derek's dad was not as impressed. He leered at them for a moment before returning to the conversation that must have already been underway when they arrived.

"This is your final warning. Jerry is going to send some of the boys down if you don't come back with us."

"We could probably get him to lay off you until the season starts next year if you needed to finish some things out," Derek's mother said. Erica could tell that she was someone used to placating unreasonable people. The sweetness in her tone was a little too hopeful, too performative. Erica tried to catch her eye, but the older woman avoided it.

Derek shook his head. His voice came out thin and weary like he knew the answer before he said it. "You should come out here. Get out from under Jerry and the rest of them. You know that what they have going on up there isn't right."

"How many times do I have to tell you it was an accident!" Derek's father shouted. The couple in the corner, who had been trying a little too hard not to look at them, gave up and gathered their scarves, bags, and cups.

"Mom. Anna. You know that's not true," Derek pleaded. Anna's eyes hadn't yet left the table, and she made no indication that she heard him.

"I don't know, baby. None of us were there. We should give Jerry the benefit of the doubt," his mother responded.

"Even if it was an accident, it happened because they were all boozed up. Like if they keep us in whiskey and girls they don't have to pay us shit. I'm making way better money here." Derek looked to Kyle for backup. "Right, man?"

Kyle looked startled at being drawn into the conversation but recovered quickly. "Oh yeah, great money."

Xander stiffened next to Erica. She thought she knew why. He hadn't come to defend Kriners and convince Derek's family to live off logging money. She thought she felt the ground below her shift. She elbowed Xander's side, but he didn't flinch.

Derek's father was shouting again. "It's not just about the money. It's about the roof over our heads! You want your sister to be homeless?"

"Of course I don't fucking want that. If anything, I'm hoping she won't get back on that plane with you!" Derek's demeanor changed when his attention shifted from his father to his sister. "I can find us a place here, Banana. Do you want to stay?"

Anna lifted her big, dark eyes when her father yanked her arm. "She's fifteen!" he yelled. "She's coming with us if I have to use her as goddamned bear bait!"

At this, Derek lunged across the table and grabbed his father by his shirt. Kyle immediately thrusted his arm between them, and Xander jumped to his feet. Derek's mother and sister shuffled to the corner of the bench, but they weren't cowering. Erica wondered how many times a similar scene had played out.

"You fucking asshole!" Derek was yelling. "If you would get a fucking job maybe you wouldn't have to live off your kid."

"What's the point of having spawned a freakshow if I can't make a little money off him? What else are you good for?"

This time it was Derek's father who tried to swing at his son, but he barely made it an inch off his seat before he was slammed back down. Woody tendrils wound themselves around his thighs to keep him rooted to the bench and made their way around his forearms. Everyone noticed them at the same time, and Derek's mother and Anna jumped up from the table.

"The fuck is this?" the man yelled. The tendrils pulled his arms into his chest and strapped them to his torso. "Where did you pick up this trick?" he stammered at Derek, not registering that he might not be the only one in the room who was more than they appeared.

"I've made some friends," Derek said. All eyes moved to Xander whose green eyes were blazing as if someone had lit a candle in his skull.

"Enough!" Erica said. She jumped off the bench and peeked out the tent flap. The couple was gone and no one else was coming, but that didn't mean they wouldn't. "This is not a productive conversation. What's going to happen is you two," Erica said to Derek's mom and sister, "are going to come to my house with Derek to have a real discussion."

"You are not taking my family away from me, bitch!" The last word turned into a strangled yell as the tendrils holding Derek's father tightened.

"Watch your mouth," Xander hissed.

"Xander. Enough. Seriously." Erica stared at him until he loosened the clenched fist he was holding at his side just enough for Derek's father's lips to stop turning blue. "Kyle, can you babysit Mister—." Erica stumbled, realizing she didn't know Derek's last name.

"Kelly," Derek said helpfully.

"Can you babysit Mister Kelly for us while we try to sort this out?"

"I swear to fuck's sake that if you three take one step out of here without me, so help me, I will—."

"You'll what, Dad?" Derek was still sitting across from him, his demeanor greatly improved by having his father restrained. "You think this is how you convince me to come back home? I don't know why Mom and the others stay, but the minute Anna turns eighteen, I'll come home one last time. To make sure she never has to set foot in that house again."

Derek's mother let out a noise between a cry and a whimper and clutched Anna's wrist as if she was about to run away on the spot. Erica flagged her attention as verbal jabs continued to be thrown across the table. The two backed slowly away from the table to join Erica by the entrance.

"Will you come with me?" Erica asked.

The woman gave her an appraising look, though more than half of her attention was still on her husband. "He will be so mad."

"Will he hit you?"

"Oh, no, not us," she said, her face drooping as she looked at Derek. "Probably just more of this all the way home." Anna nodded at her mother's side. Her almost black eyes were large in a way that would almost have been comical had they not been so sad, like the caricature of a kicked puppy.

"Can I ask you a question?" Erica prodded, trying to keep their attention away from the scene at the table. When neither answered, she continued, "Do you think anything will improve if Derek comes home? I know it will be worse for him, but will it be any better for you?"

Derek's mother's eyes snapped to meet Erica's. Erica already towered over them, but she threw her shoulders back and straightened her spine. Anna winced, but her mother didn't look away. Erica was reminded of elementary school staring contests, though she didn't remember getting the feeling back then that her opponent was able to read her like a book. Maybe she had judged this woman too soon.

"We'll go. But only if you answer a question for me too." Erica nodded, trying to keep her face neutral. She pointed to Xander. "What exactly is he?"

Erica smiled. "That can be one of the things we discuss."

CHAPTER 13

Extracting themselves from the Coffee Stop was not easy. Erica learned Derek's parents' names—Brian and Kim—as he yelled and she cajoled while Erica tried to herd them toward her car. Xander wanted to stay with Kyle and Brian to keep the latter under control, but Erica had a feeling that a large part of Kim's willingness to come along was her curiosity about him. In the end, they figured that Kyle had enough muscle to get Derek's father somewhere that he could throw a fit in private once the rest were far enough away for Xander to release him.

As they drove, Erica asked Xander to call her grandmother so she knew they were coming. Granny and Joe had been discussing whether he needed her to run the cash register after Xander left, so Erica wasn't sure if she would be at home or at the store. It turned out Granny had gone home, and they walked through the door to the smell of freshly brewed coffee and chocolate chip cookies baking in the oven. Tulip was nowhere to be found, which meant Granny must have locked her away upstairs in preparation.

"Derek!" Granny exclaimed as though she hadn't only met him once on Thanksgiving. "This must be your family!"

Derek introduced his mother and sister, and Granny got everyone settled in the living room. She grabbed Erica's arm and gently guided her to the kitchen after gathering everyone's drink preferences.

"What precisely is it that is being mediated in there?" she asked as she poured coffee into mugs.

"It's a long story," Erica said, "but essentially we're trying to save them, or at least Derek, from his abusive dad." She poured a glass of orange juice for Anna. After shoving the carton back in the fridge, she made a move to hasten back into the living room, but Granny stopped her.

"I think we should let them work it out themselves, don't you? At least until the cookies are ready."

"But Xander is out there." Erica's adrenaline was pumping, and she wasn't sure if she was being protective or envious.

"I don't think he'll impose himself too much on their conversation."

Erica let out a little laugh, and Granny raised her barely-there eyebrows knowingly. It was true that around strangers Xander was about as talkative as his tree in the cemetery. As much as she didn't want to miss out on the action, this wasn't her fight. She had a very recent, very painful experience inserting herself into situations where she was out of her depth.

Granny put her finger on her lips and nodded in the direction of the living room. They listened intently while leaning up against the counter. They could only make out the cadence of the conversation, not actual words. Derek and his mother were both pleading their case but neither was giving in. It didn't sound like the arguments Erica was used to having with her own mother. Those escalated to yelling on both sides very soon after they started.

The kitchen timer—not the one on the stove but an old plastic egg timer in the shape of a chicken that Granny always insisted was somehow more accurate—buzzed to tell them the cookies were ready. Granny pulled the metal sheet out carefully and moved the hot cookies to a baking rack.

"One more round, I think." She spooned spheres of dough out of the mixing bowl onto the cookie sheet. Erica drummed her fingers against the countertop, itching to be in the midst of things but giving in to Granny's better judgment. Her phone buzzed.

Xander: Where are you?

Erica smiled and showed it to Granny. "I can't read that without my glasses, love."

"Xander is wondering where we are."

"He can stand the suspense for a little longer." Erica giggled and texted him back.

Erica: Granny is holding me hostage in the kitchen.

Xander: I feel like a hostage.

Erica put her phone back in her pocket. She took the now-empty bowl of cookie dough from Granny and rinsed it in the sink. She had just poured out some dish soap when the tone of the conversation in the living room changed. Granny and Erica raced into the other room to find little Anna standing up and giving them all a piece of her mind.

"Why are you pretending we can go back to normal? When have we been normal? It's not normal that Derek can turn into a bear. It's not normal that Dad doesn't work. And what's this guy's deal?" she shouted without taking a breath. Her voice was as high as Erica would have expected, and it didn't help her impression of her as a yappy puppy.

"I'm a dryad," Xander said, clearly trying to be helpful. Erica shot him a look, shocked he said it that easily.

Kim made a sound of interest, but Erica cut in. "Anna, you're right, it's not normal. You probably had a longer time to get used to this than I have, but I can understand why you're angry. If it helps, you're Derek's number one priority. He's here to make sure you have options."

"What do you have to do with anything?" Anna asked. Her tone was sharp and biting, deservedly so. She was right. Erica held her hands up in defeat and turned her attention to Derek, encouraging him to speak with a lift of her eyebrows.

"I said it a million times today. I can't go back there," Derek said. He sounded tired and fought to look his mother in the eye. "Even if they don't kill me, which, okay, seems unlikely, I can't go home. I can't turn out like Dad and the rest of them. I got to be me."

"Can't you be you with us? In Kodiak?" Kim attempted.

"What if I could convince Dad that you didn't have to work for them?"

Derek's hands balled into fists that he rubbed up and down the thighs of his ever-present black jeans. "That wouldn't happen. You know you're lying that you think it could work." He turned to address Anna, his face softening as much as his tone. "Banana, stay. They're not going to call the cops on us. The high school here is shit but Oregon has good colleges."

Anna opened her mouth, but Kim cut her off. "That's not going to happen. So you can put that out of your mind right now."

The siblings both sighed. Derek diverted his eyes to his lap, and Anna sat down on the end of the couch farthest from her mother. Erica walked to where Derek sat on the blue recliner and put a hand on his shoulder. To her surprise, he laid his hand on top and squeezed. She was about to try to initiate conversation again when the chicken timer binged from the kitchen.

"I'm going to go get us some cookies," Granny said cheerfully. "And when I get back, I would love to hear more about where you're from, Kim." The whole room stared at Granny as she left, trying to process the casualness of her tone as if she hadn't heard the rest of the conversation.

"My grandmother, it turns out, is a stellar politician," Erica said to no one in particular.

Granny called Erica to help her bring out the drinks they had left in the kitchen. Erica brushed a hand along Xander's shoulder and tugged his sleeve on her way out of the room, encouraging him to join her.

"It's been nice to learn that no one's family is perfect," Xander said once they were in the kitchen gathering up mugs and cups. Xander could carry two each in his big hands.

"Of course not," Granny said. She piled a plate high with cookies and pulled the roll of paper towels off its holder. "We all have our problems."

When they came back in, each member of Derek's family was looking at a different corner of the room, as if pretending to care about the shabby decor was a better alternative to having to talk to each other. Erica and Xander handed out drinks, and Granny followed behind with cookies. Xander reclaimed his seat on the red recliner, and Erica opted to lean against his legs. This left only the spot between Kim and Anna on the couch, which Granny took without a moment's hesitation.

"Kodiak is a beautiful place, I've heard," Granny said, her whole attention on Kim. "Are you from there?"

Kim shifted uncomfortably, cradling her black coffee in her hands. "Why don't you just ask what you really want to ask?"

"I don't know what you mean," Granny said, her politeness never faltering.

"You want to know why my kid is a bear."

Granny shrugged. "It's just one piece of information among many that I would be interested to learn about your family."

The women held each other's gaze in a bemused sort of way. Erica didn't know how to explain that this wasn't Granny attempting to be rude. She was sincere in her line of questioning and probably would have been just as happy talking about how many hours of sunlight they got during the summer as to how Derek came to be the way he was.

"Just tell her the story, Mom," Anna said. Erica thought that Anna could probably tell it just as well.

Kim set her mug on the end table and relaxed on the couch. The resemblance to Derek was stronger than ever. "We think the bear gene comes from Native Alaskans, but the truth is that pretty much when white people showed up on Kodiak, they took everything over like they always do. I couldn't tell you if I even have any Native blood. I didn't know about Jerry Whitlock and his family's history of cultivating werebears until Derek came along."

"Cultivating?" Granny asked, her eyes wide.

"It sounds nicer than breeding, doesn't it? But it's unpredictable. It runs in families, but it's not like you can draw a little square and figure out your odds of a werebear. You could have ten kids and maybe two would have it. Or none."

"Tell them about the first time Derek turned," Anna said.

She hadn't touched her orange juice but had chocolate and crumbs on her lips.

"He was two days old. He was screaming, but I was doing something for one of the older boys. When I looked back in the bassinet, there was this tiny fuzzy thing where my baby was. Have you ever seen a newborn grizzly? Not cute. Half-naked, eyes closed. I thought one of the kids swapped it out as a prank. I was screaming at everyone, and this animal was whining. I tossed it outside and looked everywhere for Derek. Two hours later I go, and my baby is asleep on the porch. I lost it on the kids again, but I knew they had no idea what was going on. Then it happened again, and I realized something was going on when he cried."

"It's anger. It makes it easier to change," Derek said. He was looking between Erica and Xander and Granny, a worried look on his face. For Erica's part, she didn't feel as though anything could surprise her anymore. She shrugged at him and nodded as if it all made perfect sense.

"We let him smoke pot as a teenager. Parents of the year, I know, but imagine if every time your kid was pissed at you, you wound up with a three-hundred-pound bear tearing up your living room."

"Come on, Mom. I got it under control before that. I even got to go to school for a little bit."

"You did. You were a good kid," Kim conceded.

"Until dad found out," Anna piped in. She wiped the crumbs off her lips with the back of her hand and looked to her mother to finish the story. Kim brought her coffee cup to her lips and shook her head once. Anna explained, "Mom made us keep it a secret from everyone, including Dad. But Beau, our oldest brother, slipped up one day. Dad hit Derek until he changed. And then he figured out who to tell."

"Your father doesn't have the most sense sometimes," Kim said, so quiet that Erica almost didn't catch it.

No one spoke as they filled in the blanks for themselves based on what they already knew. Erica thought about how hard it must have been for Derek to hide such a big part of himself out of fear of his father. Fear that wound up being justified.

"You said something a while back about the lore around werebears. What does it say about how they came to be?" Xander asked.

Derek leaned his head back and looked at the pattern in the textured ceiling. "This is just what Jerry says, so who knows if it's anywhere near true. But they say the first werebear wasn't a man that turned into a bear. The legend says that a bear found a beautiful woman in the woods and fell in love." Erica held in a comment on bestiality as Derek continued. "Supposedly their kids were able to shapeshift between forms. I did some research later and shapeshifting is a big deal in Native culture, but it's thought of as more spiritual. Not quite this literal."

Xander nodded. From her spot on the floor, Erica looked up at his strong chin, his jaw set. She knew what he was going to ask.

"Do you have any lore about me?"

"Nah, man."

"I heard something," Kim said. Xander snapped his attention to her. Erica saw Kim clock the unnatural greenness of his eyes for the first time. "It's not Kodiak lore. I'm not sure where I heard it. I didn't grow up with Native stories. That came after everything with Derek. But there are legends of spirits who protect the forest and whisper to the trees."

"Do you know what happens when the spirit dies?" Xander inched forward in his seat, pushing his knees into Erica's back.

"Supposedly the forest dies."

Erica could feel his entire body tense at this comment. She shifted onto her knees to look at him and watched the wild conclusions he was drawing dance across his face. She took his hands in hers and rubbed his palms. "Later," she whispered.

He looked down at her and then back to Kim who was watching them closely.

"What did you say you were again?" Kim asked. Her mug was empty, and she set it on the end table with a sharp thud. Erica tried to warn him with her gaze, with her touch. He had already given enough away.

Xander let go of her hands. "Do you want to see something?"

The afternoon wrapped up quickly after Xander entertained them with the orchid in the corner of the living room, a remnant of Keith's funeral flowers only kept alive by the constant presence of a dryad in their house. He coaxed stem after stem out of the lush green leaves, the ends of which exploded into fat, white flowers. Kim asked him about the extent of his power, but he remained modest and made it sound as though it was limited to these kinds of tricks. Erica knew the nonchalance was a ruse by the way he wouldn't meet her eye.

Derek texted Kyle after accepting that he was at a stalemate with his mother and felt confident that if his father had more up his sleeve than yelling at him at a coffee stand something would have manifested by now. Kyle was entertaining Brian at the Diner off the highway, which was busy enough this time of day that he couldn't make too much of a scene. Derek thanked Granny for providing them sanctuary and ushered his family toward the door. Erica offered to drive them, but Derek was feeling okay. She made him promise to text her when he had safely deposited them all at a hotel or an airport and was back home, though she wasn't sure where home was for him.

Derek did text Erica later that afternoon, mostly to lament that he had not been able to figure out how to get Anna to stay. She would much rather have given more attention to that conversation than the one she and Xander were engaged in from the moment everyone left. Xander was convinced that bringing down the bear dryad had doomed the entire forest.

"It explains so much," he said, his hands in his curls, pacing the few steps her small bedroom allowed. "Things haven't been right since then. I haven't been right. What if it's some kind of curse? What if I'm dying?"

"You're stronger than ever. I don't think you're dying." Two hours ago, Erica had been holding and soothing him, but as Xander had been spewing these same concerns the entire time, she was now settled into her bed scrolling through her phone. When he threw himself at her feet, stretching his long body across the width of the mattress, she was hopeful he had finally worn himself out.

The room was quiet for several minutes before Erica took her eyes off her phone and saw Xander watching her.

"What?" she asked.

"I'm stronger than ever."

"I know. I just said that." Erica lifted her phone back up, but Xander reached out and put a hand over the screen. He moved catlike up the bed until his face was within inches of hers.

"The power. How in tune I am with the forest. The need to get out there and undo the damage Kriners is doing. My eyes." Then Erica knew where this was going. She dropped her phone and put her hands on Xander's shoulders, shaking her head. It didn't stop him from saying it. "I'm supposed to replace the bear dryad. The forest is dying without me."

Erica's heart pounded, and she wanted to deny, deny, deny. She pushed her forehead into his, hard, as she tried to formulate the words that would allow them to maintain this precarious balance they had struck. The one where she got to pretend that they had the same needs and desires and plans. The one that felt like it was slipping away the closer she got to college, and he got to being set loose upon the forest without her to distract him.

"You can't know that," she whispered. "It's an old wives' tale. Folklore. Stories."

"That's what I am, Erica. Something out of a story. Plus, I feel it. I've been feeling it. Since the minute I was conscious again. Something shifted, and I've spent weeks trying to make sense of it."

She pushed against his shoulders even harder, but she was no match for him. Without registering how he did it, Erica found herself on her back with Xander on top of her, staring down at her. She crossed her arms behind his neck and filled her hands with fistfuls of his hair.

"What are you going to do?" she whispered on the exhale.

"I think I'm going to start by talking to Alden."

He kissed her then, and Erica wondered how something could feel so comfortable, so familiar, so homey, and at the same time so hopeless.

CHAPTER 14

Erica called Joe the next morning and asked if she could take a half-day and come in after lunch. She drove to Roseburg ostensibly to buy Christmas gifts and school supplies, but also to give herself a break from everything Juniper Falls. Derek texted her as she was driving that his family was headed back to Portland for their flight. She sent him a couple of appropriate emojis then contemplated shutting her phone off. Between Derek and Xander and Granny's debate that evening, she was in critical need of a few hours to herself.

She had her finger on the button but, before the screen went dark, she had another idea. It was barely nine in the morning, and she might be in class, but it was worth a try. She scrolled to Robin's contact and was surprised when she picked up on the second ring.

"Hey." Robin sounded like the call had woken her up. "I was hoping you would call. Madison and I were just talking a couple of days ago about when we were thinking you would show up."

"Probably not until that Sunday before classes start. Things are a little crazy here."

"With your boyfriend's uncle?"

It took Erica a minute before she remembered the lie she told Robin about why Xander was stuck in Juniper Falls. "Oh, yeah, that and my grandma is running for town council. My parents are coming for Christmas. Work. You know, life."

"I do not know. My life is very boring."

"That's not true," Erica said, though she supposed she didn't know Robin well enough to be sure. "But I was calling to see if you needed me to pick anything up for the room. Hot plate? Mini fridge? What are dorm rooms supposed to have?"

"You've been here. There might not be enough room for the stuff you already have. If you're contemplating extras, I'm going to need to have a yard sale."

Erica laughed. It was good to be reminded how much she liked Robin. "So just the basics then?"

"Comforter. Pen cup. Maybe a book," Robin confirmed.

"I will carefully consider my single book." Robin didn't reply, but the pause was not awkward. She imagined Robin sitting at her fluorescent desk and wished she was there. "Are you going home for Christmas?"

"Yeah but San Francisco isn't a very festive place. We usually decorate on Christmas Eve and it's all down before New Year. My parents pretend it's a tradition, but they just can't find the time to do it when it's not a company-mandated holiday."

"I'll have to bring you out here next year, then. You should see our store. The definition of festive."

"That sounds great," Robin said. She sounded sincere.

They chatted a little longer about nothing before Robin told her she had to go, or she would miss the omelet bar. They hung up, and Erica was left craving eggs and cheese. She felt lighter than she could remember in a long time. Weeks. Maybe months. The irony was not lost on her that what had seemed so oppressive over the summer—a new room, new classes, new friends—was now not only inevitable but something she looked forward to.

She couldn't put her finger on what had changed. Maybe it was just having more time to process or meeting Robin at orientation. But she knew it was also Xander. He treated college and her life beyond college as a given. He brought out a different side of her, turned her into someone stronger and more assured than she was used to. Or maybe it wasn't Xander at all but Juniper Falls and the independence it afforded her. Maybe it was Granny's gentle support and unshakable trust. Whatever was responsible, Erica found herself ready to start at Cascades.

First, she had a few more hurdles to jump. She had been talking with Granny about how they were going to navigate introducing Xander to her parents. It was going to be bad enough to tell her mother that she had a serious boyfriend. That he lived with them was going to send her over the edge. It was the truth, though, and Erica was getting tired of lying even if by omission.

As likely as it was that her mother would blow up, Xander also felt like a bomb about to go off. She didn't think he slept last night. She had drifted off next to him despite his tossing and turning but sometime around three in the morning, she'd had to physically pull him back into bed to stop his pacing. He was a little too eager to see her go this morning, and she thought she knew why. She would put money on him stalking a logging site despite their agreement. She could only hope he talked to Alden first. She would leave her phone on just in case.

Erica's trip to Roseburg had been restorative if not particularly productive. She bought presents for her family and, being unable to get omelets out of her head, treated herself to a second breakfast at a great little cafe in a strip mall. She ran out of time to stop for dorm stuff, so she was going to have to rely on whatever her mother bought her for Christmas. Erica had sent her a list several weeks ago and tried to have a conversation about sticking to a color theme and who was going to buy what. Danni had told her not to worry and promised everything she received would be tasteful. Erica figured she could fill in whatever didn't show up under the tree and crossed her fingers that there wouldn't be too much pink.

When Erica got back, Granny followed her around the store practicing her talking points for the evening's debate, her usual entourage of gray-haired women being otherwise engaged in drumming up last-minute attendees. Granny left about an hour before the store closed, and Erica rushed through cleaning and reconciling the tills before rushing home to shower and change. Xander was nowhere to be found. She texted to see if he had already made his way to town hall. He had not, but he assured her that he was right behind her. Erica fought back the urge to ask where he was and replied with a heart emoji that she hoped he interpreted as support.

Erica walked the few blocks back into the heart of Juniper Falls. Town hall was two buildings down from the library and had the same brick and concrete facade as all the local municipal buildings. Erica entered the low-ceilinged main chamber and was impressed by the turnout. The room could comfortably hold sixty, but there had to be at least a hundred people. Granny's supporters had done better than even she had expected. Erica wondered what Bobby Hendricks—the mayor, Cora's father, and staunch Kriners supporter—thought of the turnout.

Large, square pillars broke up the room and made it hard to find anyone. Granny, of course, was up front leaning on the long, low desk where the council usually sat. Erica caught Granny's eye and waved. Granny beckoned her over, but she demurred, not wanting to join in the spotlight.

She was thinking about finding chairs for her and Xander, as they were in limited supply compared to the size of the crowd, when she felt a hand on her upper arm. She turned to find Derek wearing a worn black peacoat over his usual ensemble. His hair was slicked back.

"What are you doing here?" she asked as she gave him a one-armed hug.

"Your granny was so nice to us yesterday that I figured I'd show some support." Derek was blushing, which was not a look she was used to seeing on him.

"Can you even vote?"

"Nah."

They laughed, and Erica scanned the room for anyone else they might know. In the corner, she spotted a splash of red that could only be Cora whispering something into Kyle's ear. He smiled and put a heavy arm across her shoulders. To Erica's surprise, Cora didn't shrug him off but leaned into him.

"Is that a thing?" Erica asked, pointing them out to Derek.

"That's kind of always a thing on and off."

"What!" Erica looked around to see if she had been too loud, but the general clamor of the room masked her outburst.

Derek chuckled. "They've been hooking up regularly since she was legal."

Erica's mind spun at how she could not have known this piece of information. Cora even pushed her toward Kyle when she first arrived. "Did you know when you guys were dating?"

"Oh yeah," Derek said on the inhale with a shake of his head.

"Doesn't that break some kind of bro code?"

"In which direction?" Derek shrugged. "Cora isn't the kind of girl that bro code applies to. She's going to do what she's going to do."

They watched as Kyle and Cora blasted each other with their respective charm offensives—her slapping his arm and giggling, him touching the small of her back when he leaned in to whisper. Erica had first-hand experience with how effective their tactics were when applied to other people. But between the two of them, it looked like ping pong. No one scored. The ball just kept bouncing endlessly between them.

"It's like watching a teenage soap opera," Erica said.

"I don't know. I think the real soap opera is this." Derek stuck out his thumb and his pinky and shook it between her and the door. Erica looked in the direction he was indicating and saw Xander striding toward her as if he couldn't see anyone else in the room. She felt herself straighten up, widen her eyes, and spread her lips into what she could only imagine was a stupid smile. "See?"

"Shut up. At least this is genuine."

"What's genuine?" Xander asked as he slipped an arm around her waist and kissed her neck.

"You. Me. Not that," she said, pointing her chin at Kyle and Cora.

Xander's eyebrows went up for a split second, but he looked relieved. "Well good. Maybe it will distract him from you."

"Unlikely. Derek says it's been going on for a while."

"I think they scratch an itch for each other," Derek said.

"Gross," Erica said. The three of them watched as Cora's mother interrupted her and Kyle by putting her hand on Kyle's forearm. It was obvious where Cora learned her moves. "You don't think he'd tell her, do you? About you guys and your, uh, special abilities." Xander squeezed her side at the suggestion.

A mischievous look passed over Derek's face. "She is *really* good in bed. A man could find that persuasive."

"I didn't need to know that."

"But you kind of always suspected it, didn't you?"

This was a point Erica could not dispute, so she just bobbed her head, her expression between a grimace and a frown. She looked at Xander who was staring at Kyle and Cora with alarm. She scanned him head to toe, looking for signs that he had just come in from the forest, but he was neat and put together in a Henley she hadn't seen before and jeans. She was about to say something about how nice he looked when the screech of a microphone rang through the room, and they were forced to turn their attention to Granny and Muriel who were seated behind the long desk.

Erica was disappointed but not surprised to see that also behind the desk, a few seats away, sat Mitchell Watters looking smug in a dove gray suit that likely cost more than some cars in the parking lot. He tapped a small stack of crisp, white note cards on the table. The sound, picked up by the microphone, reverberated through the room.

"I would stand up, but I'm pretty sure this thing is bolted to the table," Mitchell said, miming pulling on the microphone. There was a smatter of polite laughter.

Erica stood on her tiptoes and craned her neck. Sure enough, it was easy to spot big Bobby sitting in the front row and laughing the loudest at the bad joke. Erica was annoyed at herself and the rest of the campaign team for just assuming Bobby himself would moderate. Mitchell continued to try to work the crowd, but they weren't particularly responsive. Erica recognized a lot of them as regulars at *Farm & Feed*—good, steady locals who might not take kindly to an outsider, even one with money.

Granny was given the opportunity to introduce herself, and Erica squeezed Xander's hand, the only outlet for the pride she felt as Granny put her passion on display. She laid out her plans for leveraging municipal dollars to attract new services, how to reallocate funds to protect the most vulnerable populations, and what the town meant to her after spending over forty years there. Then it was Muriel's turn.

"I am Muriel Lambert," she said. Her mouth was too close to the microphone, causing it to boom and squeak. She smiled wide and said no more.

Mitchell looked expectantly at her. He waved his notecards in a gesture that was meant to encourage her. Erica got the impression she was acting like she couldn't see him.

Mitchell had no choice but to push forward. "Okay, thank you, candidates." He shuffled his note cards. "Muriel, I would like to start with you. There has been a lot of discussion around this election about how to attract new business to Juniper Falls. Can you tell us about your ideas?"

Their intel was that this was Muriel's big talking point. Mitchell must be nervous if he was trotting it out first thing.

"I would like to hear Vivian's thoughts on this," Muriel said, once again with her mouth almost on the mesh of the microphone.

Mitchell's face at that moment would be burned in Erica's memory forever. His facade of being effortlessly in charge dropped. His jaw went slack and his eyes squinty. He stared at Muriel, trying to figure out what was going wrong. Granny looked equally as surprised but regained her composure quickly and began running through the details of her platform.

The entire debate went this way, not that it could be called much of a debate. Muriel ceded her time to Granny at every opportunity, often nodding along with her talking points. Erica and Xander traded baffled glances, none of them quite sure what was going on. Derek was preoccupied with this phone, his show of support not extending to taking an actual interest.

It only took three questions before someone, a burly man in a canvas jacket and cargo jeans, yelled, "What's going on here?" and Mitchell, shuffling through his note cards, was forced to acknowledge that he wasn't in control.

"It seems Mrs. Lambert is choosing not to participate in this debate," he said, almost succeeding in regaining the usual smoothness of his voice.

"The fact is that Mr. Watters is trying to buy this town like he tried to buy me," Muriel said.

"Mrs. Lambert," Mitchell warned. Muriel put up a hand in his direction and for the second time that night, Erica snapped a mental picture of Mitchell that she would treasure forever.

"No. This town is only getting one side of the Kriners story. The truth is that Juniper Falls and its residents can have a more prosperous future without cutting down the trees that make this part of the world so special. Kriners tried to find a reliable old bag like me to tell you all that their way is the only way. But it's not. Vote for Vivian Schueller!"

Erica would have loved for the applause throughout the room to have matched the fervor of hers and Xander's and Derek's too once he caught on. But there wasn't so much of a roar as a smatter, and several people, mostly men, left while muttering under their breath things like *hoax* and *fraud*.

"I think this event is over," Mitchell said, abandoning his place and making his way toward Bobby.

Erica rushed to the desk, dragging Xander behind her. Granny was already admonishing Muriel when Erica gave her a big hug from behind that made Granny jump.

"Erica, can you believe Muriel?" she cried, patting her hair back into place. "What made you decide to do that? Everyone is going to think I'm behind it!"

"No, they won't," Muriel said, laying a hand on Granny's arm. "The paper will be all over it, and I will set them straight."

"Who all knew about this?" Granny asked Erica. "You didn't, did you?"

"Definitely not but way to go, Muriel!" Erica said, too loudly because Mitchell's head snapped around to look at them.

"It was my own little secret," Muriel said, making direct eye contact with Mitchell.

"Well, what's done is done, I suppose," Granny said. "Hopefully we can do some damage control before Tuesday."

That was when they noticed the little line forming in the aisle between the rows of chairs. It wasn't Granny's usual group, who were mostly milling in the back, waiting for the signal to head to the house to debrief. There were a handful of people Erica didn't know waiting patiently to talk to Granny.

"See you at home," Erica whispered and gave her grandmother one last squeeze before releasing her. Granny shook out her shoulders and beckoned the group toward her.

On their way out, Erica noticed Joe talking to Kyle, Cora, and Cora's mother, the last three each with a sour expression on their face. Joe gave Erica a big thumbs up, which she returned with a wave before Kyle put his hand on his father's wrist and said something to him that Erica couldn't make out across the room. Derek must have left already, but she wished he was there to try to help her make sense of what she was seeing. Two days ago, she and Kyle were a united front helping Derek with his family, and today he was determined to align himself with the Hendricks and, by extension, Mitchell. Kyle might be pro-Kriners, but it seemed impossible that that position could make him anti-Granny, his father's lifelong employer.

Erica almost asked Xander what he thought, but he was distracted by something at the front of the room. Erica followed his gaze to see that none other than Mitchell himself was watching them.

"What's his deal?" Xander asked.

"No idea," Erica said. She grabbed his hand. "Let's go home."

CHAPTER 15

Granny won. It was not a landslide victory, and less than a quarter of the town's registered voters even bothered to turn out for the off-season special election. Even with the debate making front-page news in the local paper, Muriel's stunt couldn't undo all the shiny signs with her name splashed on them that Kriners scattered all over town.

"My other plan was to concede to you," Muriel said later that night, champagne glass in hand.

But she didn't need to. Granny's extra twenty-eight votes were enough to secure her spot.

Once the news was out, all the women who supported her campaign and their husbands and those of their kids who still lived in Juniper Falls converged on the house. Derek showed up with a keg of beer that Xander helped him set up on the front lawn. Joe—though conspicuously not Kyle—brought a large sheet cake that read *Happy Holidays* and was decorated with holly, but no one minded. Other food and beverages and people appeared out of thin air. The house filled up in a way it hadn't since Keith's funeral though the atmosphere couldn't have been more different. It was loud and chaotic and full of life.

Erica was thrilled to have something to celebrate without the slightest reservation. Watching Granny move among her friends, red solo cup in hand like she was seventeen instead of nearly seventy, Erica knew her grandmother felt the same. Even Xander couldn't escape the vibe. When Derek produced a wireless speaker and blared dance music, Xander pulled Erica into the middle of the room so they could lead a group of Social Security recipients in moving to the beat, not that either of them could dance. They did their best and laughed at themselves alongside everyone else. Erica reveled in Xander's touch, in the light in his eyes, in the easy way his body slid against hers, and fought back the voice in the back of her head that said this was as good as it was ever going to get.

The party burned bright and died fast, which was not surprising given its demographics. The core group of women who had been there since the day downtown when Granny decided to run encouraged Erica and Granny, both more inebriated than they would have owned up to, to go on up to bed and let them clean up. One of them gasped when Xander followed Erica up the stairs, but another politely elbowed her and smiled in a knowing way that made Erica want to ask her about her own experience with young love. She fell asleep with Xander curled around her, wondering what she would say if someone asked her about this night fifty years from now.

Erica and Xander were both supposed to open the store the next morning, but Joe sent a few texts and swapped them to closing. Erica was annoyed when she was woken up by a knock on the front door and Tulip's subsequent barking. Her phone said it was just after eight. She hoped that Granny would ignore it or at worst that it was a well-wisher who would be on their way after a few kind words. She listened to the door open and could make out the murmur of a man's voice. Granny sounded businesslike, which suggested the caller would not be staying. Erica was about to let herself drift back to sleep when she heard the door close, and the voices get louder.

"Can I offer you a cup of coffee?"

"Thank you, Vivian."

Erica knew that voice, smooth as silk. She shoved Xander's shoulder. "Mitchell is downstairs."

Barely conscious, Xander grumbled. "No."

"What is he doing here?" Erica tossed the sheets off them and pulled on jeans and a sweater that were laying on her floor.

She clipped back her oily bangs to keep them out of her eyes. Xander didn't move. "Are you going to go down with me?"

"It's too early in the morning to deal with Kriners," Xander said as he pulled the comforter back around his bare chest.

"You don't even need to sleep!"

Xander sighed in a way that said he knew he wasn't going to win this battle. He found last night's clothes, and they made their way down.

Mitchell was seated at the oak table instructing Granny on his coffee preferences. "No non-dairy creamer, I assume?"

"We're a whole milk house," Erica said, bending down at the foot of the stairs to pet Tulip who was pacing and seemed as annoyed as the rest of them at being intruded upon so early.

When Mitchell turned to see who spoke, his eyes widened, and she registered a slight, upright jolt of his head. Erica wondered why he should be surprised she was there when she realized he was looking past her to Xander.

"Alexander," Mitchell said. "I didn't expect to see you here."

"It's just Xander," he replied.

Mitchell nodded slowly and kept nodding as Granny handed him his coffee and sat down opposite him at the table. Erica joined her. Xander chose to stand, placing his palm on the back of Erica's chair, the tips of his fingers resting on her spine.

They waited for Mitchell to explain why he was there. He shifted in his seat, and Erica wondered if they were making him uncomfortable or if he usually let the facade slip when his audience dropped below a certain number.

"It's no secret that Kriners is looking for a friend in the town council," Michell said at last. "I'm sure you've talked to Muriel, and you know what we are prepared to offer Juniper Falls."

"A hamburger joint and the purchase of as much timber rights on private property as possible," Granny said. She held a steaming cup of coffee in her hand and waved it in front of her as if cooling it.

"More than that, I hope. We want to develop a downtown plaza so that you don't have to host festivals in your parking lot anymore. We will help you raise a levy to improve school funding."

"In other words, pay a public relations person whose fees will get rolled into that levy in the form of taxes."

"Which they will be able to afford because Kriners is bringing living wage jobs to the town."

Granny sighed. Xander dropped into the chair next to Erica, and she thought Mitchell was trying a little too hard not to look at him. He wasn't so much staring at Granny as keeping his focus in the middle distance between them. He had slipped the middle two fingers on his left hand through the handle of his mug and tapped them in an irregular pattern against the ceramic.

"Are you married?" Erica asked, noting the lack of a ring.

"Erica," Granny muttered in admonishment.

Erica was momentarily embarrassed that her not quite fully awake brain was missing a filter. But in front of her was a man who couldn't wait a full day before pushing his platform, and she decided she didn't care. Granny made no further protest, issued no apology, and made no attempt to change the conversation. In fact, she put her mug on the table and cocked her head at Mitchell in curiosity.

Mitchell's eyebrows went up when he realized he was expected to answer. "Not anymore."

"Divorced?" Erica inquired.

"Yes. Three years ago. It was a short marriage. No children. Any more questions?" The honey in his voice was gone entirely now. He glanced at Xander as if looking for some support in this interrogation. Xander glowered back at him, and Erica thought that Mitchell should count himself lucky that things had stayed this civil.

"Where do you live?" Erica asked.

"I have a home base in Seattle, but I travel a lot. I've been down here for a few months now."

"That's it, then," Granny said, catching on to where Erica was headed. "You have no home. You don't know what it's like to truly invest in a place. To improve it without fundamentally changing it."

"You have no heart," Xander stated. His hands were planted in front of him on the table, his fingers spread. He leaned back in his chair and stared at Mitchell with an intensity that made his newly green eyes flash.

Mitchell held Xander's gaze. Erica couldn't tell if he was angry, but she could see that the words had struck him like a blow. His jaw was slack like it was waiting for his brain to catch up and know the right thing to say.

He settled on, "I knew your mother once."

This was not what anyone was expecting. Xander sat bolt upright, a deep furrow forming between his brows. Erica put her hand on his thigh.

"How?" Xander demanded.

"Kriners has been scouting the area around Juniper Falls for a long time. We thought we had a deal with the state about twenty years ago. Alina was a receptionist at town hall back then."

Xander looked at Granny, who nodded. "That's true. I forgot she did that for a while before working for the school district."

"I was sorry to hear that she died in that fire." Xander's intake of breath was so sharp, that it was almost a hiss. Erica squeezed his thigh. "I know what it feels like to lose someone."

It was the first time Erica felt like he said something real. Both the public persona and the put-upon act were gone.

"Would you like to stay for breakfast?" Granny offered.

Xander tensed under Erica's touch. She didn't think he could make it through a meal with this man without another outburst, and she wondered if the next lapse in judgment would wind up with Mitchell being strangled by a house plant.

Luckily, Mitchell was someone who knew how to read a room. "No, thank you. I think I've said enough for one day." He stood up and grabbed a scarf off the back of his chair that she hadn't noticed before. It looked soft and expensive. "I'll make an appointment with you once you're sworn in. I'm sorry to have interrupted your morning."

Granny walked Mitchell to the door and handed him his coat off the rack. Xander never took his eyes of him until the door shut behind him. Then he took off for Keith's room where he shut himself up for the rest of the morning.

After Erica had eaten and showered, Xander emerged and insisted they go on a drive before heading into work. He asked Granny for the keys to her truck. Erica wondered aloud where they were going but didn't ask again after Xander didn't answer. She was worried about him. She didn't know if it was Kriners or the mention of his mother that had sent him into a tailspin, and she couldn't find the words to ask.

They headed west on the highway. Xander exited and found his way to the logging road that she remembered from when she went with Kyle, Cora, and Derek back in September.

"I've already been here," she told him. "I've seen what they've done. Is that what this is about?"

"Just wait."

Xander blew past where Kyle had previously left his truck and they emerged into the clearing. In the full sunlight, it was even worse than she remembered—hundreds, thousands of stumps, some many feet in diameter, dotting a landscape devoid of life. When she was here last, she could still see the edges of the tree line where the logging stopped. Kriners hadn't been fully permitted then and were merely felling test areas, setting up a strategy.

Now it was desolation as far as Erica could see. Here and there a tree stood that was too small to be worth taking down, but the overall effect took her breath away.

"Are they allowed to do this?"

"I don't think it matters to them. To Mitchell. I think he became a little more human to you today, and I wanted to remind you that this is what I'm up against." Xander sat on the ground, put his hands in the soil, and closed his eyes. Cedar saplings popped up in a circle all around him. The circle spread, and Erica took several steps back before they started growing up instead of out. The saplings shot up a foot, two, three feet tall. Xander opened his eyes, and they were blazing. "I could sit here all day and I couldn't undo one-hundredth of what they've done."

You don't have to, Erica wanted to say, but she knew it wasn't true. The pain on his face, the dirt on his palms, and the way the newborn trees leaned ever so slightly toward him, all told her that he had no choice. Whether he was the guardian of the forest or whether this was just what dryads were meant to do, she couldn't possibly know.

She picked her way through the cedars into the center of the circle, stood on the tips of her toes, and kissed him. His mouth opened at the touch of her lips, and she drank him in. Her good Xander, her noble Xander, who wasn't actually and never could be hers at all.

CHAPTER 16

Erica had been dreading Christmas since she said goodbye to her mother at orientation. A very small part of her hung onto the hope that Alden and Xander would reunite so that she didn't have to own up to having a live-in boyfriend. She was beyond excited to give him the full Schueller family holiday experience with hot chocolate, cookies, brown sugar ham, and *A Christmas Story* on a loop from the time they got out of bed until they got in again. He just didn't have to do the waking up and falling asleep at Granny's house. Except that he did because he made no mention of reaching out to Alden despite his earlier proclamation.

Only Erica and Joe were manning the store on Christmas Eve. Years of experience told them to expect a slow trickle of last-minute shoppers, so the part-timers got an extra day off. Every year there was a phone call between Keith—and now Joe in his place—and Erica's mother about whether it was worth the hassle to open their respective stores on Christmas Eve. But there was always that one customer whose day they made so it was worth it. This year, they had a woman come in early and express her relief in finding them open so that her cat didn't have to settle for drinking the milk they left out for Santa.

There was plenty they could have been doing to pass the time productively. For example, they could mark down the remaining holiday items and move them to the clearance section in the back of the store. Or they could assemble the display for the seed packets that, per the laws of retail, would be arriving any day now, a full four months before they could be planted. Instead, Erica and Joe came to an unspoken agreement that they deserved an easy day, so they settled themselves onto stools behind the counter and chatted. They talked about Granny's upcoming term on the council, how empty the store always felt after the holidays, and what books Erica was reading. When they ran out of topics, Erica asked the question that had been on her mind for over a week.

"What's going on with Kyle?"

Joe slumped but played it off like he didn't understand her. "What do you mean?"

"He seemed close with Cora at the debate, and he hasn't texted me since." Erica opened the messaging app on her phone to confirm this was true. Her last correspondence with Kyle had been in the group text chain the day Derek's family showed up.

"They've been close since they were kids."

"I've heard."

Joe slid his large body off the stool and leaned into the counter. Looking at him was like staring into a time machine of what Kyle would look like in thirty years. Strong muscles, covered by fat, covered by skin that was losing its elasticity. He smelled faintly of some ointment she associated with much older people.

"Kyle likes you." Erica protested, but Joe stopped her. "Don't get me wrong. I understand why you guys don't work. You're going to college, and I don't think my son has ever read a book, even the ones he was assigned in high school. To his credit, though, I think the fact that you have is part of why he likes you so much."

Erica blushed. "I thought we figured out how to be friends."

"I think you are. But I think he also isn't that used to not getting what he puts his mind to."

She nodded at this. Having never left Juniper Falls, Kyle could be the football star forever. His imposing size, his demeanor, his high school status. They made him someone here.

"There's just—," she started. "It's complicated with Cora. The Hendricks are in deep with Kriners, and I would just rather he not, you know." She couldn't figure out how to explain it in terms that were specific enough to mean something but vague enough to not spill everything. Joe waited for her to choose her words. "He knows some things about some people that would be problematic if certain other people found out."

"About Xander?"

Erica shrugged in a way she knew didn't count as a denial. She wondered if Joe had any preconceived ideas about the Reed family before Xander began working there. She had never heard him ask about Alden. Whether the topic was taboo or the mystery was too old to bother with now, she didn't know.

"Not a lot of folks know much about Xander," Joe said. When Erica didn't take the bait to fill in the details, he added, "Kyle has a good heart, though. I don't think you have anything to worry about."

"I'm less worried about Kyle than Cora. Things slip."

"She's your friend too, though, right?"

Erica shrugged. "We are having a fight."

Before Joe could ask about what, the bell at the front door rang, and Erica took the opportunity to slip out of the conversation by heading over to greet the customer. After she helped him put together a last-minute stocking for his daughter, which included more than one plush toy meant for a dog, she encouraged Joe to take off and let her finish out the afternoon. He took her up on the suggestion with little fuss, and she was relieved to see him disappear through the office door into the parking lot. She wanted to believe that he was right, and Kyle was trustworthy. She had to account, however, for parental bias, which often resulted in holding one's child in higher esteem than they objectively deserved.

This was not the case with Erica and her mother. Erica received a text at a quarter past five. She had just locked the door of *Farm & Feed*. Her parents had done the same at the Portland store and were beginning their long drive to Juniper Falls. Erica reminded them to bring any remaining shoes and clothes from her room, which prompted her mother to reply with a pithy remark about how she was more than a delivery service.

It was an exceptionally cold night, and Erica ran back to the house to avoid letting the chill settle in. The sky was low and gray, and Erica thought it might snow, though she could only remember that happening a handful of times in Juniper Falls and never on Christmas.

When she opened the door, she was flooded with holiday spirit. A fire raged in the fireplace above which hung six stockings for Granny, herself, her parents, Keith, and Xander. All were made from old flannel shirts and most had white knit tops that came from an ancient, cabled sweater Granny had brought with her from the Midwest. Xander's, she saw, was topped with sherpa, and his name had been carefully written in all caps using a fabric pen.

Xander came out of the kitchen, smiling the big, goofy smile that was so rare and so bright that she could almost not bear to look directly at it. He handed her a mug of hot chocolate spiked with a shot of Peppermint Schnapps and topped with hand-whipped cream. He had offered to hang out at the store with Erica today even if he wasn't needed, but Granny asked him if he wanted to stay back and help her bake. To counteract some of the awkwardness resulting from spending the next two days with her parents, Xander had agreed to eat. Erica, in turn, had agreed that she would forgive him for any abhorrent behavior that followed. And Granny had used the opportunity to have a repeat of the day they spent in the kitchen making food for their picnic date.

"We made that today," Xander said, pointing his mug at the stocking. Erica leaned into him and licked whipped cream off the corner of his mouth before kissing him.

"Did you discover you like sewing as much as cooking?"

"Very much not."

Erica sniffed the air exaggeratedly. It smelled like spices— mostly ginger and mint—but also cinnamon, cardamom, and almond extract. "What all did you make?"

Xander looked positively giddy as he pulled her into the kitchen. Granny was there, Tulip at her feet, waiting to lick up spilled flour and dropped dough. It didn't look like she was going to have any luck, though, because all that was left were the dishes. The counter was strewn with cookies of all shapes and colors.

"You did a stollen!" Erica exclaimed. She wasn't a huge fan of the bread-like fruit cake, but it was a favorite of Keith's that Granny rolled out every few years to please him. Supposedly the recipe came across the Atlantic with her grandfather's German ancestors.

"Why else would I have had fruit soaking in rum on the counter for the last month?" Granny asked. She wore a prim pink apron, yellow gloves up to her elbows, and her wispy hair was in two long plaits. She looked like she belonged in a different era.

"Before you say anything, I did offer to clean up," Xander told Erica.

"He did, but I told him his help today made everything go twice as fast. He's paid his holiday debt."

Erica grabbed a gingerbread man from one of the cooling racks. It featured a rather messy bowtie, buttons, and socks in multi-colored royal icing.

"That's one of mine," Xander said. A slight blush appeared on his cheeks. "I didn't quite get the hang of the decorating."

Erica bit off the head of the gingerbread man and savored the fluffy texture and explosion of spices. "It tastes delicious," she mumbled before she had swallowed. A chunk of cookie fell from her mouth, and Tulip was right on top of it. Erica brought her hand to her mouth, horrified that Xander had seen that.

Xander laughed, a deep guffaw that he had to gasp to recover from. It was contagious, and Erica took a huge swig of hot chocolate to try to get the cookie down before she started laughing too. It went down the wrong pipe, and she sputtered, causing Xander to erupt again. Granny patted Erica on the back with her soapy, rubber-encased hand, leaving a streak of warm water down the back of her blue *Farm & Feed* polo. The whole moment was ridiculous, but Erica loved it. She wished it could stay like this, but her parents were on their way.

While Xander was in this good of a mood, she thought it was the right time to review their plan. He was going to disappear into Keith's room before they arrived tonight. He would stay there until her family visited Keith's grave in the morning, during which time he would sneak out so that he would be waiting at the door when they returned. They would play the evening by ear, but worst case, he could let himself into the store and spend the night there. Her parents would be gone before the sun was up on the 26th when everything could go back to normal.

As per the plan, Xander disappeared as soon as Erica, who had been watching the road for the last half hour, saw headlights turn down their street.

"Remember, as little noise as possible," she said, walking him to the door under the stairs.

"Erica, I'm a tree. Plus, I've got this." He held up a nearly thousand-page book he had taken out from the library earlier that week that had something to do with the origins of international trade.

"You'll be out like a light. Good thing you don't snore."

"Some of us have more intellectual curiosity than others," Xander said. He gave her a quick peck and shut the door behind him.

Granny and Tulip joined Erica in greeting her parents at their car. Her father was driving. She hadn't seen him for a couple of months, and he looked older than she remembered. A smattering of gray was working its way into his stubble and there were bags under his eyes, though this may have been from a full day's work followed by a long car ride. He wouldn't be forty until next year. Sometimes Erica thought about how weird it was that some people waited until they were older than her parents were now to have kids, and here they were, empty nesters with more than half their lives ahead of them.

"Hey, kiddo," her dad said as he got out of the car and swooped her into a hug. He was only a couple of inches taller than her, but his embrace made her feel like she was six years old. She tightened her hold on him, and he cinched up too. They made it into a game, holding each other tighter and tighter until Erica could barely breathe, and she gave in by laughing and shoving him away.

Her mother appeared beside them, arms laden with gifts. The wrapping paper was of various zoo animals wearing reindeer antlers. Danni, so precise and polished in many ways, had a bizarre affinity for kitsch that might have felt whimsical in another person but in her case was sheer bad taste.

"Are you going to help me carry these in?" she asked.

Erica went to take some off the pile, but Danni wrenched her arms away and gestured with her head toward the car. The entire backseat was covered in boxes, a couple of them huge, and Erica met her father's eyes in surprise. He shrugged in a way that suggested, you'll see.

He grabbed a few of the boxes but didn't let them stop him from planting a kiss on Granny's cheek on their way into the house. Her father's parents were still alive, but they hadn't been keen on the idea of him having a baby in his junior year of college. Whatever rift that formed during that time was irreparable. Erica remembered a brief period after they moved to Portland when her other grandparents, practically strangers, would visit from their home in Central Washington a few times a year. But that tapered off until it got to the point that no one even thought to invite them to her high school graduation. Their absence never felt like a gap or a hole to Erica. As she watched her father catch up with Granny, calling her *Mom* and putting her presents in their own special pile under the tree, she wondered for the first time if it did for him.

Erica brought a tray of almond crescent cookies and gingerbread men into the living room as Granny heated up the milk for another round of hot chocolates.

"It's too late for sugar," Danni said. She was inventorying the Christmas tree, probably searching for the few ornaments that had been in the family for decades and were supposed to go in specific places of honor.

"But it's tradition," Erica whined.

"Tradition says you should be in pajamas already."

"Pajamas it is!" her father yelled. "I'll get the bags."

Erica followed him back out to the car where he took a suitcase and a small overnight bag from the trunk.

"I bet I can guess which one is yours," Erica smirked.

"You laugh but those other two suitcases are yours and there is a garbage bag full of shoes behind them."

Erica surveyed the large bags and thought it was impossible she had that many clothes. "Did she have to bring all of this?"

"Hey now," her dad said, adjusting his tone into what Erica thought of as *parent mode.* "Can you not start off by being so hard on her? She tried to bring you what she thought you wanted in November, and you didn't like that either."

He was right. Fights occurred naturally between Erica and her mother. She didn't have to start one. "Okay, okay," she conceded.

It was more than that, and they both knew it. Danni would be on edge trying her best to make things feel like they used to even though Keith was gone. Stress was built into the situation. She didn't have to manufacture it.

Instead of putting words to awful things, her father said, "I think your PJs are at the top of the black one."

"You're not going to help me bring these in?" Erica made sure to add as much fake incredulity as possible to her voice.

"No. I am not." He leisurely swung his two pieces of luggage as if they weighed nothing as he took elongated steps toward the door.

Erica heaved her wardrobe out of the trunk and wrapped the top of the hefty black garbage bag around her hand a couple of times before grabbing the handles of the suitcases. She dragged it all up to the house, bumping the wheels on the patio steps, to where her father chivalrously opened the door for her. They were giggling and mocking each other as they stepped into the living room and were confronted by Danni waiting for them with her arms crossed.

"Granny tells me you have a boyfriend."

Granny was standing by the dining table looking sheepish. Erica racked her brain for why she would have said something. They were supposed to spring Xander on her parents tomorrow in the hopes that her mother's sense of propriety would win over her anger.

"Uh, yeah," was all Erica could mutter. She did not want to get into it now while Xander was just twenty feet away behind a thin door.

"Apparently it's serious enough that he gets a stocking," Danni fumed as she whipped one of her hands toward the fireplace.

Erica cursed herself. Of course she noticed it—nothing got past her mother, especially if it was something that could get Erica in trouble.

"Who is he? Xander?"

"He's just a guy, Mom." Erica couldn't hold onto all her bags anymore, and she dropped everything at once. A boot and a flip flop bounced out of the garbage bag. The whole family watched them fall, but no one moved to pick them up.

"Where did you meet?"

"The library," Erica lied. "He's smart. You're going to like him."

This was clearly the wrong thing to say. Danni drew a deep breath and spun around to stare down at her husband in disbelief. "I'm going to meet this boyfriend? In the only twenty-four hours I get to spend with our daughter this month? On Christmas?"

Her father carefully set down the suitcases he was holding. "Danni," he whispered as put his hands on her shoulders, trying to rub away her tension. As was often the case, his tone was flat. He was placating, not censuring. Erica wished that just once he would stop being Switzerland and take her side.

Looking back at Erica, her mother continued, "Why doesn't his family want him if he's so great?"

Erica was glad she was already facing the door under the stairs because she couldn't help but turn her eyes toward it, imagining Xander having to listen in silence. He couldn't know that none of it was personal. As much as she had tried to explain her mother to him, experiencing her was something else entirely.

"He doesn't have a lot of family," Erica said, as quietly as she could. "His mom is dead, and his uncle isn't a holiday person."

Danni furrowed her eyebrows, trying to put the pieces together. She turned her interrogation to Granny. "Do we know his family? Or did he come in with the loggers?"

"He's a Reed," Granny said simply.

"Reed? Dead mom?" The light went on. Her face went from angry to amused in a flash. "Not Alina's kid. You said you saw them at the funeral. I thought you were both full of shit." She looked between Erica and Granny. When neither of them refuted her conclusion, she laughed. "Here I was worried about Kyle Zukowski, but no, you choose the town hermit."

"Mom. Stop it." Erica scooped up the errant shoes and scooted her bags toward the stairs. She wasn't going to make it in one trip, so she dropped the shoes and focused on the suitcases.

She was halfway up when Danni started again, "I swear if this stops you from going to school—."

"Enough, Mom! Seriously!" Erica yelled. She had reached her breaking point. "It's pathetic that a guy I've known for four months is so much more supportive of what I want than you are. But for the record, he's encouraging me to go."

Erica struggled up the last few stairs before throwing in her luggage and slamming the door behind her. She whipped out her phone to text Xander.

Erica: I'm so sorry. She'll be better tomorrow.

She watched the screen, expecting to see triple dots immediately. When they didn't show up, she tried again.

Erica: I'll come down tonight after everyone goes to bed. I love you.

She stared at her phone for a minute, five minutes, maybe longer, but nothing. Her father knocked on her door and asked if she was going to come down. Her mother was already over it and ready to kick off their normal holiday. Erica didn't reply. She knew it was childish, but she didn't have it in her to play happy family tonight. There would be plenty of that tomorrow.

"Okay. I get it. Goodnight, kiddo," her dad said. She wanted to punch him. The way he let these situations happen. The way he played both sides like she and her mother were equals. But, in the end, she was the kid. Didn't she deserve better?

Erica laid down on her bed, her head swimming, wishing

she had Xander to hold her, to talk to her, to tell her it would be alright. She fell asleep at some point early in the night, still fully clothed and above her blankets. The first thing she did when she woke up was check her messages, but Xander still hadn't replied. It was the middle of the night, and she felt it was safe to check on him. She crept downstairs as quietly as she could and turned the handle of the door under the stairs, which had been greased up for the few days she and Xander had spent sneaking between each other's bedrooms before Granny told them to drop the ruse.

Moonlight spilled into the room from the window on the opposite wall. Xander was not in the bed. Erica felt stupid checking every nook and cranny of the room, even activating the flashlight on her phone to illuminate the walk-in closet. She called his name faintly, as though invisibility might be one of his as yet unexplored gifts, but she had to give in that he wasn't there.

Erica left the room, closing the door behind her, and shined her light around the living room. She decided to check the kitchen and jumped when she saw someone sitting at the table. Granny's white hair and yellow robe glowed in the faint light. Erica could smell the chamomile tea steeping in the mug in front of her.

"I saw him sneak out the window earlier," Granny whispered.

Erica sighed. She sat down in the chair nearest to Granny, which creaked but she no longer cared. "Why is she like that? It seemed worse, right? Or am I just not used to it now that I don't hear it every day?"

"She didn't know," Granny attempted, but Erica cut her off.

"It's not an excuse. It doesn't matter if she didn't know Xander was listening. Why does she get to come at me like that?"

Granny's face looked particularly pale. Erica didn't know if she should blame the lighting. Neither of them said anything. If that question could be answered, it would have been years ago. Erica tried Xander again.

Erica: I hope you're somewhere safe. I'm sorry. Please come tomorrow. Good night.

For a brief second, the dots flashed in their little bubble before disappearing again. Erica sighed. The moon was full and low, and she could see it out the window behind Granny. She had always hated the cheesy line about looking at the same moon, but at that moment, she hoped Xander was looking at it and thinking of her too. She imagined telling him about that thought and him laughing at her. He liked to kiss her when he thought she was being sentimental.

Without saying anything further to Granny, she went back up to her room where she slept alone for the first time since she returned from orientation. The bed felt cold and lonely, but a small part of her welcomed the room to spread her limbs. She fell asleep and dreamed of dark woods covered in twinkling fairy lights, and behind her, something watching, always close but never quite within reach.

CHAPTER 17

In the morning, it was as if nothing had happened. *A Christmas Story* was already playing on the television when Erica came downstairs. Granny did everyone's stockings, and Erica thanked her for the chocolate and good pens that made up most of hers. Breakfast was French toast and eggs, her father joining Granny in the kitchen as sous chef. This left Erica with her mother in the living room where she made just enough polite conversation about the goings-on at their respective stores to not trigger another outburst.

Everyone took turns getting ready in the single bathroom, each emerging in an ugly Christmas sweater and jeans. Danni had brought a wreath from one of her vendors in Portland to lay on Keith's grave. It sat between her and Granny in the backseat of the car on their way to the cemetery. "It's fully recyclable," Danni had said about the wreath that appeared to be made of old issues of *The Oregonian* newspaper. If it was the environment she was concerned about, Erica wondered why they were replacing the wreath they just left there a couple of weeks ago that was almost entirely organic, but she said nothing.

Erica kept her eyes honed on Xander's tree as they made their way up the hill to where Keith's white marble headstone looked out over Main Street. She hung back a little to talk to him, knowing she only had the length of her mother and Granny's argument before she would be missed.

"We haven't heard anything new from the police in

months," her mother was complaining, "and it doesn't seem to bother you."

"I'm at peace, love. Nothing we learn can bring him back."

"You don't want to know who murdered your son?"

"What attacked him wasn't human."

"But a human moved him!"

Granny's flat tone implied that this was not the first time they had this conversation. Erica and Granny had talked early on about the impossibility of ever telling her parents the truth about what happened to Keith. This had been easy enough for Erica because they never brought it up with her. But Granny must have been fending off questions behind the scenes. Erica felt familiar guilt bubble up. She sat with the feeling and discovered it was more related to Granny having to play defense than that she particularly felt like she owed her mother a sense of closure. She wondered for a moment if that made her a horrible person, but the thought was quickly chased away by her mother's voice.

"You would think that as his mother—."

There was more after this, but Erica had reached Xander's tree, and the others continued down the other side of the hill. She leaned against the trunk, its cracked and dimpled bark digging into her shoulder.

"I swear she's better behaved when other people are around." She ran her hand across the bark and picked at a rough edge before realizing what she was doing.

It was hard to have a conversation with a tree, even when you knew someone was listening on the other side. She tried to fill in the blank with Xander's facial expressions, his gestures, and his laugh.

"I understand why you left, but I hope you come today. I have a present for you. A few, actually." She and Granny had wrapped the bracelet she bought him back at the Harvest Festival in gold paper, and Granny showed her how to make a red ribbon bow worthy of social media. She had also picked him up some clothes in Roseburg that she hoped would cover his wrists and ankles.

Then her time was up. Her mother was looking around for her. If she lingered, she was going to hear about it.

"I love you. Come," she whispered. She ran down the hill to avoid being scolded, mentally crossing her fingers that he would listen.

When they pulled into the driveway after finishing up at the cemetery, there was a plant sitting on the welcome mat by the front door. This wasn't entirely unusual as people liked to leave cuttings for Granny to put in her garden, but it was well outside of growing season. As she approached, Erica recognized the rounded edges of the leaves.

A miniature oak, about two feet tall, sat in a square ceramic pot surrounded by moss. It was several inches thick at its base, and its bark was as gnarled as that Erica had just been touching. About a third of the way up, the trunk split into a dozen or so branches, each dotted with a handful of dark green leaves. A fat, full-size acorn drooped from one branch, looking ridiculously out of proportion. It was a bonsai version of Xander's tree, and it was beautiful.

Erica squatted to look closer at it and noticed a card sitting at the base of the trunk. It read simply, *Erica.*

"Who is it from?" her mother asked, narrowing her eyes at the tree like it was somehow suspicious.

"I'm not sure," Erica lied. If this was here, it meant that Xander was not coming. She couldn't bear to say his name and risk reminding her mother that she expected him to. She picked up the heavy pot. "I'll put it away."

She let her dad open the door for her, and she ran the bonsai up to her room. She placed it on the vanity and admired it in greater detail. It looked old, but Erica knew Xander could force years of growth to happen in an instant. She wondered if he grew it just for her or if it was something he had been working on since before they met. A project, perhaps, that Alden had set upon him in hopes they could find something artistic he was good at.

She took out her phone.

Erica: Thank you for the gift. I love it. Is it grown from yours?

She didn't expect him to respond, but the text came back almost immediately.

Xander: No. It doesn't have the power to bring anything back to life.

Erica stared at the backlit screen and a jolt of panic ran through her. There wasn't time to pick apart what he meant. Her father was calling her to come help with the ham. She had a whole day of going through the motions to get through. She took one last look at the tree and made her way downstairs to salvage her holiday.

In the days that followed, Erica would look at that text from Xander and extract from it all sorts of meaning. As he ignored text after text, call after call, and several in-person visits to his tree, Erica spiraled. The days until she left for college dwindled until she was counting hours instead. She packed her room and tried to convince herself that she could leave without seeing him if she had to.

With less than three days until she was due at the Cascades campus, Erica sat in a fold-up camping chair between Xander and Alden's trees. She was bundled in a down jacket and fleece-lined boots and wore fingerless mittens that Muriel had hand-knitted and dropped by as a Christmas gift. They came in handy for being able to turn the pages of one of the history books Xander had left behind in Keith's room along with all the clothes he had borrowed during his brief stay with her and Granny. It broke her heart when she went into the room after her parents left for Portland in the early hours of the day after Christmas to see everything they had given him neatly stacked on the bed.

Erica was more absorbed in the book than she had expected to be and was hoping against hope for the opportunity to tell Xander as much when she heard the distinct sound of footsteps on dry leaves coming from behind her. She put her finger in the book and turned toward the sound. But instead of a mop of dark, wavy hair, the face that appeared was framed by thick, golden locks. Alden.

She watched him approach and neither of them said anything. She didn't get up, as though for once she was the one rooted in place. Alden walked to his tree and pressed his back into it. Erica tried to remember if she had ever seen Xander touch his.

"I received your note," he said. His expression and tone were unreadable.

"Is Xander with you?"

Alden nodded. Erica hopped out of the chair at this, whipping her head around as if she had somehow missed him. "Not here. At home."

Erica felt like a stone had been dropped into her stomach. "How is he?"

Alden shrugged. Erica could have sworn that his shoulders disappeared into his tree when he did, like a glitch in a video game. "He has a lot to deal with. Decisions to make."

Erica had asked for this audience, but she couldn't help but wonder why Alden was here. If he had Xander back and he wasn't talking to her anymore, hadn't Alden won? She had hoped they could work as a team to bring Xander some peace, but she doubted he was equally as willing to bring her on as a partner. Her tongue didn't want to cooperate, though, so she just muttered, "I want to see him."

"I don't think that's a good idea. I think he's onto something with this forest spirit business. We've been exploring it." An emotion finally worked its way into Alden's voice—excitement. "You should have seen him this last week. What he can do when he stops overthinking it."

"Overthinking," Erica said. "You mean thinking about me?"

"Not just you. All these distractions he's set up for himself." Alden stretched out his hands in front of him and opened his palms as if to indicate the weight of Xander's troubles. Then he balled his hands into fists and took a few steps toward the still standing Erica. "Do you have any idea what it's like to be staring down eternity without a purpose?"

Alden's eyes were an exact imitation of Xander's before they changed, so dark brown they were almost black. She stared into them and felt nostalgic for a version of Xander that she had known so briefly she wondered if he'd ever existed at all.

"Why can't I be his purpose? Why am I not enough?"

"Is he enough for you?"

The question was fair, but it hit deep like the breath has been knocked out of her. She dropped his gaze, but when they locked eyes again, she could see they both knew the answer. Xander was the best thing in her life so far, but he was not enough. All that time she spent waffling about college forced Erica to realize that she wanted more. She didn't know exactly what more was, but it wasn't this town, as much as she loved it. It wasn't taking over her family's store. It was something beyond that. Something she didn't have words for yet.

Her shoulders slumped, and she could no longer look at Alden. She knew that he was right about her. She was selfish. She could pretend like she was only trying to act in Xander's best interest, but that was not entirely true. She wanted to have her cake and eat it too. Go to college and keep Xander safely at home waiting for her. Xander knew it. He had told her as much in the car on their way to meet Derek's family.

"You can't live for another person. People are fickle. Fragile," Alden said. He stepped back and leaned into his tree again, looking at his hands. "I learned that the hard way more than once."

Erica's mind was moving a mile a minute, realizing what it meant, what she would have to accept, if it was true, she and Xander weren't everything her heart had been telling her. She was so wrapped up in her own thoughts that she almost missed Alden's comment. She opened her mouth to ask him to repeat himself when something else fell into place for her as well. The notebooks. The casket. Alden's willingness to trust her.

"Keith," she said. "You weren't just friends."

Alden shook his head. "I died the first time in the seventies. I didn't think it could happen again. But here I am, a walking corpse." Erica took a step toward him, her hand outstretched, planning to comfort him. He waved her away. "It's one thing to think you have forty years with someone. It makes opening yourself up worth the risk. But then they're torn away from you when the clock has barely started."

"I'm sorry," Erica murmured. This information landed on her more softly than she would have imagined. It was more than just understanding the appeal of the stoic Reed men. It had never occurred to her to question why Keith was still single in his forties but being gay in a small town was as good an answer as any. What's more, it comforted her to know that he was loved in his last days.

Alden kicked the dirt in front of him. "Xander could never recover from it, Erica. I would know. You must let him go."

Erica's head felt foggy. It was too much at once. And here was Alden looking for some sort of promise that she wasn't prepared to give.

"You're going to help him? Keep him safe?" she asked, trying to stall.

"My power is artistic. Whatever Xander took from the bear when you killed it, it's something beyond me that he has to figure out for himself."

Erica absorbed the accusation, which had come much later than she had expected. But the anger in his voice was deeper than a cheap shot. "You wish it was you," she said as the realization hit her.

Alden laughed, so brief and foreign she wondered if she imagined it. "I guess I do. Keith is dead. My store is wrecked. But it can't be me. I wasn't there. I didn't bring down the bear tree. It's Xander who has found something lasting to live for."

Something that wasn't her. Because she wasn't lasting. Whether it was today or six months or eighty years from now, she would disappear from Xander's life, and he would go on, in this place, forever.

Alden gave her one last stern look before taking a few steps back the way he had come. He had said all that he meant to. Erica was forming dozens of questions by the second about Keith, about Xander, but she knew better than to ask them.

"Please ask him to find me one last time before I go. He knows I leave on Sunday." Alden didn't make any indication that he heard her, but she hoped that Xander was listening. "If this is over, I deserve a proper goodbye."

Erica watched Alden disappear down the hill. He skimmed his hand over the top of Keith's headstone as he went, but he didn't stop to pay respects. She wished she'd known sooner that his grief matched her family's, not that he could have participated in any of the rituals around his funeral and burial, but at least she could have tried to be a kind of comfort to him. If her heart hadn't been so busy breaking for herself, it would have broken for him instead.

CHAPTER 18

The next forty-eight hours felt like the dark days after the bear dryad when Erica held a vigil at Xander's tree hoping he was still alive. She limited herself to working, reading, and making sure she was ready to leave. Derek texted her a few times with friendly check-ins that she ignored.

She couldn't put off Robin, though, whose excitement for her arrival was infectious. The carful of gifts Erica's parents brought her for Christmas had been, as she suspected, everything she needed for her dorm room and more. Thankfully, her mother had decided not to compete with Robin's rainbow explosion, which had been described to her in detail, and opted for minimalist accessories that were mostly white with splashes of sunset colors. These were now packed in her car, along with everything she brought to Granny's back in August.

Erica was tossing her toiletries and last night's pajamas into a duffle and waiting for Granny to return from her walking group when she heard a knock on the door. As she made her way downstairs, she steeled herself in case it was Mitchell Watters barging in again. Almost anyone else it was likely to be should have joined Granny on her walk. Her thrice-weekly morning ritual had become less about exercise and more of a political think tank since she had been sworn in as a councilor just before the start of the new year.

Erica was planning what she would say to Mitchell and savoring what it would feel like to slam the door in his face when she caught a glimpse of an old tan pickup parked in her driveway. She jumped the last three stairs and was at the door in less than a second. She threw it open to have her suspicion confirmed. Xander stood in front of her, looking somehow better than he ever had. He was wearing that Henley again that hugged his chest and biceps. The cuffs of his shirt and his jeans were covered in fresh dirt, which compounded his naturally earthy smell that she had desperately missed. Whether it was their separation clouding her judgment or his skin was radiating a faint light, she couldn't tell.

Xander didn't smile when he saw her. He looked pensive and hesitant like he had come here on business. Erica thought she knew what he was here to say, and she couldn't bear it. He was going to end things. The idea tore Erica in two. Tears streamed from her eyes, her breath caught in her throat, and she put out a hand to steady herself against the doorframe. Then she felt them, Xander's arms, pulling her into his chest. For the briefest moment, she thought about resisting, giving him a taste of the rejection that was the source of her tears. But she wasn't strong enough. She put her head under his chin and marveled at how perfectly her cheekbone fit in the hollow at the top of his sternum.

Erica's arms were trapped between their torsos. She snaked them out and wove her fingers through Xander's curls. She thought he might fight her as she brought their lips together, but he was as eager as she was. The kiss was sloppy and wet and punctuated by Erica's sharp intakes of breath. It was far from their best effort, but in the lonely nights far from home that were to follow, this was the kiss she would remember.

Xander's hands were all over her now, grabbing at her shoulder blades, her sides, her hips. He lifted her up, easily, as if she weighed nothing. She wrapped her legs around him, though she was in no danger of being dropped. He took two steps into the living room and used his body to slam the door behind her.

"Where?" he asked, unwilling to put her down. Erica leaned her head in the direction of Keith's room, and Xander grunted. They made it to the door under the stairs in four long strides. Xander briefly shifted her weight to one arm and used the other to get them through the door, which, once closed, he pushed her against, his mouth on her neck. Erica moaned, a more primal sound than she'd let herself make in other passionate moments. This might be the last time they would do this, and she didn't want to hold anything back.

The sound sent Xander into overdrive. He tossed her on the bed and set himself upon the button of her jeans. She sat up to help him with his, but he put one hand on her chest and lightly pushed her back down onto the bed. He loomed over her, his green eyes boring into hers.

"Patience," he said, his lips turned up in the corners.

"Not my virtue," she breathed.

Xander smiled and went back down to remove her jeans. She felt the cool air be replaced almost immediately by his breath, hot against the inside of her thighs. She came undone. How could she ever learn to live without this?

When they were both spent, having run out of ways to touch each other, Erica was lying on her side, running her fingers along Xander's temple and ear. His eyes were closed, so she was free to study his perfect face. She wrapped a hand around his chin and turned his face toward hers. He grabbed her hand, and his eyes flashed open. He brought her hand down to his chest and placed his over it. She cocked her head, questioning.

"Alden came to see you," he said.

Erica felt the prick of tears again. "Can we not?"

Xander shifted onto his side so that they were facing each other. "We have to talk about this." She tried to bury her face in his chest. He pushed her shoulders gently back. "You're leaving, and I don't think we should be together when you do."

"What do you mean?" Erica asked though she knew perfectly well what he meant. She knew that Xander likely heard every beat of her conversation with Alden. If he didn't, then Alden surely told him what she said about Xander not being enough. It was unfair to bait him into being the one to put things out in the open, but she couldn't bear to do it herself.

"Things are changing for both of us. Fast. I love you, but I can't hold you back."

"And you don't want me holding you back either." He didn't argue. "What are you and Alden planning?"

"I don't know yet." Erica gave him a hard look of disbelief. "It's the truth. I have a lot to figure out."

She couldn't stand him looking at her anymore. Erica folded herself into the crook of his arm, trying to come up with some way to salvage this. To have him gone from her life completely wasn't an option.

"I want to negotiate terms," she said.

"Terms?" Xander's voice was amused.

"Yes. I want to be able to call you."

"Erica—."

"Email?"

Xander shook his head. "Did you get the bonsai tree?"

Erica's mind drifted up to the little tree sitting on her dresser upstairs. It took her a moment to understand what it had to do with communication. Then it clicked. "You know I did."

"I don't know if it will work all the way at college, but I figured it was worth a try. Talk to the tree like you would to me. I promise to respond even if you can't hear me."

Erica fought the urge to point out that there was no way he would be able to hear her through a bonsai tree two hundred miles away and that even if it did work, it wasn't exactly two-way communication. But she had a feeling this was what she was going to get from him and all the pushing in the world wasn't going to change his mind.

"Any other terms?"

"Yes," she said, kissing his neck. "I want to be able to do what we just did whenever I'm in town."

This got a laugh out of him. "That doesn't sound much like not being together."

"I didn't say I wouldn't do it with other people too." She was joking, but Xander pulled her face to his.

"That's my term. That you will never not do something just because of me."

Once again Erica had to push back on the impulse to fight with him. Part of her wanted to scream that he couldn't tell her what to do. That he didn't get to decide how she loved him. But time was precious now and she didn't want to spend it that way. There would be no kissing and making up tomorrow. If she got angry now, that would be how they left things for weeks, maybe months.

She brought her lips up to his and whispered, "Okay."

"Promise me," he said, and she could feel the words against her delicate skin as clearly as she heard them.

"I promise." Her tongue was in his mouth before the last syllable was all the way out. She wrestled him flat onto the bed and lost herself in him.

The threat of Granny coming home and finding them in Keith's bed was the only thing that got Xander and Erica back in their clothes and into the living room. Just as it looked like he was leaving, Erica ran up to her room to retrieve a small box wrapped in brown paper and tied up with a shiny red bow. There were other boxes up there with his name on them, but she doubted he would accept them.

"I got your Christmas present, but you never got mine," she said, handing it to him.

Xander eyed her warily and tugged on the end of the ribbon. He let the paper fall to the ground and opened the lid of the box. He pulled out the leather bracelet. Erica took it from him and clasped it around his wrist. Xander smiled and ran his fingers over the debossed acorns.

"It's perfect," he said. He gave her a light kiss on the corner of her mouth. "Thank you."

Their eyes met, and they lingered there with nothing left to do or say, willing each other to break away. It was Xander who sighed and said something that sounded agonizingly like "goodbye." Erica shook her head and put a finger to his lips. With the slightest of pressure, she pushed him toward the door. He reached around when the handle pressed into his back. She smiled at him, and his lips curled under her touch as he cracked the door open and continued to back out. Erica removed her hand, but her eyes stayed on his until the door was fully closed.

Then he was gone.

She would have to learn to be satisfied with where things stood between them. A life completely without him was impossible, but if he couldn't be her boyfriend, her occasional lover was a romantic enough prospect she could, in time, learn to accept.

Taking her leave of Granny was much easier. Granny's house had always felt like home to her, and when they pecked each other's cheeks and said see you later, they both meant it. Erica knew that if she found herself feeling homesick, this was where she would come back to and be welcomed with open arms.

"Thank you for letting me stay so long," Erica said during their final hug in front of her car.

"I wouldn't have had it any other way," Granny replied.

Then Erica was gone over the mountains. She had been right to come to Juniper Falls four months ago. She thought of all the things she would have missed out on had she pushed herself to start last quarter. Not just Xander, but being there for Granny, meeting Derek, and helping Joe. She was leaving a life that felt fuller and more her own than it ever had. With all those people rooting for her, she knew she could take her next step, and the one after that, and the one after that.

CHAPTER 19

When Erica arrived at Cascades, Robin and—to Erica's surprise—Madison, helped her move all of her things into her
dorm room. Between the three of them, they managed it mostly
in one load with a second trip for awkward things including the
bonsai tree and a small coffee maker Erica had picked up at
a thrift store. This was fortunate because the parking pass her
parents had been willing to pay for put her so far away from the
dorm she thought it might be a separate zip code.

After fielding several questions from Robin and Madison
about why she showed up with a large decorative plant, Erica
left them to sort out her closet and crossed campus to check
in with the administration office. She received her permanent
key card that let her into her dorm, the gym, and any academic
building on campus including her beloved library. She was also
given a water bottle with the Cascades bull elk engraved into its
matte green body. As she walked back to her room, she spotted
a handful of other students with these bottles attached to their
backpacks by carabiners or tucked under their arms. No one
eyed her like a lost puppy the way they had during orientation
when she wandered the campus either with a guide or consulting
a map. Carrying the water bottle and heading confidently toward
her destination, Erica finally felt like a college student.

She soon learned that her life at Cascades would consist
of endless flights of steps. She had been worried about putting on the fabled Freshman Fifteen, which she anticipated

being particularly prone to since she wasn't going to be on her feet forty or more hours per week working. But after climbing the five stories to her room only to be informed by Robin and Madison that they were going to dinner and therefore immediately making her way back down, Erica decided she didn't need to fret about her quads. It helped that Madison had decided she and Erica were swimming buddies.

"I do laps most Monday, Wednesday, and Friday mornings," Madison told her as they walked to the next residence hall over, which looked exactly like theirs but was decorated with pink ombre humps that Erica assumed were meant to represent the Painted Hills.

"I think I have Mythology at nine on Mondays and Wednesday."

Robin and Madison exchanged a wide-eyed look of horror. "Rookie mistake to take classes that early," Robin said.

"It's literally a cliche," Madison reprimanded.

"My advisor said I was fine in anything after eight! And I'm used to being up early for work. I'm sure it'll work out."

"Girl, you need to relax. You're on mountain time now." Madison was taking her own advice. She wore a hoodie and jeans, both at least two sizes too big. Erica wasn't sure she was quite comfortable with Madison yet, partly because of how comfortable Madison seemed with herself. Erica was no stranger to confident women, but she was used to them in the form of people like her mother and Cora who wielded lipstick and short skirts like weapons. Madison's brand of self-assuredness came from a deeper place, one she deemed less likely she could learn to emulate.

They made an interesting trio as they walked through the glass double doors. Robin, big, bushy-haired, and colorful in a bright yellow dress, pink leggings, and scarf covered in birds. Madison, petite and drowning in fabric, her dishwater blonde ponytail laying limp at the base of her neck. And Erica looking like a pair of legs with a head on top in her high-waisted jeans. Erica thought for sure they would draw attention as they made their way toward the cafeteria, but no one turned to look at them.

While the most popular apparel at Cascades leaned toward fresh off the trail, it wasn't strictly a dress code. Erica decided that night she would start a list of all the ways college wasn't like high school so that she could get her head in the right space.

The dining hall took up the entire ground floor of the building. Whereas Erica's dorm was beige from floor to ceiling, this one was dark green, the color of the Cascades logo.

"The options aren't as good as the SUB," Robin warned. "But it's worth not having to trek across campus for food."

Erica grabbed a tray and scanned her options. Absent were the ethnic options from the SUB and in their place was a buffet of carbs. Mac and cheese, spaghetti, mashed potatoes, French fries. There were a few chicken dishes and a vegan section that looked robust but largely untouched. Erica flip-flopped on her decision not to worry about her weight and resolved to ask Madison if she was willing to change her swim days.

They took what they wanted and searched for an open table. It was quieter here than it had been at the SUB during orientation.

"Not everyone is back on campus yet probably," Robin said when Erica asked about the typical decibel level of the dining hall. "But it's not usually too crazy here. It's mostly freshmen and sophomores in this part of campus."

Erica nodded. Robin and Madison had been info-dumping on her since she arrived, and it felt strange to be the center of a conversation to which she had nothing to contribute. She shoved a forkful of mashed potatoes in her mouth and found them to be exactly as salty as one would expect mass-produced food to be. That wasn't to say they were unpleasant. Quite the contrary—she couldn't wait for the next bite. A careless thought drifted through her mind about how she was going to describe them to Xander when she realized she probably wouldn't. She wasn't sure how she would explain herself to Robin if she was caught whispering to a tree about potatoes.

"What's the matter?" Robin asked, genuinely concerned.

Erica realized she was staring into space. "Sorry. I sort of just remembered that my boyfriend and I broke up."

"Oh no," Robin said, though this time the emotion was a little less real. "What happened?"

"The usual, I guess. I'm here. He's there. We're going in different directions." It was the truth even if it was missing a novel full of subtext.

"Who broke up with who?" Madison asked through a mouthful of pork chop.

"Madison," Robin admonished.

"It's fine," Erica said. It felt good to talk to girls her own age about boy stuff. Granny was always a willing audience, but she was well past the days of teenage crushes. Even if Cora would talk to her, she doubted she'd be willing to hear about Xander without saying *I told you so*. Who did that leave—her mother? She would rather poke her eyes out with her potato-topped fork. "He broke up with me, I guess. It's just hard though because I get it. But I love him and he's my best friend and we had sex, like, this morning."

Robin's eyes widened at this statement, and Erica wondered if she was scandalized. Madison just laughed.

"Christ. Straight people."

Now it was Erica's turn to laugh. "Excuse me?"

"Madison is asexual and so she thinks she's above it all."

"Asexual and aromantic," Madison clarified. "That doesn't mean I don't love hearing about other people's drama. I just have no interest in participating."

Erica mentally added Madison to the list of people she wasn't going to be unloading on for her boy troubles. "I'm familiar with the concept, but you're the first person I've met who identifies that way."

"We're frustratingly uncommon. Though from what I can gather from forums and Reddit posts, every one of us winds up friends with some hopeless romantic," Madison said, looking at Robin. "Like the universe has to fill the void created by our apathy."

Robin blushed hard. Erica was surprised. She kept getting the impression that Robin was annoyed when she brought up Xander.

"Hopeless romantic?" Erica repeated.

"That's unfair. I think it's more like I've had all this time to build it up in my head. I went to a STEM high school and I'm not the prettiest." Erica tried to object here, but Robin shook her head. "It's fine. It's just facts. But when you're almost twenty and a virgin, you've spent so much time thinking about it that reality can't help being a disappointment."

"I keep telling her to just make a Tinder profile," Madison said. She speared what remained of her pork chop and swiped it through Erica's mashed potatoes.

"I get that. I think it's part of what makes it so hard with Xander. He made me feel like I was part of a great love story. I don't know how you move on from that."

Madison rolled her eyes, but Robin was looking at her intently. "What does it feel like to be in a love story?"

Erica tried to keep her face passive as her entire relationship with Xander flashed before her eyes. The early meetings at the waterfall and the library. Seeing him across the bonfire at the party. Him pleading with her at the funeral. Learning he was a dryad. Watching him be cut open and somehow returning to her whole and happy. Waking up next to him in the morning. It was far too complicated for her to explain.

"Right now? Shitty. Maybe you should take Madison's advice." Erica played it off like a joke, but it was a cop-out. She knew it, and she could tell from the disappointed look on her face that Robin knew it too. Maybe someday, late at night, alone in their room, Erica would tell more of the story. A version that was more truthful without being the whole truth. When that happened, she would apologize to Robin for this moment. For now, she took another bite of mashed potato and hoped someone would change the topic.

When Erica woke up just after six the next morning to get ready for her first class, Robin threw her comforter over her head and turned on white noise that played from an app on her phone. Erica gathered her things as quietly as possible and made her way to the communal bathroom. She was much better prepared for this shower than she had been at orientation, being newly equipped with a plastic caddy and a waterproof bag for her clothes that were both Christmas presents from her mother. She decided to do her makeup and blow dry her hair in front of the big mirror opposite the toilet stalls rather than risk disturbing Robin. Back at her room, she opened the door as quietly as possible to retrieve her backpack before making her way to the cafe by the library.

Erica selected a chocolate chunk muffin, a banana, and a large drip coffee, and settled herself into an oversized leather armchair with a view of the library doors. Whether it was the time of day or still too early in the semester, the campus was eerily quiet. The library only closed for a handful of hours overnight, and the few people she saw come in and out were old enough that they had to be faculty.

She hadn't been on social media for months, her life having taken such a bizarre series of twists and turns since Keith's disappearance, but her breakfast combined with the ambiance of the pub-style cafe had her taking out her phone. Erica took several versions of the photo before realizing that what she was trying to capture was the feeling of being here, but the mixture of excitement, anxiety, and guilt muddled up in her brain couldn't be found in a filter. She thought about texting her mother whose phone calls she had been ignoring since yesterday afternoon, though she doubted she would be much help in sorting through her emotions. Instead, Erica opened Xander's favorite news app and scrolled through a few articles as she bided her time until her nine o'clock class.

Coming out of Mythology a couple of hours later, Erica was disappointed by how much it had felt like high school. The class was a general elective, and it was clear that the syllabus had been scaled back to make sure the future chemists and mathematicians would be set up for success. They were going to focus on the Greeks, which Erica had familiarized herself with while taking AP Literature less than a year ago. She wondered if her professor would know if she recycled a paper or two.

She had an hour before her next class. Though the campus

wasn't huge, it wasn't worth heading back to her dorm. Erica walked two buildings over and found a chair in the common area near her Introduction to Communications classroom. The Mythology professor had already assigned them a reading, but she didn't have the right book on her. To pass the time, she took out her only assigned textbook for her communications class, a slim paperback volume titled *Making the Human Connection*.

Erica had bought most of her books used, combing resale sites for the cheapest way to get what she needed. At the time, she hadn't connected the author of the textbook and the name on her course schedule: *Melanie Thompson*. The back cover had a small photo of a dark-skinned woman. The bio accompanying it stated that Ms. Thompson had an undergraduate degree from the University of Pennsylvania and a Master's in Journalism from New York University. A quick search on her phone told her that this was her professor.

It seemed ballsy to Erica to assign one's own book for your class but considering her entire college career to date consisted of the class she took that morning, she didn't feel she had enough information to pass judgment. Erica flipped to the introduction and read. The short essay was about Melanie Thompson's inspiration for writing the book, how she had found herself exploring the impact of low wages and poor education on enlisted families and permanent residents at an Alabama military base. Her first article came out in the 1990s, but she visited the base every year or two or five to document what had changed and more importantly what hadn't.

Ms. Thompson had won several awards Erica wasn't familiar with for that work, but the real reward, the essay said, was meeting people whose perspectives she changed by shedding light on the topic. She explained how writing is a one-sided conversation, allowing the writer to construct a complete narrative without interference. In this way, it is possible to disarm a reader, anticipate and address counterarguments, and remove some of the bias that comes along with looking someone in the eye when you talk to them.

It was a view Erica had not considered before. Most of the

reading she had done to this point, other than textbooks, was fiction. Unlike Xander and his biographies, Erica's awareness of the world around her came largely from eavesdropping on conversations between the adults in her life. Erica left her finger on the final page of the introduction and closed the book. She stared straight ahead as a wave of panic rushed through her. Was she ignorant? Was everyone she was going to meet in college smarter, better informed, and more worldly than she was? That familiar feeling of insecurity that had stopped her from coming in the fall crept into her mind, and she felt herself spiraling.

"You okay?" a female voice asked from somewhere above her.

Erica snapped back to the present to find a chic woman in a blood-red pantsuit standing in front of her. She was tall before factoring in her matching heels, and the curls piled on the top of her head pushed Erica's eyes even higher. Even if she hadn't been holding a stack of syllabi, Erica would have known this was Professor Thompson. The same level of competence permeated through her book cover, her writing, and her person. She was someone who would smell a white lie from a mile away, so Erica didn't bother.

"I'm contemplating whether I'm smart enough to take your class."

Professor Thompson's eyes widened, and she laughed. "With that level of self-awareness, I am sure you will be fine. What's your name?"

"Erica Wright."

The older woman shuffled through her papers until she came to a class roster. She scanned the page, then flipped it over, her eyes trailing to the bottom. "Freshman? Undeclared?" Erica nodded. "Well, Miss Wright, let's open your mind, shall we?"

Professor Thompson flung out an arm in the direction of her classroom. Erica packed up her bag and followed her into the room. It had about forty of those chair-and-desk combos that made Erica feel like she was eight years old again, which didn't help her flagging confidence. She took a seat in one immediately across from the desk where the professor had set down her papers and was searching for something in its drawers. She located a dry erase marker and wrote her name and the title of the class on the whiteboard at the front of the room.

"You know," she said, her back to her, "I was once eighteen and sitting in my first communications class wondering if I was good enough." She turned around and looked straight at Erica. "And you know what? I am. I have a suspicion you are too."

It sounded like an invitation, though the tone suggested a challenge. Erica knew she had no choice but to prove her right.

CHAPTER 20

Over the next three weeks, Erica established a schedule with the goal of helping her make sense of her new life. She had four hours of classes each day Monday through Thursday with Friday through Sunday totally free. She swam with Madison three days per week. She spent Sunday afternoons after Robin left their room for a pastry and a fancy coffee talking to the bonsai tree. She told Xander about the good—Robin, Communications, the beauty of the campus—and the less good—her other classes, the food, how crowded she felt most of the time.

Nothing about her college experience so far was bad but much of it was empty. Even with a significant amount of reading to do and struggling through her Business Calculus homework, Erica found herself with more free time than she could ever recall having. She picked books out of the fiction section of the library that weren't to her usual taste, discovering Japanese and Italian authors whose mastery of prose survived translation.

To avoid boredom and the overthinking that inevitably accompanied it, Erica called her mother begging her to let her get a job.

"I don't understand. You always whined about having to work at the store," Danni protested.

"When I was eight and you wouldn't let me be a Girl Scout."

"Why can't you just enjoy it when we try to do something nice for you? Maybe if you don't fail your first quarter, we'll talk about it."

Erica hung up and fell back onto her bed with a sigh.

"Do you want to run into Bend tonight and see a movie?" Robin asked. It was Saturday afternoon, and Robin was working on a technicolor design project that was supposed to simulate art produced by artificial intelligence.

"I would love that."

"Should we invite Madison?"

Erica made a face that Robin didn't see since her eyes were glued to her enormous monitor. She liked Madison best when they were engaged in an activity and their conversation could easily be steered away from political rants. Madison was an environmental science major with a lot of left-leaning views that Erica agreed with but didn't feel the need to discuss at length on a daily basis. "Maybe just the two of us?"

"Sure. Find us something to watch."

Erica was on her second movie trailer when a text popped up on her phone.

Derek: Hey so I was wondering if u wanna show me around ur collage sumtime next week

Her first reaction was to be surprised by the request, though she probably shouldn't have been. He had recently asked her to put in a good word for him with Granny to work at the store. With Erica and Xander having left at around the same time, there were big gaps in the schedule. She knew Derek was a hard worker, and he already had a good relationship with Joe through Kyle. She was thrilled to get him away from Kriners. She was happy to recommend him. The pay was lower, but they gave him more than full-time hours to try to make up the difference. They had been texting each other regularly since then.

Though she had come to consider him a friend, Erica had to admit she had an ulterior motive for keeping in touch with Derek. A few times a week he would drop a hint that he'd seen Xander, maybe even that they'd hung out. She never asked him directly, not wanting to be the clingy—she could barely bring herself to think it— ex-girlfriend. She had to think of a better term. Former girlfriend? Once and future girlfriend? Regardless, Derek was her only lifeline to Xander.

She was working on a reply to his text when his call showed up on her screen.

"Hey," she said.

"Hey yourself. I saw you typing but thought I would plead my case."

"You don't have to but let's hear it."

"You know Anna? I was telling her about your school, and she wanted to know more about it. I thought you could show me around? Give her a video tour?"

It felt like an excuse, but Erica understood the need to take a break from your life. Plus, even with Robin and Madison and trying to talk to new people in her classes, she was lonely. No one she met at Cascades had ever heard of Juniper Falls let alone could understand how crazy the last few months had been for her. Going from dryads and werebears to too many hours alone with her own thoughts was an isolating transition.

"When are you off next?" she asked.

"Really?" Erica could hear the excitement in his voice. "I was thinking I could come down early Wednesday and stay until Thursday morning."

"I get out of class at two," Erica said. "I don't think I can put you up in my room, but it's a co-ed floor, so you could probably sleep on a sofa in the common area."

"I'm not picky."

They worked out the rest of the details, and Erica was elated about the idea by the time she hung up the phone.

"What was that about?" Robin asked as soon as Erica said goodbye. This was interesting enough to warrant peeling her eyes away from her project.

"My friend is going to come by for the day."

"Not Xander?" Robin asked, and Erica couldn't tell if she was relieved or disappointed.

"No, Derek." It would never be Xander. A vision burst into her head of what him on campus would be like. Introducing him to Indian food at the SUB, walking through the greenhouses, hours spent reading in the library. But it passed faster than it came, a fleeting fantasy.

Robin had said something that she missed. "What was that?"

"I asked if he's cute."

Erica smiled.

As planned, Derek was waiting for Erica outside the Communications building on Wednesday afternoon. It was snowing lightly, and Derek's all-black ensemble stood out against the flurries. She had warned him it was colder here than in Juniper Falls, and he had taken her advice of bringing a decent jacket.

"The roads were okay getting here?" she asked upon arriving at where he was leaning against a concrete pillar.

"I grew up in Alaska. Oregon snow is nothing."

Derek leaned in for a hug, which Erica had not been expecting. They did a bit of a shoulder bump accompanied by an awkward back pat. Erica could feel her cheeks flushing. She had never spent time alone with Derek, and, as much as she liked him, she wasn't sure what to talk about. Opening with questions about Xander felt desperate and asking about anyone in his family other than Anna was full of pitfalls.

She opened her mouth to attempt another softball, but he wasn't looking at her. He casually surveyed their surroundings, his hand still on Erica's elbow.

"This place looks even more like a lodge than it does online," he observed. A group of students wearing stocking caps and sheepskin boots passed by them and entered the building. "A lot of basic white girls to match."

"Hey, watch who you're calling basic," Erica scoffed. To punctuate her point, she pulled a teal knit hat with a snowboarding company logo out of her messenger bag. It had been left behind at her parents' store years ago, and she'd stolen it when no one came looking for it after a week. She didn't know how to snowboard, but Derek didn't know that.

He grinned and held his hands up in an apology. "Not you. Duh." Erica laughed at the mock incredulity in his voice and allowed herself to relax.

"What do you want to see first?"

"What's worth seeing?"

Erica led him to the library where Derek impressed her by wanting to explore every corner. He explained that he had spent his whole life in small, rural places, and this was the closest thing to real architecture he has ever witnessed. He was transfixed by the way the light from the atrium made the whole building glow without any of it hitting a stack of books directly.

Derek asked her to show him where the chemistry books were, and she led him to a long aisle on the second level. He snapped a picture.

"Anna is a future scientist. She wants to invent the next plastic, but, you know, the good for the environment version."

"She would get along with my friend Madison."

"Yeah? Making friends already?" Derek asked as he browsed titles like *Non-Standard Applications of Inert Gasses.*

"You sound surprised."

Derek had his back to her, but she could hear the smile in his voice. "I like you, but you don't try that hard to be someone people like in general."

Erica *tsked* and slapped his arm lightly, but she didn't disagree with him. "I didn't realize we were psychoanalyzing each other. My turn?"

"No thanks."

They continued their tour around the library, then Erica walked him over to one of the science buildings. Most of the classrooms looked like the ones Erica had sat in, in high school—waist-high, black-topped worktables intended to allow four students to crowd around a Bunsen burner. The volume of generic, warm wood was overwhelming from the bases of the desks to the many cabinets that lined three of the four walls. It made her feel nostalgic.

When they were back out in the fresh air, Erica thought she heard someone calling Derek's name. She wondered who here would know him, then her answer manifested in a pink parka. It was snowing harder now, but Cora came into focus as she approached where they stood under the covered walkway that connected the buildings in this part of campus.

"You're the last person I would expect to see at a college," Cora said to Derek. Then turning to Erica, "And you're the last person I would expect to see with Derek. Does your boyfriend know he's here?"

"Hi to you too," Derek said. Erica didn't bother to reply. She probably deserved the cold shoulder. She hadn't bothered to look up Cora in the two months since orientation or after they both started at Cascades. She could blame it on having a lot on her mind and being worried about slipping up and saying the wrong thing. But the truth was she didn't want to hear Cora's passionate defense of the logging industry or her take on Granny's election.

"Rumor has it you quit Kriners. I bet Kyle misses you."

"Nah, we had drinks this weekend. I'm working for his dad. No hard feelings."

Cora pouted and tried again, "You heard that Mitchell is putting up cameras to catch whoever is vandalizing the sites, though, right?"

Erica heard the accusation hidden in the comment and fought to keep her face neutral. Cora suspected her, and likely Xander by extension, of being involved in the downtown incident. Erica wondered if Kyle had let something slip as they spent time together over the holidays. She couldn't help but check Derek's expression and hope Cora didn't notice.

The confusion on his face told her that if there was ongoing vandalizing, and it was perpetrated by Xander and Alden, Derek didn't know about it. She wished she could ask Cora if things had changed after the Harvest Festival, but she couldn't figure out how to do so without raising suspicion. She was pretty sure Xander was just growing trees, but they hadn't talked specifics the one time she'd seen him since he returned to Alden. They had been otherwise engaged.

None of this was as important as the fact that Mitchell was concerned enough to put up cameras. They had to warn Xander. Erica's hand clamped around the phone in her pocket, wishing she could walk away from this conversation and call him immediately.

"We should go," Erica said, ignoring Cora's satisfied smirk.

"You never told me what the two of you are doing here together."

"I'm sure you'll make up a good story to tell people."

Cora's eyes widened and she wobbled on the wide heels of her fur-topped boots.

"Oh, burn," Derek smiled. "See you around, Cora."

Erica took off toward her dorm. She was pretty sure Robin would be in a lab, and she couldn't think of anywhere safer to call Xander. Derek shuffled along behind her, thankfully not asking any questions. They passed several beautiful buildings that, if she was a better host, she would have shown him, but they could wait.

The snow was coming down so hard that Erica felt compelled to stamp and shake it off in the foyer, losing precious seconds. She flew up the stairs and through doors until she and Derek were safely in her room. She whipped out her phone and was dialing before Derek could get out, "Dorm rooms look bigger in TV shows."

Erica gestured toward Robin's floral chair, inviting him to sit as the phone rang. Derek ignored her, opting instead to inspect the rainbow explosion that was Robin's side of the room. She paced as the phone rang four, five, six times before an automated message told her the mailbox had not been set up. She grunted in frustration. She threw her phone on the bed and then her body followed it, being careful to leave her feet, still in their wet boots, planted on the floor.

"Why isn't he picking up?" She was so anxious, that she could feel her blood pressure rise. She pulled off her stocking hat and worked on the zipper of her jacket.

"You guys did say you weren't going to call," Derek said, rearranging the gel pens on Robin's desk. He was not having the same reaction as Erica.

"You know that?"

Derek nodded and took the seat he was offered. "He knows he's doing some risky shit. He and Alden are working out ways to make it less risky."

"Like what?" Maybe if she knew Xander had a plan to protect himself from Mitchell she could bat back this feeling.

"We didn't get that deep into it. We mostly talk about you."

Erica's heart leaped into her throat. She tried so hard not to miss him. To think of their separation as the best thing for them. But she had too much time on her hands here, which evolved into a loneliness that was hard to shake. She fought the tears that rose and wondered when she had become so prone to crying.

"Can you try him?"

"He knows, Erica. I mean, you guys used a trail cam to catch the bear. I'm sure he's thought of it."

She sat up and flashed her wet eyes at Derek. "Please." It was more than the warning now. She needed to hear his voice. "I won't say anything."

Derek took his phone out of his pocket slowly as if giving her time to change her mind. When she didn't, he pulled up his contacts and hit the call button. Xander picked up on the second ring. Erica was annoyed by the confirmation that he had ignored her.

"Hey, what's up?" came Xander's deep voice.

"Hey so I'm doing that campus tour thing with Erica," Derek said. He paused but the line remained quiet. "We ran into Cora, and she said Kriners is putting up cameras. They said it's to catch vandals, but, you know, dude. We just thought you should know."

More silence, then, "Is Erica there?"

"Yeah," Erica said just barely loud enough to be picked up by the phone.

"Okay. Thanks for letting me know."

Erica held her breath to stop herself from saying everything that was rushing through her head—how worried she was for him, how she missed his touch, how desperately she wanted to debrief with him at the end of every day.

"We're going to get back to it, then, man," Derek said.

"For sure. You guys have fun." Derek's thumb was hovering over the hang-up button when Xander added, "Erica?"

She flew off the bed to be closer to the phone. "Yeah?"

"I hope everything is going well with school."

"It is. Thanks. You too. With your stuff."

Erica heard him exhale, a warm, soft sound. She wanted to close her eyes and lose herself in the memory of what his face looked like when he made that exact noise. But she didn't want to weird out Derek.

"Okay. Bye."

The call disconnected. Derek made a face that asked her if she'd gotten what she wanted. But Erica was lost in Xander's words. *I hope everything is going well with school.* He couldn't hear her. Those afternoons spent whispering to the bonsai tree had made her feel better, but that illusion was shattered now that she knew he couldn't hear her. A glimmer of anger rose in her. How dare Xander create the illusion of connection and shatter it so casually? She wanted to vent to Derek, but Robin appeared clutching at the chest of her aqua-colored, knee-length winter coat.

"Oh hi," she said, startled by finding her room occupied. She opened her arms to welcome Derek but quickly clasped them around herself again. Erica cocked her head as Robin unzipped her coat and wrestled her laptop out of it. "Sorry, it was snowing and there wasn't room for it in the bag."

As if she felt this statement needed proof, Robin dropped her backpack off her shoulders, and it hit the floor like it was filled with rocks.

"Robin, Derek. Derek, my roommate, Robin."

"The interior decorator," Derek said, casting his eyes around at the many textiles and patterns that were strewn about in a way that seemed random. Erica knew by now was very intentional.

"The coder," Robin clarified. She set the laptop on the desk. Her face screwed up as she ran her fingers over the pens that sat there. "Are these organized in ROYGBIV?"

Derek nodded from the chair, and Erica raised her eyebrows at the smile that crept its way onto Robin's face. Erica was going to have to swallow her anger toward Xander. Derek's attention had moved on to something far more interesting.

CHAPTER 21

Erica was not the slightest bit surprised when Robin opted to join her and Derek on the remainder of their campus tour. Robin, with four more quarters of experience living there, proved to be a much more adept guide than Erica. Erica wished she had ditched her formal orientation and opted for Robin's version. Even after several weeks of living together, Robin had not yet introduced Erica to all her favorite nooks and crannies at Cascades. But she brought Derek to them, one by one, with a rundown of her daily routine that he appeared very interested in. Erica wondered a couple of times if she should find a reason to leave the two of them alone, but since they had known each other less than an afternoon, she thought it might be too presumptuous.

Several hours later, they found themselves back in Erica and Robin's room discussing dinner plans. Derek had heard from one of his logging buddies that there was a brewery in Bend that was well known for not carding, and he suggested driving them into town.

"It's dumping snow," Erica said, gesturing to the window. "And Bend is like forty minutes away."

"I told you, I'm a pro at driving in the snow."

"Can your car handle it?"

"I think it's a great idea," Robin interjected. "Let's invite Madison. She's from Montana. Between the two of them, we should be fine, right?"

Erica was outnumbered. She gave in. She rode in the back of Derek's old hatchback, which smelled more than a little bit like feet, trading knowing smiles with Madison as they listened to Derek and Robin play get-to-know-you.

The drive was less precarious than Erica had been expecting. There was less snow the closer they got to Bend, and it barely stuck to the highway. Arid Mountain Brewing was on the south side of Bend farthest from the campus in a nondescript suburban strip mall. Looking up at the neon sign mounted on the faux stone facade, Erica wondered why they bothered coming all this way.

Walking in, however, was an entirely different experience. The walls were reclaimed barn wood and all the fixtures, including the huge tanks of beer visible in the far back, were bright, shiny copper. The tabletops were resin over beaten copper, and the black leather chairs had cowhide seats. Everyone seated looked like they had come straight in from skiing with wind-swept hair and cheeks pink from the cold.

Erica followed behind Derek and Robin who had not stopped talking—about their families, movies, memes—and thought about the odd pair they made. Robin was taller, broader, and more colorful than Derek. They couldn't have more different backgrounds either, Robin having grown up affluent in San Francisco and Derek just above poverty in Kodiak.

Madison must have been thinking something similar because she whispered to Erica, "You did this?"

"I did nothing. I could not have expected this."

"Is he a good guy?" Erica could hear the trepidation in Madison's voice.

"Honestly, one of the best. I've had to trust him with some kind of massive stuff, and he came through."

Madison nodded. Robin chatted with the hostess who guided them to a table. Just as Derek predicted, she put down four menus and told them to order their drinks at the bar with no mention of identification.

"First round is on me," Derek said. "Any preferences?"

Erica and Robin both shook their heads, having no idea

about beer. Madison, on the other hand, surveyed the menu quickly and said, "Get me the hazy IPA." Erica tried not to look impressed.

Robin watched Derek walk away. When she deemed he had gone far enough that he wouldn't hear, she turned to Erica. "Oh my god, tell me everything you know about him."

"What? I think he already has." She was pretty sure that was true except for one rather large and hairy detail.

"No but what's he *like*," Robin prodded. Her hands were clasped in front of her, and she was leaning halfway across the table.

"Derek is pretty much what you see is what you get. I'm surprised you guys are hitting it off so well." Robin looked hurt, and Erica quickly course corrected. "No! I just didn't have you pegged as someone who was into lumberjacks."

"He's the first lumberjack I've ever met in a band t-shirt and ripped jeans," Madison said.

"How many lumberjacks have you met?" Erica threw. All three of them laughed, but Robin quickly put back on her serious face.

"But really. What should I know? Any red flags?"

Erica considered the question. There were lots of ways for her to approach it. To some people, Derek might be a walking red flag, but she saw him more like a diamond in the rough. "I mean, he hasn't had an easy life. He has a rocky relationship with his family. I couldn't tell you if he graduated from high school. But he has the biggest heart. He's been a good friend to Xander through some tough stuff."

Robin beamed. Erica should have known that she wasn't someone who cared about the optics of who she was dating. In that way, she and Derek were the same: two people who took those around them at face value. Erica thought of all the times she had ignored Derek's calls and texts, and he never once called her out on it. It struck her how lucky she was to have these people in her life to learn from.

Derek approached the table deftly carrying four very full beers. He set them down on the table and passed them out. "A hazy IPA for the lady who knows what she wants. Blondes for the two of you because I don't know if you can drink anything else. And an oatmeal stout for me." Erica eyed Derek's beer that was so dark it looked solid. He raised his glass and said, "Cheers to new friends."

They shouted "Cheers!" and clinked their glasses together. Cold, pale liquid splashed onto Erica's hand, and she used a napkin to clean herself up. The waitress arrived then. Erica thought she was looking at them suspiciously, so she did her best to look like she drank beer all the time. They put in an order for loaded French fries, chicken wings, and other appetizers for a family-style meal.

The waitress left, and Derek asked Madison if she liked attending Cascades.

"Oh, um, yeah," Madison said, caught off guard by his sudden interest.

"Why did you come here from—," Derek fumbled, looking to Robin to save him.

"Montana," Madison and Robin said at the same time. Madison continued, "Yeah, well, people are a lot more open-minded out here. Like, they believe in climate change unlike in Bozeman. And Cascades has good science programs. My parents kept going on about their job placement stats when we visited."

"Mine too," Erica said.

"Tell them what your parents do," Robin said, raising her eyebrows at Madison who shot her back a dark look.

"They work in mining," she sighed.

"No!" Erica couldn't believe it.

Madison put her head in her hands. "Yeah, imagine trying to be an environmentalist when your parents work in admin for a goddamn mine."

"They're still paying for your degree, though," Robin said, patting Madison on the arm. "So at least that mining money is going toward something good."

"Cheers to mining and logging paying for college tuition," Derek said.

They brought their glasses together again, this time with less gusto.

Erica asked Robin about how her big group project in her software engineering class was going, and from there the conversation flowed among the four of them. Derek asked a lot of questions that were mostly answered by Robin and Madison. Erica found herself sitting back and enjoying how easily her worlds merged. She had gotten used to thinking of college as something separate from her real life but having Derek here helped her see that it was all part of one continuous narrative. It made her question whether she and Xander had put everything into terms that were too black and white. She wished he could be here, experiencing this perfectly normal but spectacularly pleasant evening with people who had no preconceived notions about him spread by a small-town rumor mill.

She had been so overwhelmed by hearing his voice and the revelation that followed that she only just realized that he hadn't said anything about their warning. She hoped this meant that he had it under control. Maybe he could sense the cameras on the trees and disable or avoid them. She could hope.

The food arrived and brought Erica back to the present. As the waitress the placed the plates in front of them, Erica caught Derek's eye. He mouthed you okay? and she pursed her lips and nodded. He cocked his head toward Robin and lifted his eyebrows, which she took as him asking if their flirtation was upsetting her. She immediately shook her head and tried to give him a stealthy thumbs up.

"What are you two miming about?" Madison asked. She and Robin had divided the food onto four smaller plates, and they each placed one in front of Erica and Derek.

"Nothing," Erica said too quickly, causing the other girls to stare at her dubiously. They were headed fast toward a misunderstanding, so she decided to tell the truth. "I was just thinking about how nice it would have been if Xander could be here."

"I thought you guys broke up," Robin said.

"We did. He just doesn't get out much because of the whole sick uncle thing." She had filled Derek in on her story about Xander via text before he came. "Juniper Falls is such a small town. We don't have anything like this. It would have been a nice treat."

Robin and Madison bobbed their heads, but she could tell they weren't interested. She didn't blame them. She never was much interested in listening to her high school friends lament about their breakups. Erica commented on how good the wing sauce was and asked Robin how she liked her beer and let the topic of Xander drop.

After finishing their food, they decided against a second round. The snow was still light but steady. Out the window, Erica could see that the tire tracks they had made on the way in had been filled back in. The three girls split the bill for the food. They gathered their coats and walked back into the storm.

Derek was as good of a driver as he claimed to be. They made it back to campus without incident. Overnight visitor parking was about as far away from the dorms as possible. The four of them put on hats and wrapped scarves around their necks before getting out of the car.

"I can sleep in the car if I need to," Derek offered.

"That's insane. It's below freezing," Erica said.

"I don't want to get you in trouble with anyone."

"I don't think it's going to be a problem. Right?"

Robin shook her head. Madison said, "There are boys I don't recognize passed out on the couch in the TV room all the time. You'll be fine.'

Derek grabbed a puffy sleeping bag and a backpack out of the back of the car, and they made their way across campus. Erica looked for an in and when Derek and Madison began discussing football, she grabbed Robin's arm and held it for a moment as the others continued ahead.

"Do you want me to take the couch tonight instead?"

Robin's cheeks were already red from the cold and the color deepened with the question. Her eyes went wide. "Oh my god. No. Erica. No."

"Okay, if you're sure. I wouldn't be a good roommate if I didn't check. Rumor has it he's a surprisingly good kisser."

"Who told you that?" Robin yelped. Derek and Madison turned around to look at them. Derek held his hand out for Robin to catch up, but Erica waved them on. She had to stare daggers to get them both moving again. In the time that took, Robin had worked herself up into a silent freak out.

"Cora," Erica said.

"Cora! High heels Cora?" This answer did nothing to calm Robin down. Erica had pointed Cora out on campus once her first week. Robin had inquired about the nature of their fallout, which Erica chalked up to generic girl stuff.

"Yes, I'm sorry! I thought I told you that's how I met him!"

"You said you met him through that other lumberjack you used to date."

Erica wanted to object to the idea that she had ever actually dated Kyle but now was not the right time. "Robin, calm down. You're twice the person Cora is."

"Physically maybe."

"Hey," Erica said, putting her face right in Robin's. "You are amazing. I was very nervous to come here but meeting you and knowing you would be there to help me has made this whole thing one hundred times easier. Sure, Cora is hot. But you are also hot and not stuck up. Derek likes you. He would be crazy not to. Whatever you want this to be—a hookup, a friendship, a relationship—I support you."

Robin looked like she was going to cry. Erica's mind raced for what else she could say. She had been putting her foot in it with everyone all day, though, so she wondered if it would be better to stop talking. That impulse proved to be correct when Robin threw her arms around her and hugged her tight. This was becoming a thing, the hugging, but Erica didn't mind.

"Can I maybe just text him for a while first?" Robin asked as she let her go.

"Yes. Absolutely."

They squeezed hands and kicked up snow as they rushed to catch up with Derek and Madison. The latter was eyeing them to figure out what had just happened, while Derek had to struggle maintain the laid-back demeanor that usually came so naturally to him. Erica reminded herself to research whether bears had exceptionally good hearing.

The rest of the night passed uneventfully. After hanging out as a group a bit longer in the common area, Madison less than subtly suggested she and Erica go to bed. Robin and Derek had been slowly closing the gap between them for the better part of half an hour, and if what Robin needed was a snuggle and maybe a deep kiss, Erica wouldn't stand in her way. She said goodnight to them and didn't stay up long enough to hear Robin come back into the room.

CHAPTER 22

Classwork picked up after Derek's visit. Erica's English and Mythology classes bored her. Sometimes she would scroll through the upper-level English course summaries, wishing she was discussing American Literature through 1865 or reading books by authors she had never heard of listed in the syllabus for the seminar on Colonial Stories. Rehashing the basics of essay writing was much less fulfilling. When it came to Business Calculus, she could see how the content could be useful if she pursued that path, but the prospect of spending the next three and a half years talking about economic growth and decay was bleak. Every week it became clearer that Communications had her heart.

Her interest was fueled by more than the magnetism of Professor Thompson, though Erica couldn't pretend that wasn't part of it. She was the first woman Erica had met who was the person her mother tried so hard to be—someone whose competence was apparent in everything from her crisp pantsuits to her precise way of speaking. What she said was as compelling as the way she said it. Erica wanted the professor to notice her, but the brisk pace of class impeded her ability to distinguish herself.

In class on Monday, the students broke into small groups and completed a communications style assessment. They each took a quiz and discussed their results with their peers. Erica had come out firmly in the Conscientious style. She scanned the keywords associated with her results—systematic, logical, reserved.

"Cautious," said Professor Thompson. "Often to their own detriment. Conscientious communicators can easily find themselves in an endless loop of analysis paralysis."

Erica found herself annoyed that a thirty-question quiz had pegged her so accurately. After all, she just spent the last year waffling about attending college and had not yet declared a major. And she was clinging to a boy who had rejected her and who she had said out loud would never be enough. She looked at the words in the Dominant category—decisive, efficient, results-oriented—and figured that's where Professor Thompson would fall. She wondered if it was possible to will herself to become a different kind of person or if, at eighteen, she was stuck with who she was.

The assignment given at the end of class was to prepare a three-minute speech about the most impactful day of your life. The twist was that it had to be delivered in a way that would appeal to someone with a different communication style. Erica was sure of two things immediately upon hearing the task: first, that she would talk about the day she heard of Keith's disappearance, and second, that she would test her speech out on Robin. Robin was a Steady personality if ever there was one. She also was a good sounding board to make sure Erica explained the impact that Keith's death had on her without saying things that might lead to questions she could half-answer for Robin but didn't want to have to try to field in front of a classroom full of strangers.

Erica spent the next several days putting her outline together and carefully choosing her words. When she came to the parts that she knew she couldn't say to anyone else, she whispered them to Xander's bonsai tree despite knowing no one was listening on the other end. This didn't stop her from checking her phone for a text just in case she was wrong. No text from Xander ever appeared.

It didn't help that Robin and Derek had been texting and calling constantly for the last week and a half. Erica never wanted Robin to get a hint of the envy that swelled inside her when the other girl's phone would light up and her face melted into bliss personified. She was happy for them, though she couldn't help wondering how they had so much to talk about. It wasn't exactly a case of opposites attract, but it felt akin to that and forced Erica to think about the complex nature of like and love.

It was late morning on Saturday, and Erica's speech was set for that Wednesday. Erica knew by now that Robin was rarely functional before ten o'clock. She had already swum with Madison, had a big breakfast, and returned to their room with two to-go cups of coffee before Robin began her day.

"You're up!" Erica said, throwing the dry bag holding her wet swimsuit onto her bed. Robin groaned. Erica knew it was her slamming their door on her way in that had woken her, but it was late enough that she didn't feel guilty about it. "You said this morning would be a good time to help me with my speech?"

"Need coffee," Robin whined.

Erica put one of the cups on Robin's wallpapered desk. "Hot and ready!"

Robin extracted herself from her sheets. She wore a flannel pajama set patterned with tiny pink flamingos on a white background. The oddly large lapels of her top were rumpled, and Robin's hair flew wildly in every direction. Erica knew the right thing to do was to let her gain full consciousness before forcing her to provide a critique, but Robin had a way of zoning out once she was sitting in front of her computer that she wanted to avoid.

Once Robin was upright, Erica pulled the typed copy of the most recent version of her speech out of her backpack. She had printed it, double-spaced, in the library on her way back from the pool that morning.

"Okay. I'm going to start. Remember you're commenting on both the content of the speech and my delivery." Robin nodded, showing much less enthusiasm for the project than she had when initially approached. Erica sat on her bed, checked her posture, and took a deep breath. "Two weeks after my high school graduation, my mother told me my uncle was missing."

"Wait a second," Robin interrupted.

"What?"

"You can't just jump into the story like that."

"But it's a good storytelling device. It's meant to grip the listener right away." It felt callous to say, but it was true. Her *Making the Human Connection* textbook had told her as much. She had watched enough episodes of true crime television to know this was how they all started.

"Maybe, but you're supposed to be writing this for me, right? I want to know something about him first. What he meant to you."

Erica wanted to argue, but she had specifically asked Robin for her feedback. She jotted a note down to prove she was listening. "I'll change it. I'm going to keep going, though?"

"Sure," Robin said. "Pass me that coffee first."

Erica dislodged herself from her speaking position, handed Robin the coffee, and settled back in with another deep breath. "When he didn't show up for three weeks, we started to worry. The police found his car, and my mom decided to drive to Juniper Falls to help look for him."

"Stop, stop. You are taking so much for granted here. Where is Juniper Falls? Why is your mom important?" Robin beckoned to Erica to give her the speech. Erica rolled her eyes but handed it over and sat next to her on the bed. She was quiet while Robin scanned the pages. "This is a lot of facts and not a lot of feelings. Show me the personality profile you want to write for."

"Hang on." Erica was getting tired of all this up and down, but she went to her backpack and pulled out the binder with her Communications notes and handouts. She flipped through until she found the profiles. She opened the binder with that satisfying click of the rings and plucked out the requested pages. "Here."

Robin steadied her coffee between her thighs so that she could flip through Erica's speech and her notes at the same time. "Right here," she said, pointing to the Steady quadrant. "You want to play on my fear of instability. And friendliness. You have to make the connection so that we understand why you losing that support system was so important."

It was easier with the sheet in front of her to see how she had missed the mark. "Why are you so good at this?"

"All computer science majors are required to take public speaking. Cascades is big on trying to force us nerds out of our shells."

Erica looked through her speech again. "Should I even bother reading the rest of this?"

"Why don't you rework it, and we'll try again tonight. When I'm awake."

Erica collected her papers and put them on her desk. She pressed the power button on her laptop. As she waited for it to load, Robin crawled back under her covers.

"What are you doing?"

"Having a proper wake-up. It's barbaric to get out of bed without at least half an hour of scrolling through Insta."

It wasn't the first time Erica thought that Robin could benefit from a few weeks of having to wake up before dawn to unload pallets. It might give her a little perspective. But then she admonished herself for sounding like her mother. Maybe if Erica had more time to herself growing up, she would be as confident in who she was and what she wanted as Robin. Instead, she was stuck with a conscientious personality, forced to overanalyze every decision and terrified of making the wrong one.

Robin workshopped Erica's speech with her on and off all weekend. It improved with each iteration until Erica was sure she had nailed the assignment. Several of her classmates gave their speeches on Monday, and she was taken aback when Professor Thompson asked for real-time feedback on their performance. One girl gave a passionate speech about scoring the winning goal in a soccer tournament final when she was twelve and looked like she was going to cry when another classmate told her he missed half of it because she didn't speak loudly enough.

Erica wasn't the only person talking about a dead relative, but the other student's speech was about a grandparent and coming to terms with his mortality. She found it a little too tidy to appeal to the impulsive Influencer audience he claimed to be targeting.

On Wednesday, Erica didn't even hear the speeches before hers. She was so focused on running through her delivery in her head that she almost missed her name being called by Professor Thompson. She slowly rose from her seat and made her way to the lectern. Professor Thompson sat at a desk in the front row and gave Erica the same reassuring smile everyone received as they took their turn. Smoothing out her notes and bringing her head up to look at the class, Erica was struck by how different the outlook was from the front of the room when you were standing and everyone else was sitting. She felt exposed yet powerful. It made her stand a little straighter and take a deep breath.

Erica began with Robin's suggestion to tell them about what Keith meant to her before jumping into what happened to him. It was when she got past the part about finding his body, how it felt both inevitable and unfathomable, that she picked up speed.

"Keith had one last gift for me, though. I met some unusual friends of his. They gave me a different perspective on death. They—he—taught me to be brave and how to trust myself. I fell in love for the first time. Then I lost that too. But because of everything I learned from them and from Keith while growing up, I could handle it. I finally felt like I could stand on my own two feet.

"And now I'm here, and it's going okay. I'm not saying that Keith had to die for me to get here. In fact, I think all the time about how maybe if I had talked to him more about how I was feeling about Portland and college and, I guess, growing up, that he could have helped me figure it out sooner. But that's not how it worked out. That's been a lesson for me too. That things don't always go how you planned, but you have to take the best parts of what you're given and move on from the rest.

"That's what I'm doing. Living my life with the best parts of the people I love. For Keith."

The last part had not gone quite as she rehearsed. It was like she knew what she wanted to say without thinking about it.

She held each side of the lectern tight as she willed the tears she could feel were forming to stay inside. She had veered a bit too far from the deliberate and stable delivery she had been hoping for and didn't think crying would win her any points.

"Okay," Professor Thompson said, her tone not telling Erica anything about her opinion on what she just heard. "Does anyone have any feedback for Erica?"

Erica looked out at her classmates. She didn't see the emotion she was feeling reflected in any of their faces. A girl raised her hand tentatively. Professor Thompson pointed at her, giving her permission to speak. "Did you ever find out how Keith died?"

"The police said it was a bear attack."

The room was quiet.

"We're looking for feedback on content and delivery," Professor Thompson reminded the class.

"I thought it was good," said Kaitlyn, a girl who often sat with Erica in the front row. They usually paired off or joined the same group during activities. Erica appreciated the show of support.

"No one else?" Professor Thompson scanned the room. "Alright, then. Thank you, Erica. Looks like Reagan is next."

Erica took her seat and listened to the rest of the speeches. The ones her classmates chimed in on were usually really good or really bad, and the low participation following hers probably meant it was middling. It was a disappointing result after working so hard and exposing so much.

She made sure to say something nice after Kaitlyn's speech, which was the final one of the day and about her parent's divorce in her junior year of high school. Erica and Kaitlyn were congratulating each other on their respective performances when Professor Thompson interrupted.

"Girls, it's almost time to register for next quarter, and I wanted to invite you both to sign up for my Writing in Communication class. I think you'd enjoy it."

Erica fought the urge to jump up and down. Who cared that her classmates weren't impressed if her professor was. She and Kaitlyn mumbled excited yeses and thank yous as Professor Thompson tapped her knuckles on the desk and went to talk to another student. They made big eyes at each other but didn't exchange a word until they were outside the classroom.

"Are you a Communications major?" Erica asked when they reached the corridor.

"No. Undecided." Kaitlyn hitched her red and black plaid backpack over her arm. She had a punk vibe with her pleated skirt and pink tips at the end of her bleached blond hair.

"Me too! I thought I was the only one!"

"Girl, hardly."

Erica watched Kaitlyn walk away, and a strange realization washed over her. Kaitlyn didn't look remotely embarrassed to admit that she didn't have everything figured out. All this time Erica had felt so alone in her aimlessness, but what were the odds that she was the only teenager at Cascades who didn't know what she wanted to do with the rest of her life? Having met another one opened the possibility that there were more. Which, of course there were.

Professor Thompson had praised her and wanted her to continue in her classes. She might be on the path to finding the thing she was good at. And if this wasn't it, she had more than three more years to go. High school had been the end of something, but this was the beginning. And the thing about beginnings was that she wasn't required to know yet how it all wrapped up. In that moment, standing in the hall alone yet surrounded by other students whose lives she didn't know, who might be musing on these exact worries, she decided to mean what she said in her speech and go easier on herself.

CHAPTER 23

Returning to her dorm after class, Erica set up an appointment with her academic advisor to register for her next quarter of classes. She was used to high school semesters that dragged on for half a year and even then she was lucky if two of her classes changed. She had barely scratched the surface of the subjects she was currently taking, and another four weeks didn't seem like enough time to master them. She marveled at how her days could feel so slow but the weeks so fast.

Checking her phone, she saw a text from Madison inviting her and Robin to a board game meet up on Saturday. Thinking about weekend plans made Erica realize how long it had been since she was home. Madison had a fondness for games with too many pieces and equally as many ways to win. A trip to Juniper Falls would be a good excuse to avoid having to spend longer learning the rules to something than actually playing it.

She called Granny who picked up on the first ring despite the jumble of voices in the background.

"Hello, love. Are you not in class?"

"I'm never in class. I was thinking about coming home for a few days this weekend." Erica could pick out Muriel's voice asking loudly, *Who's that?*

"This weekend?" Granny sounded distracted. "I don't know. We have a big non-profit coming into town next week to talk about expanding local resources for pediatric and preventive medicine."

Delivering on campaign promises already. She expected no less from Granny. While Erica was disappointed, she also wondered if she could have handled it if she'd shown up in Juniper Falls and Xander refused to see her. Maybe it was for the best. "Call me when you're less busy, okay? I want to hear all about it."

"I will. Study hard. I love you."

"I love you too."

She hung up, and her phone reverted to her contacts screen where her mother's name sat at the top of her favorites. She hadn't been to Portland since August. After declining to go home for Thanksgiving, she had not technically been invited again, but she imagined that even her mother's cold heart was hurt by how long she had stayed away. Erica stared at the phone until the screen went dark. Maybe she would offer to come up for a few days during spring break. She had some time to think about it.

Turning her attention back to her laptop, Erica proofread her English paper that wasn't due for another week. Her mind wandered, landing on the bonsai tree sitting in a weak pool of light that came through the room's only window. She'd been neglecting it since she found out it wasn't connected to Xander. The leaves drooped from lack of water and the acorn had fallen off. Erica had saved it, though, putting it in a little box and shoving it in the back of her desk drawer just in case Xander was wrong about it having no special properties. She knew she shouldn't take out her frustration on an innocent tree. She grabbed her water bottle from her backpack and dumped the remainder of its contents on its roots then laid down on her bed.

She looked at the little bookshelf hanging above her. For as much as she loved reading, she didn't own many books. Most of the ones she read growing up technically belonged to her parents and didn't come with her to Juniper Falls or Cascades. Between a complete collection of Jane Austen novels and the Harry Potter series sat *Wuthering Heights*, a gift from her junior year English teacher. She'd read it that summer and hadn't liked it. The characters behaved so irrationally that she couldn't find it within herself to pity any of them. Maybe if she read it now, after having loved and lost, she would understand its perpetual popularity.

She was contemplating making *Wuthering Heights* her weekend plans when the door behind her opened. Robin entered, throwing her messenger bag on the floor and herself in her wing-back chair. Erica had only recently noticed that the chair was retrofitted with rollers, and she kept meaning to ask if Robin had bought it that way or if, as she suspected, she put them on herself. Now was not the time to ask. Normally cheery Robin only got this agitated about one thing—group projects.

As Robin ranted about the guy in her group who had designated himself their project manager and wasn't a fan of feedback, Erica crossed the room to where a two-cup coffee pot sat on top of her dresser and a mason jar of homemade brownie mix sat next to a microwave on Robin's. Madison had told her at orientation that Robin's microwave brownies were amazing, and she was not wrong.

Robin beat the back of her head into the cushioned chair. "He cannot let anyone else be right."

"You should try to talk to your professor again." Erica poured the mix into two mugs and moistened them with that morning's coffee. This was her contribution to the recipe, and it took them to the next level.

"He doesn't care. He keeps going on about the entrepreneurial spirit like he's afraid to kill the drive of the next Elon Musk."

Erica popped the mugs in the microwave and set the timer for exactly seventy-five seconds. "He probably wants a cut of that sweet startup money."

Robin rolled her eyes and sighed. She took her phone out of a pocket in her backpack. "Have you heard from Derek at all today?"

"We're not on the daily communication plan like you are."

The microwave beeped, and Erica pulled the sleeves of her sweater down over her hands to take the mugs out. She put a plastic spoon in each, hoping Madison wasn't about to barge in and rant about the irresponsibility of single-use plastics. Wrapping two sweater-covered index fingers around the handles of the mugs, she carefully placed a molten brownie on each of their desks.

Sitting down, Erica noticed she did have a text from Derek on her phone. She crinkled her eyes as she opened it and saw the other recipients of the text: Kyle and Xander.

"Wait a second," Erica said.

Derek: Just got txt from Anna. She's here.

"He texted you?"

"Yeah."

"About what?"

"I—I don't know."

Erica's mind was racing. Anna was in Juniper Falls? By herself?

Erica: With your parents?

"What's it say?" Robin's impatience radiated through the room, but Erica kept her screen angled carefully away. She watched the dots flash at the bottom of the screen.

Derek: Dont no. Says to meet at diner tonite.

Alarm bells rang in Erica's head. She took her eyes off the screen and up to Robin's dejected face.

"It's a family emergency," Erica said. She looked back at the phone, wondering where Kyle and Xander were and why they weren't responding. She had to lie, but what was plausible? "Xander's family. His uncle."

Robin let out the breath she was holding. "Oh no," she said with no real conviction. A new text popped up.

Derek: she wont pick up my call.

Erica shot up, almost knocking over her untouched brownie. "I have to go."

"Where?"

Kyle: U need backup again?

Derek: Ya. 9?

"Juniper Falls. They need me." Without taking her eyes off the screen, Erica pulled her duffle bag from under her dresser and threw clothes in it at random.

"Don't you have class tomorrow?"

"It's fine. I'll email and explain." Luckily the class she would be missing was English so the creative writing exercise required to avoid revealing her friend the werebear required her assistance should count for credit. Erica tossed her entire shower caddy, still wet from that morning, on top of her clothes and was zipping the bag shut when the dots appeared again.

Xander: I'll be there.

Seeing him respond to a text in real-time made Erica's heart soar. She kept telling herself that things were really, irreparably over between them. But if that was true, how could he still make her feel like this? Erica pushed those thoughts out of her head. She had to get to Juniper Falls, to Derek, to help with whatever was about to happen.

She was aware of Robin watching her every move but trying to provide more information would dig her a deeper hole. "I'll let you know if I see Derek, okay? I'll have him call you."

Before Robin could respond, Erica grabbed her duffle and her purse and was out the door.

Once she chipped the ice off her car and made it out of the parking lot, the main roads were clear and dry. Erica left the radio on until the Bend stations cut out then synced her phone to the car and chose an upbeat playlist that didn't match her mood. The drive gave her time to make plans: one for how they should approach the Diner and another for how she was going to conduct herself around Xander.

The prospect of being physically in his presence again made her stomach churn. They had left things fine, more than fine, when they were last together. But he must have known from that first day when she crossed whatever invisible barrier marked the edge of his limits that the bonsai tree wasn't going to work. The bonsai had been a placebo she needed to swallow. Xander had chosen to maintain the silence between them under no such illusions. He had cut her off for real.

Erica turned up the volume on the stereo. Xander wasn't why she was barreling toward Juniper Falls. Or at least he was

only a small part of it. She was going for Derek, who she realized didn't know she was coming. Her phone had pinged with
several texts as she drove, but she was too worried about black
ice and the curves of the highway to check them. Maybe Robin
had told him. Erica planned to head straight for Granny who
also didn't know she was coming, but who, despite being busy,
she had no doubt would welcome her with open arms or at least
an open bedroom.

Her playlist was getting on her last nerve when she came to
her exit, crossed the river, and wound her way to Granny's yellow house. There were several cars in the driveway—Cadillacs
and Buicks—a portent of the group of gray-haired ladies she
would find inside. She parked on the street so that she wouldn't
get blocked in and made her way inside.

Sure enough, five women turned their heads when she
opened the door. They sat around the oak table, which was littered with loose paper. Granny was not among them.

"The beloved granddaughter returns!" said one of the
women. Erica wished she could keep their names straight, but
the only one she could remember was Muriel who was squinting at an open laptop in front of her. Erica set down her bag,
slipped off her boots, and rubbed Tulip's ears.

"Is Granny—?" she started, but another woman pointed to
the kitchen. Erica could smell the yeasty warmth of fresh-baked
bread. Sure enough, when she rounded the corner, Granny was
standing in an apron tapping slowly on her phone next to a pair
of round loaves steaming on a butcher block cutting board.

"You text now?"

"Not if I can help it." Then, only just registering the voice
she was hearing, Granny put the phone on the counter and
embraced Erica. "What are you doing here?"

Keeping her voice low, Erica explained about Anna and
the Diner. "They don't know I'm here. I should probably call
someone."

Granny frowned and squeezed Erica's bicep. "I wish you
would have called me before you left. I would have asked you if
you were sure this was your fight."

Erica took this like a punch to the gut. She wasn't sure if Granny meant it to be accusatory, but the comment conjured for her the last time she acted rashly and took charge of a situation that wasn't hers to commandeer. That decision left physical and emotional scars that were still healing, and yet it hadn't once occurred to her to ask Derek before rushing to his aid. But he'd texted all three of them, hadn't he? Why would he have included her unless he wanted her there?

She was about to make this case to Granny when Muriel popped into the kitchen. Muriel pointed to the loaves. "Can I grab those?"

"Absolutely not. They will collapse if you cut into them now. I'll be out in a minute." Muriel shrugged and retreated. Granny sighed. "I swear I couldn't do what I do without them, but you've never encountered a bigger bunch of busybodies."

Erica took the opportunity to avoid having to defend herself. "How is the mobile clinic going?"

"I think we can do one better than that. There is a doctor who is willing to come two or three days a week. She says she can bring a nurse and sign people up for the Oregon Health Plan."

"That's amazing. You're amazing." Erica hugged Granny again. Her phone buzzed as she released her. She had several unread messages in the group chat and a missed call from Derek that must have come in when she was out of cell range. "I'm going to go throw my stuff upstairs and then I'll be out for a bit."

Granny nodded, her face still sad and searching, but Erica didn't have time to argue. She smiled at the women in the dining room as she passed through to retrieve her bag from where she had left it by the front door. She took the stairs two at a time. Opening the door to her room, she hoped that she would be hit with Xander's wet earth smell left upon the sheets she hadn't washed before she left. But Granny had tidied everything up. The room looked almost exactly like it had when she'd arrived in August. Erica wondered if she looked the same or if someone could tell at a glance how much she had changed in the last six months. It made her sad to think they couldn't.

She sat on the bed and opened the text thread.

Derek: called my parents and they rnt picking up

Xander: What about your brothers?

Derek: nope

Kyle: meet at my place? 7:15?

Derek: ya

Xander: Sure

There was about an hour when the chat went silent. Erica hoped that Derek was calling Kyle and Xander during this time to calm his nerves but, in her limited experience, that wasn't the way boys operated. She imagined him trying to help customers at the store in between sneaking off to the storeroom to place another call to a family member in Alaska. She read the next text.

Derek: E, Robin says ur coming??

The time stamp on the missed call fell between this text and the one after.

Derek: ne1 hear from erica? X?

Xander: No but she's probably on the road.

Erica loved that he knew her well enough not to doubt that she was coming. She loved them all a little bit for not try-ing to stop her. She had the least to offer—at least Kyle was bulky and intimidating—but there appeared to be no objection to her joining them. Technically she had half an hour before their proposed meet-up, but her adrenaline was pumping too hard to wait.

Erica: Sorry. Just got to Granny's. Heading to Kyle's now if that's OK.

All three of their initials popped up next to the blinking dots then disappeared. One by one their texts came in.

Kyle: I'm here

Xander: On my way.

Derek: just gotta close up

Erica grabbed her purse off the floor and made her way quietly down the stairs, hoping to avoid a conversation as she shoved her feet into her boots. Granny met her eyes as she opened the door, but she made no attempt to stop Erica from slipping out. Either the temperature had dropped since she arrived, or she hadn't noticed the cold on her way in. It was at least ten degrees warmer than on the other side of the mountains, but still very much jacket weather. Erica pulled on the purple puffer jacket she had tossed in the passenger seat mid-drive and made her way to Kyle's. She was the first to arrive, and he had the door open before she had made it onto the porch.

"So this is crazy," he said by way of greeting.

A rush of unexpected emotions hit Erica all at once. She hadn't seen Kyle since the debate and hadn't talked to him since the run-in with Derek's parents. Her mind formulated questions about his relationship with Cora and his continued employment at Kriners. She wasn't sure that if it was up to her that she would continue to put her trust in him. But this was Derek's crisis and if he wanted both of their support, Erica would defer to his judgment.

"You don't think they really have his sister, do you?" she asked.

Kyle shrugged. "I guess we're going to find out."

Erica kicked off her boots and tried to think of a neutral topic. Kyle looked equally uncomfortable, which made her even more suspicious of him. She imagined the relief on his face was mirrored on hers when a knock on the door saved them from the awkwardness. Knowing it could only be one person, Erica capitalized on the brief second it took Kyle's brain to switch gears to open the door.

There stood Xander in his usual hoodie and jeans, his hair back to the close shave it had been when they met. All the nerves and confusion and worry that she had built up in her head and all her anger at him for misleading her about the bonsai dissipated the moment the corners of his mouth turned upward at the sight of her. Erica jumped at him, throwing her arms around his neck and nuzzling her face into the soft skin behind his ear that smelled exactly like she remembered. She heard Kyle mutter something behind her but all she registered was Xander's arms closing around her back, holding her inches off the floor.

"I missed you," she whispered.

"I missed you too." His voice was melodic with laughter.

Xander lowered her to the ground and kept one hand on the small of her back as she turned toward Kyle. "Do you mind if we catch up while we wait for Derek?"

Kyle sighed and waved them into the living room. Erica barely registered his annoyance. She had so much she wanted to tell Xander about school, about Communications and Professor Thompson, and how strange it was to share a room with someone who wasn't him. She reached behind her back and took Xander's hand, leading him to the tan couch they had sat on back in November. Kyle did not join them. This half-hour before Derek got off work might be the only time they would have just the two of them until, well, Erica didn't want to think about it. She held Xander's hands in her lap as she told him about her classes, the snow, early morning swims with Madison, and how Robin was entirely smitten with Derek.

"I think the feeling is mutual," Xander said, a conspiratorial smile on his face.

"I need you to meet her. I was thinking about bringing her here for spring break."

Xander didn't reply to this. She pretended not to notice that he wouldn't commit to seeing her again. She asked him what he was reading. The time passed too swiftly and then Derek was at the door looking harried, his eyes wide but not landing on anything.

"I'm worried, guys," he confided as they all stood in the entryway.

Erica waited to see if anyone was going to take the lead. She looked between Derek, Xander, and Kyle, hoping one of them had a stroke of genius and would lay out a plan for whatever they might find at the Diner. The last time Erica had put herself in charge, it ended disastrously. She was hesitant to do so again. But she hadn't driven all the way here to not have the outcome be Anna leaving safely with Derek.

"I have an idea," she said when she could no longer stand the silence. Three pairs of eyes landed on her face, and she started to explain.

CHAPTER 24

Erica walked into the Diner at half-past eight. She wore a waxed canvas jacket and a black beanie that sat low on her forehead, both belonging to Kyle's dad. Joe had arrived home as the four of them sat in his living room arguing over the finer details of the plan they were forming. He greeted them one by one, made himself a sandwich in the white kitchen, and retreated down the hall to his room. She wasn't sure if Kyle had given him the heads up or not, but either way he seemed wholly unconcerned to find them there.

They had raided the coat closet for her disguise, which also included the paperback copy of a Tom Clancy novel she was carrying, the only book they could locate in Joe and Kyle's house. The logic applied was that if Derek's dad was the mastermind behind this latest attempt to ambush him, Erica was the one he would be least likely to recognize or have described. He hadn't gone to her house after the events at the Coffee Stop, plus he didn't seem like the kind of man who thought much of women. In case he remembered some details, however, they covered her up and sent her to the Diner in Xander's truck, which she parked and stashed the keys under the seat.

The shaggy-haired waitress gestured to the nearly empty assortment of booths and tables, letting Erica pick her seat. The only other patron was a tired-looking middle-aged man sitting near the window who she figured belonged to the tractor-trailer sitting in the parking lot outside. She chose the booth nearest the entrance and cracked open the book somewhere in the middle. Her eyes skimmed the lines, but the words didn't register.

The waitress offered Erica a menu. She ordered a black coffee, scrambled eggs, and toast without looking at it, then handed the waitress a twenty-dollar bill and insisted she keep the change. The woman gave her a strange look but didn't argue. She returned seconds later and placed a plain white mug of steaming coffee in front of Erica who took a sip of the bitter brew and waited.

She heard the bell on the door of the attached convenience store ring and listened to the footsteps that came her way. Xander and Derek waited for the waitress to seat them. Kyle was outside in Derek's car. If things went how they were supposed to, he would be her getaway driver.

Erica could feel a pair of eyes on her, probably Xander's from the way it made her blush, but she didn't turn around. He and Derek were offered the same instructions she was, *pick a seat*, which they did on the far side of the Diner, both sliding into the same bench facing the window. Erica was glad she could watch the backs of their heads. She wasn't sure that in their place she would have been able to stop herself from sneaking a peek behind her, which might ruin their ruse.

After the boys received their coffee, the room went quiet. The last time she was here the jukebox would play a random song even if no one made a request. Now there was no music to hide the hiss and clank of her eggs being cooked. Erica tried to pay attention to her book, but every unexpected noise—the scrape of the older man's fork across his plate, Xander mumbling something to Derek, the abrupt arrival of her order—made her jump.

Erica ate slowly. She checked her phone at five minutes past nine. She nibbled on a piece of toast and checked again. Only two more minutes had gone by. Anna was late if she was coming at all. They had talked through all the possibilities, including the very real one that someone had taken her phone and Anna wasn't the one sending the texts to Derek. If Anna didn't show, Erica was supposed to leave, walk to where Kyle waited in the car, and let Derek and Xander handle things themselves. She had seen Derek take on a bear four times his size and Xander bend a hundred-foot tree, but the voice in the back of her head that said they needed her didn't want to listen to reason.

At more than a quarter past, Xander broke and looked over his shoulder to make eye contact with Erica. She smiled so imperceptibly she doubted he could see it. She was halfway through a shrug when they heard the bell next door. Their eyes went wide. Erica's phone buzzed.

Kyle: They're here. Two guys and Anna.

In the split-second Erica had taken to look at her phone, Xander's head had snapped forward. She retreated like a turtle into her oversized jacket and trained her eyes on her book as she listened to the heavy footfall and deep voices of the men who made their way into the diner. They stopped just feet away from her.

"You see him?" one of them asked.

Derek got out of the booth and slouched toward them, a rehearsed smile on his face. His eyes were trained on the group behind her and didn't once fall on Erica. "Liam! I didn't know you'd be dropping off Anna for me, man. Long time no see. Who's your bro?"

"You know Evan."

"Yeah? Holy shit. Little Evan Lewis. You made some gains, man."

Erica heard a slap of flesh that might have been a handshake or a fist bump, which was promising. Xander had thrown his arm across the back of the booth and was watching Derek and the others.

"Is that your boy? With the?" asked a second voice. Erica wished she could see whatever gestures accompanied this question. Xander's face was so scrunched up in distaste that she had to fight not to laugh. She assumed they were mocking the hand gestures that usually accompanied him manipulating a tree or a flower.

"Yeah, but we're not looking to get into all that. You're just here for a friendly chat, right?" Derek asked. Only because she had spent so much time with him recently could she hear the edge in his tone. There was a grunt from one of the newcomers and then a pause. Erica couldn't read anything on Xander's face about what was going on. Then Derek's voice again, "Come sit with us. I'll buy you a coffee and get Anna some dinner. You feed her?"

Anna was with them after all. The four of them walked past, their thighs almost touching the chrome edge of her table. From what she could see out of the corner of her eye, Derek's acquaintances were huge. One looked to be Derek's age, early twenties, tall and athletic. The other was younger and shorter but so laden with muscle he could only zip his heavy jacket half-way up his chest. She assumed that one was Evan.

Derek tried to get Anna to sit next to him, but Liam tugged on her arm.

"Hey!" Derek protested. Liam dropped Anna's arm but pushed her into the bench where his friend was already seated. He got in after her, boxing her in.

Erica could see their faces clearly for the first time. Anna didn't look scared so much as annoyed. The guys had the cut jawlines and grim countenance of football players about to run a particularly challenging formation and the vacant eyes that come after taking too many hits.

The waitress appeared next to Erica. "You need anything else?"

"Another cup of coffee."

"You've got it," she said, but instead of going back to the kitchen, she headed for Derek's table. To Erica's dismay, she flicked a switch on the jukebox on her way and the voice of Frank Sinatra filled the Diner. Unless a screaming match broke out, she wasn't going to be able to hear what was happening. Though that might help her with what she had to do next.

Her job was to get Anna to the bathroom. This would involve attracting her attention without making others suspicious. If it took too long, Derek had promised to kick Anna under the table, but that was a risk Erica was hoping they wouldn't have to take.

Erica's first move was to yawn and stretch her arms over her head. Evan was the only one who looked her way but only briefly. Their attention was on the waitress who had just handed Anna a menu. Bad timing. Erica picked up her book and managed to read a couple of pages before daring to look up again. The waitress had gone. The table's attention was on Derek now. Xander leaned against the wall, and she could see his face in profile.

Erica thought she saw Anna's eyes drift in her direction but there was no recognition. She tugged on her earlobe as if this was some secret signal between them, which of course it wasn't. Without moving her head, she flicked her eyes up to see Evan and Anna watching her. She dropped her hand. Her phone rattled against the Formica tabletop.

Kyle: Any movement?

Erica: Not yet.

As she texted, she held her phone at a height that let her watch the others. Evan was looking back at Derek, but she still had Anna's attention. Bingo. Erica jerked her head to the door. Anna squinted at her. Erica scooted to the end of the bench, maintaining pointed eye contact with Anna. Before she got up, she took a pen from her purse and wrote *BATHROOM* in capital letters at the top of a napkin. She put the napkin in the book with the word sticking out the top, hoping it could be interpreted as a note to the waitress not to clear her table.

Not daring to call attention to herself now that she was moving, Erica didn't check to see if Anna was following as she went through the doorway into the dusty mini mart. She stayed along the back wall covered in refrigerated cases of soda and beer before ducking into an alcove with two doors, each bearing a black enamel sign with white lettering. The one on the left read *Employees Only* and, on the right, *Restroom*. Erica tried the handle. Locked.

She swallowed the bile that rose in her throat. She would not panic. In as few steps as possible, she made her way to the counter. She stole a brief glimpse into the Diner and saw Liam was standing, hopefully to let Anna out. Erica slapped the counter to get the attention of the cashier, a teenager with oily hair wearing a sweat-stained polyester polo shirt. He looked annoyed by her rudeness and continued stocking the cigarette packets cradled in his left arm.

"Be right there," he said.

Erica grasped her stomach with both hands and bent over. "It's an emergency."

The cashier sighed and put the cigarettes on the countertop. Erica looked at the entrance to the Diner and then back at the cashier, scrunching up even tighter like she was in pain. He handed her the key from next to the cash register. It was attached to a long wooden dowel by a metal chain. She ran back to the bathroom, shoving the key in the lock, and shutting the door.

Erica stood in the darkness behind the door and waited, hoping that she hadn't been seen. She was breathing so loud she worried she would be heard from the other side of the door. As she tried to calm herself, the knob turned, and Anna flicked on the fluorescent light. They both jumped, but Erica stepped forward and pressed the tips of her fingers onto Anna's lips. She used her other hand to slam the door shut and flip the lock.

"The fuck?" muttered a voice outside the door.

Evan? Erica mouthed. Anna nodded.

Erica took her phone out of her pocket, opened an app, and typed. *Are you okay?* She showed the screen to Anna who scrunched her face and gestured for Erica to hand her the phone. She did so and was struck again by the sense that Anna's primary emotion during this entire fiasco was annoyance.

They won't hurt me, Anna typed. She passed the phone back to Erica who dropped her shoulders.

They might hurt Derek. She turned the screen at Anna. Her eyes shot to Erica's, and they stared at each other. Erica cocked her head, hoping to convey that Anna knew she was right. She watched the younger girl think this through, neither of them dropping their gaze. Sadness relaxed Anna's features into a frown.

Erica brought up her texts and messaged Kyle. *Pull up to the curb. Anna's coming.* She hit send then kept typing. *I'm going to distract him. Wait until you think it's safe then run. Kyle is in Derek's car.*

Anna's eyebrows shot up as she read. She shook her head. Erica shrugged—what else were they going to do? Anna held her hand out for the phone as a text message popped up. They both read it.

Kyle: Not you?

Erica put the phone in her pocket. "Ready?" she whispered, her hand on the doorknob.

Anna was still shaking her head when Erica stepped into the alcove, right into Evan. He took a step back and glanced toward the bathroom door. She quickly shut it behind her.

The seam of one of his jacket sleeves had given way to the strain put upon it by his bicep, and fluffy white stuffing was showing through. Erica tried not to look at it.

"Hi," she said as casually as she could for how hard her heart was beating. "How was the flight?" Evan made a guttural noise of confusion, so she added, "From Kodiak," as if that was the part he was unsure about. She took small, careful steps toward him, and he continued to back away from her until they were in the main part of the store. She appreciated that it took him a moment to figure out what was going on until, kicking a display of chips with his heel, it clicked.

"Who are you?" Evan puffed his chest out and came toward her. She stood her ground, hoping the height she had on him worked in her favor.

"A friend of Anna's. Just making sure she's okay."

Evan didn't seem to want to touch her though his fists were balled at his sides. She swayed to block him when he tried to move past her. "She's fine," he huffed.

"I'm not sure." Erica put the fingertips of her right hand on his chest. He looked down at them then up at her. She tried to force her face into a sympathetic smile like they were both on the same team. "You have Derek now. Let me take Anna home."

He shook her off but considered what she said. "Jerry didn't say we had to bring her back."

"She'll go home with you, I'm sure. But I don't think Derek plans to go without a fight. I don't want her to have to see that." Erica cringed internally at the fake honey in her voice. She put her hand on him again, this time on his bicep like she was putting her money on him in the impending tussle. It was hard to flirt in men's clothes. She took her hat off and shook out her hair, her long bangs falling over her eyes, allowing her to peek out at him from behind them.

This was the wrong move. Evan's eyes widened. "You're tree boy's girl."

Erica's heart skipped a beat. Acting on instinct, she shoved him with as much force as she could conjure into the chip display. She screamed for Xander at the top of her lungs. The pegboard snapped and Evan fell, scattering multicolored bags in every direction. Erica had no idea what to do. Evan was on the ground, his legs shooting out from under him every time his foot slipped on a bag. She swept the contents of a nearby shelf onto him, sending donuts and snack crackers raining down as he swore.

Xander, Derek, and Liam appeared behind her. "What the—," she heard Liam say as he tried to make sense of what he was looking at.

This was the moment Anna chose to streak past them from the alcove. Liam made to go after her, but Xander and Derek each grabbed an arm. Erica kicked a still prone Evan hard in the shin, jumped over him as he roared in pain, and followed Anna.

Anna was already opening the car door when Erica got outside. "Go!" she yelled at a bewildered-looking Kyle. He opened his mouth, and she said it again. "Just go!" Erica just saw him shake his head and put the car into drive before Anna had even closed the door.

Erica watched the taillights of Derek's hatchback fade down the highway and wanted more than anything to breathe a sigh of relief that they accomplished their goal of getting Anna to safety. But the way the four bodies behind her came barreling into the parking lot told her it wasn't over yet.

"Where is she?" Liam and Derek asked together.

"Gone," Erica told them. She couldn't help but smile at Derek.

"You've got to be fucking kidding me." It was Evan. His sleeve was completely torn now. Stuffing fell about it like snow.

He stepped toward her, his palm open and raised. Erica closed her eyes and prepared for the impact. It didn't come.

Erica heard a strangled yell. She opened her eyes to see that Evan's arm had what appeared to be grass coiling around it like a dozen tiny snakes. She followed the path of the grass down to a crack in the pavement. She looked at Xander whose eyes were glowing.

"You want to play?" Liam growled. He unzipped his jacket and tossed it on the ground.

"Not here!" Erica admonished, scanning the exterior of the building for cameras. Xander tilted his head toward the forest. Erica and Derek exchanged a glance and nodded. Without another word, all three of them took off at a full sprint into the trees.

CHAPTER 25

Liam and Evan had been smart enough to kick off their shoes before they came after them. Erica wished she wasn't running for her life so she could pause to laugh at the absurdity of three men ripping off their clothes as they ran. Even with Xander clearing a path for them, it wasn't easy to undress on the move. Or in the dark of an Oregon winter.

Erica and Derek had been neck and neck when, pulling his second foot out of his black skinny jeans, Derek tripped and rolled out of sight. Erica stopped to look for him, forcing Xander to throw up a wall of trees in the direction they came. He whipped his head around, looking almost panicked until a grizzly bear shot out of the darkness. It positioned itself between Erica and the tree barrier then looked back at Xander.

"We're doing this here?" Xander asked. The grizzly grunted, steam rising from his nostrils. Erica had only briefly glimpsed Derek's bear form once before, but she knew him immediately. Skinny and shaggy with a pronounced hump on his shoulders. Xander pushed his arms out and every living thing down to a single blade of grass glided into a jagged semicircle.

Xander grabbed Erica's hand. "You need to stay out of this." Before she could argue, a nearby fir bent down and scooped her into its branches. She felt her fingers slipping from his as her feet left the ground.

"Not too high!" she yelled, and the fir stopped moving, suspending her ten feet in the air. Erica could hear the bark crack as the tree settled into its new position. She was incredibly uncomfortable, twigs and knots poking into all her soft spots, but she stopped struggling when she saw two massive bears break through Xander's barrier.

They were nowhere near the size of the bear dryad, but they were still larger than Derek. The darker, denser one had to be Evan while Liam was a sight to behold. She hadn't found him remarkable as a person, but as a bear he was muscular and graceful, the moonlight glinting off the red tones in his fur.

At first, the three bears did nothing more than grunt and pace. Derek hadn't told her whether they could communicate in this form, but Erica could have sworn it looked like a negotiation. Derek was careful not to let them get too close to either her or Xander. The bear she thought to be Evan took an almost playful swipe at Derek. In response, Derek reared up and came down hard, planting his paws in front of him. Erica's mind flashed immediately to Xander being on the receiving end of such a hit and the blood and pain that followed.

The bears were still. Erica heard a rustling come from all around. She looked at the ground and watched as it was taken over by a cover of dense, waxy leaves. Long, spiky brambles crept under her like a little wall of soldiers.

With nothing that she could interpret as a warning, Derek and Liam rose onto their hind legs and clashed while vines shot at each of Evan's legs, pulling him, splayed, to the ground. Evan's claws tore the vines to shreds while the other two lunged at each other, their mouths perpetually open. The sounds coming from them were unlike anything Erica had ever heard—low and deep, almost alien.

Evan tried to come at Derek from behind when a tree, a foot thick, came swinging at him, hitting him in the chest. He fell back with a thump and lay still. Erica yelled for Xander to stop, but he didn't turn around. She could only see his back and his hands as they danced instructions to the greenery around them.

Derek and Liam were still thrashing at each other. Erica didn't know if real bears fought standing up, almost boxing with their front paws, but the werebears were. She watched as

Derek got his claws into Liam's shoulder and tore off a chunk of muscle and fur. Liam screamed in a way that was half-human, half-animal and made the hairs on the back of Erica's neck stand up. Derek wiped his paw on the ground and took a few steps back.

Erica thought that had to be it. They had been bested. Kyle had Anna, and they were no match for Xander and Derek. There was nothing to do but retreat.

She was wrong. Evan stirred and got to his feet. This rallied Liam. Shoulder-to-shoulder they charged Derek. Erica watched in horror as Liam's white teeth, eerily bright in the moonlight, came within inches of Derek's throat. They were stopped by what looked like a javelin that made its way straight into Liam's wounded shoulder with a bone-shattering crunch. Liam collapsed and vines encased his body. Evan looked at his fallen friend, giving Xander enough time to wrap enough of him in brambles that he couldn't move. Evan tried to yank a paw, but the brambles squeezed, and Erica hoped his fur was thick enough to protect him from the thorns.

It should have been over, but the vines and branches kept crawling up the bears' bodies. Liam attempted to right himself with his good front paw, but Xander whipped it out from under him and he fell again on the injured shoulder. There was a final roar, and Erica watched Liam's body shrink, his bloody fur retracting into his skin. It made no sense to watch. There was nothing in nature to compare it to. For the first time since she had fallen in with these unusual people, she understood what she was seeing. Magic.

Erica had been so entranced by Liam's transformation that she missed Derek's. He was standing naked in front of Xander and bleeding from a gash at his hip.

"Enough, dude," she heard him say. But Xander stayed still, feet planted, slowly curling his fingers toward his palms. Liam lay panting in a pile of leaves that inched their way up to his chest toward his neck.

"Xander!" Erica yelled from above him. He didn't move. "Push him!"

Derek obeyed, shoving Xander and knocking him momentarily off balance. In response, Xander wrapped a vine around Derek's ankle and pulled him to the ground.

That was too far. Erica struggled against the branches that suspended her above the fray. She couldn't find purchase for her feet to pull herself up so her only option was to drop. She grabbed onto a thick branch near her waist with both hands and rocked side to side, trying to widen the hole her legs stuck out of.

Xander didn't seem to be paying attention to her. Derek had managed to get up and went to Liam, trying to pull the vines down that were wrapping themselves around his throat. They crept up Derek's arm even as he yelled *enough!* over and over.

Erica heard a crack, and she dropped. She only managed to keep her grip on the branch for a second, but it was enough to slow her fall and stop her from breaking a leg. Even so, she hit the ground hard and landed in the brambles that led to Evan. She felt a thousand tiny pricks through her jeans and all over her hands. Pushing through the pain, she ran at Xander, screaming his name, and tackled him from behind. They fell to the ground and rolled, her landing on top of him.

Below her, Xander's face was like stone. His jaw was set. His eyes blazed. They were locked straight ahead, not seeing her. She grabbed his shoulders and shook him as he spread his palms on the ground and the earth beneath them rumbled. Without knowing what else to do, Erica clamped her hands over his eyes, laid her body across his, and put her mouth right in his ear.

"Stop. You're going to kill them. This isn't you. You're Xander Reed. The love of my life. This isn't you."

She felt the muscles beneath her relax. Continuing to talk to him, Erica lifted her eyes to the two nude figures laying just feet from her. Derek's eyes were wild, but he didn't look like he was in pain. He nodded at her as he tentatively tried to lift his arms and the leaves slid off him. He lunged for Liam again, and this time was able to snap the tendrils cutting off his air supply. Liam took a deep, gasping breath.

Erica tentatively took her hands off Xander's eyes. They snapped to hers, and she willed him to come back to her.

Instead, he pushed her off him and darted into the trees. Erica only made it three steps in the same direction before branches shot out from the bare trunks all around her, forming an interlocking barrier that made it impossible for her to follow in his path. She yelled after him, terrified of him alone out there in that state.

Someone was yelling back but it wasn't Xander. Derek was calling for her to help. "We need to get Liam to a hospital. I think he's in shock."

Evan was human again and kneeling over Liam. Only then did the awkwardness of the situation hit her. She tried very hard to look only at faces.

"You guys get him up," Erica said. "I'll look for your clothes." As worried as she was for Xander, there was a more pressing need. Xander could take care of himself physically. He had just proven that. How he would cope otherwise, she had to wait to find out.

They walked back out the way they came, Derek and Evan supporting Liam between them. All animosity seemed to have vanished. Erica kept herself a dozen paces in front and used her phone as a flashlight to search for articles of clothing. She managed to find all three pairs of boxers but only two pairs of pants, two shirts, three socks, and Derek's boots. Only Evan was able to put on a complete outfit as they stood at the edge of the forest looking at the Diner. The shoes and coats he and Liam had left there were gone, presumably to be rifled through by the convenience store attendant to figure out who to go after for the mess they caused.

Moving as fast as they could and drawing as little attention as possible, they deposited Liam in the backseat of his rental car. The dome light came on as they opened the door, and Erica slapped it off with a glance toward the Diner. It was past eleven now and several more tractor-trailers had come in, so they had a little bit of cover.

Erica took off her coat, and the evening breeze hit her sweat-drenched t-shirt. She shivered as she wrapped the coat around Liam's wound, trying hard not to look at the mess of red, white, and yellow. Derek typed the name of a hospital into Evan's phone and explained that while it was an hour away, they were going to wind up there regardless because the little emergency room in Juniper Falls was going to have no idea what to do with a wound like that.

"Tell them it was a logging accident. Put it on Kriners' tab," Derek said. He shut the door, then tapped on the window. Evan rolled it down. "And dude? Call me."

The look that passed between Derek and Evan was sad and loaded with something Erica wasn't sure she understood. Half an hour ago they were enemies literally at each other's throats. But when they had walked into the Diner, Derek had greeted them like old friends. She realized they must have grown up together, worked together, witnessed the same exploitation of their were-brethren. They were all pawns in someone else's game.

Derek, half dressed, watched Evan and Liam leave with a look of deep sadness on his face. Erica got into Xander's truck, once again turning the overhead light off, and waited until Derek was ready. When he slipped into the driver's seat, she motioned to where he could find the keys under the seat. Erica couldn't believe no one had come into the parking lot to confront them, but maybe little fights broke out at the Diner all the time. The people who worked there had the world-weary look that came with not always seeing the best of humanity.

This line of thinking didn't help Erica's mood. She leaned against the door, trying to process everything she had just witnessed.

Neither spoke until Derek had exited the highway and crossed the river. Sitting at a stop sign, he asked her, "Do you want me to drop you off or do you want to drop me off?"

"Drop you off."

He nodded and took a right. They arrived at Kyle's house. The lights were on in the living room, and Derek's car sat in the driveway. He promised to text her before getting out of the truck, leaving it running. Erica undid her seatbelt and slid behind the wheel.

She thought about driving to Xander's tree to try to talk to him, but she had no coat and was bone tired. There was a bed for her at Granny's. She would recalibrate in the morning.

CHAPTER 26

A long shower and a fitful start to her sleep put Erica to bed later than she expected. It was mid-morning when she finally awoke to the sounds of several text messages from Derek telling her that Anna was well, and Liam had made it to the hospital. Notably absent was anything from or about Xander.

Granny had been waiting for her at the table when she got home the night before, and she received the most abbreviated version of events Erica could muster. She was there again this morning but didn't push for more information. Erica made herself a light breakfast, told Granny where she was going, and left. The drive to the cemetery was second nature now. She could do it in her sleep.

She parked Xander's truck in the gravel lot and was halfway up the hill when she saw Alden. He sat on the dewy ground, leaning against his tree like he was waiting for her. Erica's heart sank. He was either here to intercept her or he didn't know where Xander was either. She hoped it was the former because the latter couldn't mean anything good.

"It's no use. I don't think he can hear us," Alden said as she approached.

"What does that mean?" Erica felt the acidic taste of anxiety bubble into her mouth.

"I think he's shut himself off from it, but I can't say for sure."

Erica placed her hand on the jagged bark of Xander's tree.

"Hey," she whispered even though she knew it was impossible to hide it from Alden.

"I said he can't hear you."

"I know. Just in case." She put her back against the tree, leaning her head against it and keeping both palms on the trunk. She knew she must look stupid, but if Xander could feel her, it was worth it. "You know what happened?"

Alden nodded. "I didn't see what you idiots did, but I felt it until he put the barrier up. I haven't been able to find him since."

"You're worried?"

"Isn't that why you're here too?"

Erica shrugged. She couldn't hold her position anymore. She squatted so she was eye-level with Alden. "Do you know what he did?" Alden stared impassively at her. "He got rough with one of them. Squeezed him like a snake until—." She couldn't say it. She didn't want to relive that moment.

Alden didn't look particularly surprised. He sighed and tilted his head back. Erica couldn't be sure it wasn't a trick of the light, but it looked like the tree gave no resistance. It yielded to his body like it was made of foam. "He gave in, then."

Erica furrowed her eyebrows. Gave in to what? She studied Alden, the way he sat on the ground like a broken doll. His face had a sunken appearance that was new.

Then she realized. "You don't think he's coming back."

Alden sighed again. "I knew it was coming even if he didn't. I just thought he would take me with him."

Erica stared at him. This is what Alden thought it would come to. No more cabin in the woods. No more friends. A full embrace of the wild. A complete loss of humanity. She couldn't let that happen. "You're giving up on him?"

Alden shook his head. "It's not like that. He's more powerful than me."

"I've seen what you can do. It requires a lot more finesse than throwing trees around. It's beautiful." Erica thought back to the maple fox in Alden's sculpture garden and how it looked ready to pounce.

"Beauty isn't power, Erica. I've built a craft over decades.

He's been chosen. Given a gift."

"The gift of what? Walking the woods alone for eternity? You think he wants that?"

"I don't think he has a choice. You saw to that."

The accusation took Erica's breath away. She stared into Alden's chocolate eyes, the exact color Xander's were before the bear dryad, before he defied death a second time, before he tested the extent of his power. The first time they kissed, she had promised him a future. Had his fate been sealed since that day? Was the idea of them—happy, whole, and together—always just that, an idea? A tenuous thing never to be realized, like so many ideas before it.

Erica lowered her eyes to the ground and willed them to stay dry. She had no defense. Alden had told her not to get involved, that she was out of her depth. And so she had lost Xander again in a way she hadn't seen coming and yet only she could have prevented.

She jumped when her phone rang from within her jacket pocket. She ripped it out, hoping to see Xander's name on the screen. It was Derek.

"Hey," she said, trying not to sound like she felt.

"You should come to the store now."

"What's going on?"

"That guy from Kriners is here. The slick one. He says he can take us to Xander."

Erica almost dropped the phone. Her eyes darted to Alden who had heard. He jumped to his feet.

"We'll be right there."

She hung up. Without saying another word to each other, Erica and Alden ran down the hill. Alden shot her a look when he saw Xander's truck. She tossed him the keys and hopped in the passenger seat.

Cora had warned them that Mitchell had cameras all over the forest. Scenarios for what he knew and how he could have subdued Xander played through Erica's head as Alden navigated the twists and turns of the roads that led to the *Farm & Feed*. Neither of them said anything. Alden wasn't the type to have the radio playing, but they would have only made it through a song, maybe two, before the midnight blue barn came into view. A red Kriners truck with the ax logo emblazoned on the doors was parked alongside a handful of other cars.

Erica wasn't sure that where Alden left the truck was technically a parking spot, but she wasn't about to argue with him. She threw off her seatbelt and was three steps toward the store when she realized Alden wasn't following. She was about to encourage him when she remembered; Alden didn't do public spaces. She returned to the truck and knocked on the driver's side window, which he slowly cranked down.

"You're not going in?"

Alden's face betrayed his internal war between helping Xander and not being seen. A sheen of sweat was forming on his forehead. "Find out where he is," he said through clenched teeth.

"What if he won't tell me?"

"He needs to tell you."

Erica was confident that Mitchell wasn't just going to say where Xander was. If it was going to be that simple, he'd have told Derek. But they were wasting time. She spun around and made her way toward the glass doors and into the store.

Mitchell was standing at the counter with Derek and Joe, all three looking tense and not speaking. A handful of customers milled around. Erica had to consciously slow her steps as she approached the front of the store so as not to draw too much attention.

"Where is Xander?" she asked in as demanding a whisper as she could muster.

Mitchell tugged on the sleeve of his beige shell-neck sweater. He was impeccably dressed as always but something was off. His hair wasn't quite as smooth or his shoes as shiny. "I was hoping you would let me take you to him."

Erica's eyebrows shot up and she caught Derek's eye. From the shrug he gave her, she knew he didn't trust him either. She studied Mitchell. His face was inscrutable, but there was a twitchiness about him that she hadn't seen before. "I don't know how you're holding him, but you're in over your head."

"I think you're probably right about that."

"This conversation may be better suited for a private location. Erica, maybe you can take Mr. Watters to the office," interjected Joe. He smiled reassuringly at an older woman who was cautiously approaching the counter. Erica wondered how much explaining Kyle had to do about the sudden appearance of Anna in his house last night and if that had something to do with how blasé Joe was acting.

She headed for the storeroom so Joe could ring up the customer, but Mitchell took several steps in the direction of the front door. "I would rather you come with me," he said.

"That's not happening."

The woman looked between them. "Is everything all right?"

Not wanting to cause more of a scene, Erica sighed and followed Mitchell. Derek looked like he wasn't sure if he was supposed to stay until Joe shooed him out, which Erica was grateful for. In the parking lot, Erica could feel Alden's stare boring into her from where he sat in the truck. He had materialized a baseball cap from somewhere and pulled it low over his forehead.

"Is that—?" Derek started, but Erica elbowed him.

"Look, I know you think I'm the bad guy, but you couldn't expect me not to try to figure out what the hell happened out here in October." Mitchell pointed in the direction of Main Street.

"It wasn't Xander."

"I've got it on tape."

"The bear?" It hadn't occurred to Erica before, but it was inevitable that someone pulled out a phone and took a video of a gigantic bear ripping apart a quaint community gathering.

"Not that. We paid people off for those videos. Last night. Xander running through the woods, trees falling all around him. Your friend Kyle called me and told me which cameras to watch, though he didn't prepare me for what I would see." Erica's eyes flew open wide, and she looked at Derek who appeared equally as shocked. Her mind raced, and she wanted to interject, but Mitchell was still talking. "I went out there because I couldn't understand what I was seeing. When he heard me, he started making this sort of fort. Twigs and weeds in every direction. I had a machete, but I couldn't cut it down faster than it grew. I've never seen anything like it."

A car door slammed behind them, and Erica just made out a flash of blond hair before Alden was upon them. "Keep your voices down," he hissed, his head down and eyes hidden. "In the truck. Now."

Still reeling from Kyle betraying them to Mitchell, Erica followed him back to the truck. To her surprise, Mitchell came with them. She traded looks again with Derek. If Mitchell had seen the werebears, surely he would have commented on it. They must have gotten lucky that the cameras that picked up Xander were far enough away from the fight to miss the main event.

At the truck, it was immediately apparent that they weren't all going to fit. "You and you," Alden said, pointing to Erica, then Mitchell, then the fraying bench seat.

Erica hesitated. Driving to some unknown destination with two men who, to the best of her knowledge, hated her, was not the wisest idea. She would be safer with Derek around.

"Derek could ride in the bed?" she proposed.

"I am not getting pulled over."

Derek grabbed Erica's hand and squeezed it. He nodded toward the truck. "You'll be okay."

She wanted to ask him how he knew, but he probably wouldn't have an answer. She steeled her nerves and reminded herself that she was heading to Xander. If nothing happened on the way, she was always safe with him. Erica climbed into the truck through the passenger door. Mitchell followed in after her.

"You know the old mill?" Mitchell asked, carefully locking in his seatbelt without touching Erica. Alden nodded. "Head there. I'll guide you."

Erica questioned the life choices she was making to continually wind up in trucks with men driving into the forest. She had no idea where the old mill was, which would not be helpful if she had to call someone to come find her. She resolved to pay attention and keep track of every turn. This proved not to be easy once Alden broke his silence and started needling Mitchell.

"If you aren't telling the truth about this, we're going to have a problem."

"No problems here."

"Oh, there are problems. Your morally bankrupt company ruins everything it touches. What happened at the Harvest Festival was your fault. Your total deviation from the sustainable logging practices you lie about on all your advertisements woke it up."

Erica expected Mitchell to squirm, but he was still and calm in his reply. "Woke what up exactly?"

"You saw it," Alden spat.

"But what was it? What is Xander?" Neither Alden nor Erica answered him. Kyle was a snitch, but he hadn't told Mitchell everything. Just when she was feeling smug about all the things she knew that Mitchell didn't, he revealed something she could never have expected. "I'd like to know. He is my son."

Erica was glad it was Alden who was driving. Had it been her, she wouldn't have been able to help swerving into a ditch or slamming on the breaks. His son? She whipped her head around to look at him, but they were so close she had to lean into Alden who shoved her with his shoulder.

"Bullshit," Alden said.

"Not quite. Alina and I were seeing each other, casually of course, when Kriners was first looking at the Umpqua region almost twenty years ago. When we met in front of your store back in November and he told me who he was, I admit I was taken aback. I thought they had both died a long time ago."

"Alina never mentioned you." Erica thought she could hear Alden's teeth grinding together.

"She mentioned you, though. Her older brother, Alden. But you look like you could be my kid too. How is that?" Alden took a hard left and stepped on the gas. They headed toward the river on a road Erica wasn't familiar with. Mitchell continued, "I visited Alex a few times over the years, but Alina didn't want to tell him who I was. We had a, shall we say, disagreement over whether she should continue the pregnancy and ended our relationship before he was born. The last time I saw him, he was five."

"Xander said you felt familiar," Erica said. She looked for Xander's features in Mitchell but couldn't find them. It was like his genes knew how little his father wanted him and took as little from him as they could.

Alden grunted as if in pain. Erica thought she understood. It was difficult to connect someone she loved so deeply with someone she reviled.

Mitchell either did not register or was not deterred by their discomfort. "Imagine my surprise when my newly rediscovered son showed up in footage right before my security cameras went down. And then what I saw last night with my own two eyes."

Erica's shock was wearing off. The more Mitchell talked in his slow tones like he was explaining something simple to a child, the more it was replaced by something new: fear. Mitchell had Xander on camera. Multiple times.

"I thought I was going crazy when I would show up to places I knew we had cleared and the trees were taller than the ones we took down." He paused here, training his eyes on Erica to gauge her reaction. "I know what he's doing. The question is how."

Alden brought the truck to an abrupt stop. "We're here."

In front of them was a long, low building constructed with metal sheets that were in the later stages of rust. Shrubs and long grass ran several feet up the walls. Behind it was a sort of two-story square silo in similar condition.

"What is this?" Erica asked.

"You're dodging my questions, but this is the sawmill the residents of Juniper Falls built forty years ago hoping it would attract exactly the kind of industry you all are so intent on pushing out today."

"Why would Xander come here?"

"He didn't. You'll need to take a right, Alden. We'll drive in as far as we can."

Alden's face was set like he was going to yell or worse any minute, but he did as he was directed. They let the question of Xander linger as Alden did his best to keep the truck in the barely-there ruts. The sound of crunching rocks and broken twigs rang unnaturally loud in the thick silence of the cab. Erica was very aware of every slight motion made by the men on either side of her. If they were headed into a trap, she hoped Alden was ready for it.

"We'll have to stop just up here and walk," Mitchell said, pointing to where the road terminated in a dense line of trees.

"Just point me in the right direction."

If Mitchell was surprised by this, he didn't show it. He drifted his arm toward Erica, and she pressed herself into the seat to avoid it. Slowly, inch by inch, the trees shifted just enough to allow them to pass through.

"Fascinating. You too, then?"

They continued at a pace that made Erica wonder if Alden was showing off. They could have walked faster. Mitchell pulled out his phone and swiped to an app that looked a lot like the handheld GPS Erica used to locate the place associated with the coordinates in Keith's journal.

"You might want to go a little more to the—," he began.

Alden cut him off. "He knows we're here."

The confidence in Alden's voice made Erica believe that Xander had finally dropped his guard, which she hoped meant he would come save her. Though, if she was being fair, Mitchell hadn't made a threat at any point in this whole ordeal.

Just when Erica's impatience was hitting its peak and she was getting tempted to ditch the truck, a massive dome of plant life came into view. Brown branches and green vines snaked over each other like they had minds of their own. As they got closer, she could see flowers popping up only to be shredded and drop to the ground when they were passed over by some thorny briar. The ground was littered with petals—tiny pink ones, delicate white triangles, thick yellow half-spheres, and many, many more.

"It hasn't gotten any bigger than it was this morning," Mitchell said in a voice that sounded almost bored. Erica unbuckled his seatbelt and pushed him out of the truck. He made a sound of protest, but she was already racing Alden to the dome.

Alden planted his feet. She could tell he was trying to affect it but there was no visible response. He put out his hand, and a branch flicked it, leaving behind a small streak of blood.

"I tried that too," Mitchell said. He held up the back of his hand, which sported a scratch that was only just forming a scab. "I tried talking him down. I told him about our, shall we say, connection."

"You did what?" Erica yelled. The sound coming off the dome was not loud, but the rustle and snap was rapid and constant. It rattled her nerves.

Xander was already vulnerable and in pain from his run-in with the werebears. While she was sure now that Mitchell didn't know about that, her heart broke for Xander. It was too much at once for someone whose whole life up until a few months ago had been so quiet and consistent.

Erica walked partway around the dome. It was so large that she lost sight of Alden, which for some reason made her nervous. She retraced her steps until she could see him again. Despite the reaction Mitchell and Alden had both received, she could come up with no other course of action than to reach out. She steeled herself for the whip she figured was coming and stepped forward with both hands in front of her. She was met with no resistance. The dome pulled back. Erica turned around to look at Mitchell and Alden. Each had a better claim on Xander than she did, but it was Xander's heart that hurt. She was the best salve for that wound.

Erica took a few steps into the opening, and the dome closed behind her. It was unnerving having no way back, but while the foliage lashed around her, none of it touched her, short of dropping petals at her feet. She didn't have far to go before she came upon Xander sitting cross-legged and eyes closed between two ancient cedars. He was filthy, his torn jeans and his stretched hoodie covered in dirt.

She called his name. He didn't respond. His stillness was unnatural. She wondered if he was breathing. She bent down and ran a finger along the inside of his wrist where his hands sat limply on his knees. He felt warm but lifeless at the same time. Erica got on her knees so that their eyes were level.

"Xander. Love." They didn't use pet names with each other, so she stole the one Granny used for family. It felt right. "I need you to wake up." There was no change. She took his hand, lacing his fingers between hers. "I know you've been through it, but Derek isn't mad at you. And we'll figure out this stuff with Mitchell. You knew this would happen. Okay, not the father part. That's weird. But so what? He knows about you. That just means you can take him head-on."

Erica sighed. Xander had the crease between his eyebrows that she was so fond of smoothing away. She did so now, but it stayed stuck steadfastly in place. She only had one more trick up her sleeve that worked last time he had gotten drunk on his power. She kissed him.

It was like kissing rubber. She pushed her face into his until she could feel his teeth on the other side of their lips. The sensation was not pleasant. She began to pull away when Xander's hand darted out and grabbed her waist. His mouth came alive, his tongue slipping between her parted lips, and she wanted to shriek with joy. She inched forward toward him until he pulled them both back onto the forest floor. There was a rock digging into her side, but she barely noticed.

When at last he opened his eyes to look at her, she realized the incessant rustling had stopped. Mitchell and Alden must have noticed too because Erica could just barely hear them calling out her and Xander's names.

"I almost killed them," Xander whispered. He dropped his head onto her chest, and she wrapped her arms as far around his wide shoulders as they would go. "I lost control. I could see what I was doing but it was like it wasn't me. I was a missile pointed at a target and let loose."

"They picked the fight. They deserved it." Erica didn't entirely believe that. She knew Xander went too far. But this living dome was a testament to how much he regretted it.

Xander shook his head. "The bear dryad was killing people at the end. Not just Keith but those loggers. I can't let that happen. I want to save the forest, but I can't be that."

Erica stroked the soft baby hairs at the base of his neck.

She could hear the hurt in his voice, the ever-present conflict between what he was and what he wanted to be. She wished, for maybe the millionth time, that she could ease that burden.

A particularly loud shout made its way through the dome and Xander sat up abruptly. "Is that Mitchell?"

Erica grabbed his arm. "He brought us here."

Xander groaned. She knew it was too much at once, but an idea started to take hold in her mind. "Mitchell says he's your dad."

"Can we do one crisis at a time?" Xander threw himself on the ground, no longer touching her. She felt the lack of him instantly, all the way down to her core.

"You really didn't remember him?"

"Everything from before I died is spotty at best. The only memories I can really hold onto are of my mom."

Erica knew she would have to unpack that hurt with him later but for now she had to plant the seed that could solve so many of their problems. "What if we could get Mitchell to pull Kriners out of Juniper Falls?"

Xander narrowed his eyes. "Why would he do that?"

Laying down next to him, she put her finger on his forehead, but instead of stroking his nose, she gave a little push. "You. He doesn't have family. No wife. No kids. If you're all he's got and you're not going to back down—." She paused like it was a question. He nodded. "Then maybe we can convince him it's not worth the fight. He's spending all this money hushing people up about what's happening here. Maybe it's a win-win."

Xander stared up at the fortress he had made. He reached for her hand and flipped it over, running his finger across every scratch on her palm. "I did that?"

"No. I knew what I was falling into."

"The thorns that I grew."

"Xander," she sighed.

He brought her palm to his mouth and kissed it. "I wish I could heal you."

"It's okay. That's enough."

They laid side-by-side, Xander holding Erica's hand to his

chest until Mitchell and Alden gave up on yelling their names. Erica's mind whirled with a plan to get Kriners out of Juniper Falls if only they could win over Mitchell. But it was just a distraction from what was really bothering her.

"Alden thinks you're going to disappear," she whispered.

He squeezed her hand. His silence told her everything.

CHAPTER 27

Xander eventually agreed to leave on the condition that Alden and Mitchell didn't bother him. There would be a time for questions and explanations and awkward reunions, but that time was not now. Erica rode with him in the bed of his truck to Granny's house. She invited Alden and Mitchell back the next morning. It was odd seeing them ride off together, two enemies that she hoped she could unite in the common goal of lessening Xander's heartache on his way to fulfilling his destiny.

Heeding Erica's warning, Granny had made herself scarce and they arrived at a quiet house. Erica led Xander straight to the shower to wash off the debris from a night spent outside. He emerged from the bathroom clean and barely able to keep his eyes open, a pair of Keith's old sweatpants she'd found for him low on his hips. He threw himself on Erica's bed and opened his arms for her. She crawled into them despite it being barely past noon. Though her head was overflowing with what they would say tomorrow and the sudden realization that she never emailed her English professor, she slept better than she had in weeks.

Hours later, she tiptoed downstairs and sent a series of text messages. The one to Kyle read only, *I know what you did,* and then she blocked him. She would confront him eventually, but she had more important matters to attend to first.

Xander slept until the evening. When he woke up, he called for her, and she slipped back into bed with him. They kissed and touched and made slow work of loving each other until they were sated. Not wanting to spoil the moment with phones or films, Erica pulled a battered copy of Rebecca from the nightstand and read it to Xander until he fell back asleep.

In the morning, Erica woke early to help Granny make a big breakfast. She ran the waffle maker while Granny cooked bacon and cheesy scrambled eggs. As she requested, people began showing up around nine. First was Mitchell wearing a sport jacket over an open-collared dress shirt like he knew instinctively he was walking into a negotiation.

"I've never met two women who were so intent on getting the better of me," he said after he and Erica exchanged pleasantries and Granny seated him at the table overflowing with food.

"I'm going to take that as a compliment," Erica called from the living room where she was watching Alden come down the driveway.

"You should."

Alden said nothing to her and sat across from Mitchell. The feeling between the two men was not as adversarial as it had been in the truck, and she wondered if they had spoken after dropping off her and Xander the night before.

Derek arrived, ten minutes late, with Anna in tow. She was less skittish than the last time she was in this house, and her owlish eyes fell right on the food.

"Help yourself," Erica said, and Anna loaded up a plate without so much as looking at anyone else in the room.

Derek chuckled. "Sorry."

"Don't even worry about it. Is she okay? When is she going home?"

Derek dragged a hand through his hair. "I don't think she is. The family is pretty pissed about it, but I don't know what they can do. Jerry Whitlock and his crew appear to have gotten the message."

"What about Liam and Evan?"

"This is crazy, I know, but they might stay too. They're pretty pissed that Jerry sent them to get thumped. They're starting to see the light."

Erica considered asking if he knew what he was getting

into, but then, did any of them? Instead, she asked, "Did Kyle tell you he called Mitchell?"

Derek's eyes flashed. "What? No?"

He tried to ask more questions when Alden interrupted. "Where's Xander?"

Erica squeezed Derek's bicep in a promise to talk more later. She approached the table where Granny was now also seated and initiated the conversation she had been rolling around in her mind since the day before. "I'm going to go wake him up but here's the thing: when he comes down here, when he tells you what he wants, we need to listen carefully. I think we all have come to Xander with our own agendas. I know I have. But it's his turn now." Alden betrayed no emotion. Mitchell and Granny both nodded at her, the latter with a sad smile on her face. "We need to be there for him. Before it's too late."

In her room, she shook Xander's shoulder. His eyes fluttered open, and his lips spread into a slow smile as she came into focus for him.

"Everyone is downstairs. Come on. We need to figure this out." Erica pointed to a neatly folded stack of Keith's clothes at the end of the bed.

"Who is everyone?" he asked, pulling a t-shirt over his head.

"Everyone." Erica gave him a meaningful look, and he sighed. "I'll meet you downstairs."

When Erica sat at the table, deliberately taking the vacant seat next to Mitchell so that Xander wasn't forced to, the mood was uncomfortable. The adults were largely addressing their questions to Anna who was oblivious to the awkwardness of the situation. Erica thought she was remarkably nonchalant for a girl who was just kidnapped and told she probably wasn't going home. She was going to have to set aside an afternoon to get to know her.

Xander joined them several minutes later, walking straight up to Derek who stood and hugged him.

"I'm sorry," Xander said, a hitch in his voice. "Are you okay? Are they okay?"

"I mean, I don't think Liam is going to be throwing any more punches but that's probably good for him."

Xander only then seemed to see the other people at the table. He gave Derek a look of contrition, as if he wasn't quite done with his apology but understood it would have to wait until later and sat down next to him. Xander eyed Derek's full plate of food. Erica momentarily felt guilty for tempting him. But for the people at the table who did eat, Granny believed that full bellies were an important component to winning people over to your side.

"Okay, so," Erica started. Now that the moment had come, she suddenly had stage fright. She glanced around at the faces at the table, an equal number friendly as unfriendly, and decided to just spit it out. "We want Kriners out of Juniper Falls."

Alden shot a smug look at Mitchell who sighed deeply, set down his knife and fork, and leaned back in his chair.

"Erica, you know I can't do that."

"We're at an impasse, then. Your *son*—," she emphasized the word. Granny gasped, and Derek's mouth dropped open, half-chewed waffles visible. "—Can't stop what he's doing. And I think you're in the best position to understand the consequences if he gets caught by someone other than you."

"Surely we can compromise." Mitchell made a triangle with his hands and set them delicately on the table in front of him. His expensive watch flashed, and Xander's eyes flickered in response.

"No compromise," Xander said. His voice was weaker than Erica had expected.

"Xander," Mitchell said in a manner meant to placate. "You can't expect me to just stop logging because you say so. Do you know how many millions of dollars have been spent to get here?"

"That doesn't sound like my problem," Xander replied more forcefully.

"It is if you want to keep playing these games. You're one person, extraordinary as you are, against a whole corporation."

"Two people," Alden interjected.

Mitchell opened his hands to acknowledge Alden's point.

"The thing is, Mitchell," Xander said, mimicking his tone, "it may be just the two of us, but I have something in my corner you could never understand. I am tied to this forest and it to me. The forest picked me, a human, to fight this human threat. I believe that now. You're right that I've been playing games so far. But I can wage a war if that's what will make you understand you're not wanted here."

Erica didn't know what to feel. Pride at Xander taking a stand. Deep sadness over what that stand meant. He had told her the same thing two months ago, but she hadn't been ready to hear it. Now she knew Alden was right. There was only one way for this to end, and it wasn't the two of them spending vacations in her bedroom upstairs.

Mitchell stared at Xander then looked at each of the faces around the table as if waiting for someone to call April Fools. When he ended on Erica's steely gaze, he threw his hands up.

"I'm not saying I'm in on this. But if I consider putting some things into motion, I'm going to need all hands on deck. Except maybe yours," he said, pointing at Derek. "Who is this person?"

"I used to work for you, man."

Mitchell shook the distraction from his head. "We are going to have to create so many obstacles for Kriners that they have no choice but to leave. I'm going to lose my job." The last comment was a throwaway that no one acknowledged. They all had so much more to lose.

"What kind of obstacles?" Granny asked.

Mitchell sighed. Across the table, Erica and Xander locked eyes and smiled.

AUTHOR BIO

Kelsey Parpart grew up in Washington state before moving to Oregon then Alaska and finally settling in the Blue Ridge Mountains of North Carolina. She holds a bachelor's in English from Washington State University and is a graduate of Portland State University's Book Publishing program. When not writing, she works in marketing in the engineering and construction industry and makes slow but steady progress on building her dream hobby farm. The White Oak Trilogy is her first series.

If you enjoyed this book, please leave a review on Amazon or Goodreads.

www.ingramcontent.com/pod-product-compliance
Lightning Source LLC
Chambersburg PA
CBHW061237310726
48971CB00007B/2108